Dying to Crochet

Bendy Carter

PublishAmerica
Baltimore

ISBN: 1-60610-109-9
PUBLISHED BY PUBLISHAMERICA, LLLP
www.publishamerica.com
Baltimore

Printed in the United States of America

For my true friend always
Veronica Gatson Ruben
I love you too, always have and always will.
Ronnie you will never be forgotten.

Acknowledgments

I want to thank my family for their love and support while I penned this work of fiction.

Police Chief Tony D'Andrea, Judge Ben Z. Grant, Karl Krohn M.D., Kyle Krohn M.D. and B.J. Herrin M.D. for answering my legal and medical questions in preparation for this book.

I also want to thank Carol Partch of Simply Fibers Ltd in Springfield, Missouri, the yarn shop depicted in this story, for allowing me to observe life as it is in a yarn shop. And thank you to Jim Gaw of Trainland Hobbies, also of Springfield, Missouri, for allowing the use of his store.

Thank you to Kathleen Sams, Terri Geck and Joan Barnett of Coats and Clark for supplying the yarn and hooks for the models.

Thank you to Shirley Lykins for all her last minute help, when I needed it most.

And a special thank you to all the professionals in the crochet world who gave their support, encouragement and time to make this book a reality.

Prelude

◆—

Veronica lay in bed thinking over the events of the past few months.

She wasn't looking to fall in love. She was just minding her own business, strolling down the tree lined streets. Veronica loved to take walks, especially that time of year. It was the season of Apple Fest otherwise known as autumn to people not familiar with Marionville, a small town with five apple orchards.

Trees were in full color and the streets were strewn with falling leaves. The heat of summer had finally passed and a fresh, cool, crisp breeze was gently blowing. It couldn't have been a more perfect day for a festival.

Craft booths and food vendors were abundant on the city's streets. Veronica loved the aroma drifting from the downtown square. The sweet smell of apples was everywhere. Apple brownies, apple pie, apple cider, apple preserves, if it could be made with apples one would find it on the square.

Veronica stopped a moment and looked down admiringly at the warm bundle she was carrying in her arms. She carefully lifted the cotton cloth back to take a peek. Perfectly sweetened apples baked in a rich golden flaky crust. One of her best, she thought, as she replaced the cover.

The highlight of Apple Fest, for Veronica, was always the apple pie baking contest. She loved to bake, especially pies.

The pies were judged in the morning then, at the grand ceremony that afternoon, monetary prizes were awarded followed by the pies being auctioned off to the highest bidders.

As she neared the fire station where the pies were to be judged, she heard the excited cries of young children watching the parade go by. Veronica watched the little ones diving toward the ground to grab the candy being thrown toward them from the costumed people on the various floats. Being a small town, she knew most of the children.

Veronica worked Monday through Friday at the daycare center, a place for children to go after school until their parents got off work as well as a place for children not quite old enough for school. She loved playing games with the children. They would usually greet her with a big "hello" and a hug when they saw her coming, but not today. Today, candy was their only focus. Veronica couldn't help laughing out loud as she watched their frenzied activity.

She hated to leave, but the pie had to be delivered on time. Veronica continued down the busy street, past the parade watchers and into the fire station to register her pie. As she looked around the room she noted that competition was going to be steep. There were at least fifty pies already entered and more would be arriving shortly. After she signed her name, gave all her contact information and placed her pie in the appropriate age category, twenty to twenty-nine year olds, she headed back out to watch the remaining floats go by.

Veronica arrived outside just in time to see the Missouri Fox Trotting horses, a sign that the parade was coming to an end. The fire trucks slowly drove by throwing the last of the free candy toward the eagerly awaiting children. She wished she had been able to see a little more of the parade.

Veronica stood on the sidewalk a few minutes listening to passersby say how great the floats had been before suddenly remembering that the parade always ended at the park just a few short blocks away from the square. She wondered if she walked down to the park if she would get a chance to see some of the floats before they were taken away. It was worth a try.

As Veronica hurried toward the park the wind persistently blew her long raven hair across her face. She brushed her hair back with her hands then watched as the wind lifted up the colorful fall leaves from their resting places creating a masterpiece of color right before her eyes. As she continued walking, she was mesmerized by the beauty of the colors; vibrant yellows, reds, greens and purples. Then it happened. Her whole life, changed in an instant.

Perhaps it would not have happened had she not been looking at the leaves. Perhaps if the wind had not been blowing so hard against her back or perhaps even a simple change of shoes and her whole life would have been different. Veronica often liked to ponder these things. But the simple fact was, it did happen. Her shoestrings came untied and she fell. In more ways than one she would soon discover. For as she lay sprawled on the payment her future came rushing to her aid.

He was a handsome man, over six feet tall with gorgeous wavy black hair. He swept her onto her feet then swept her back off them. Veronica had never believed in love at first sight before, but then again, she had never met Jack before either.

"Here, let me help you."

"Thanks, but it really isn't necessary." Veronica tried to take a step forward but started to fall again.

"Yes, I can see it is not necessary," he said as he picked her up.

Jack gallantly started carrying Veronica back to the square. "Uh, I appreciate your being my knight in shining armor, but was just wondering, do you have a name?"

"Sir Jack," Jack replied as he gently placed her on the

grassy hill in back of the gazebo. "And who might you be?" Jack asked in his best imitation of a British accent.

Veronica continued the game, "Why, Lady Veronica, of course." Veronica looked down and began examining her slowly swelling ankle.

"I'm going to get some ice and a towel from one of the vendors. I'll be right back." Jack gently placed his hand under Veronica's chin and turned her face toward him. "Will you be ok?"

Veronica tried to smile, "Yes, I'll be fine. It's just a sprain. Thanks for your help."

Jack stood up, bowed and tipped his hat. "Anything for you, milady," he said before departing on his mission of mercy.

A few minutes later, he returned with a bag of ice wrapped in a green towel and gently placed it on her ankle. They spent the rest of the morning sitting on the grass talking and laughing, both completely forgetting about time and place.

"So, what do you do, I mean besides helping damsels in distress?" Veronica asked.

"I'm the manager of a hobby train shop in Springfield. I love trains. I started riding them when I was a little boy." Jack picked up a blade of grass and mindlessly started twirling it in his fingers as he began reminiscing about the past. "My dad used to take me for rides. We didn't own a car." Jack put the blade down and smiled at Veronica. "Hopefully I'll own my own train shop someday."

"You live in Springfield?"

"Yes." Jack stretched out on his side, propping himself up with his elbow. "Actually, right now I'm living in a little room in the back of the train store. The owner is letting me live there so I can save money to make a down payment on a house. Do you live here in Marionville?"

"Yes. I'm living with my aunt." Veronica adjusted the bag of ice on her ankle before continuing. "My parents were killed by a hit and run driver when I was just a little girl and I was sent to live with my Aunt Sally."

Jack sat back up and placed his arm across her shoulders, "I'm sorry."

"Trains! Is that why you came to the festival?" Veronica asked, trying to change the subject.

Jack got the hint and took his arm back down. "Yes. I was hoping to maybe find some old toy trains, but I didn't see any. After looking around awhile I decided to go jogging in the park." Jack grinned. "And what do you do, besides waiting for knights to save you?"

"I work in the local nursery. Started working there after school when I was sixteen then went full time after graduation."

"Do you enjoy selling plants?" Jack asked.

"Plants?" Veronica looked confused for a second then realized the mistake. "No, not that kind of nursery. A nursery for babies and small children!"

"Oh, I see. Do you enjoy it?"

"I love it! I love teaching and playing with the children. I hope to have several children of my own someday." Veronica looked into Jack's eyes, wondering how he would react to such a statement. No negativity, no hasty retreat, just beautiful dark brown eyes gazing back at her. "Have you ridden a lot of trains?"

"Yes, but not all of them. My goal is to ride every route in the United States, including all the little excursion trains."

"Excursion trains?"

"Yes." Veronica listened to the soothing sound of Jack's voice as he spoke, falling more in love with each passing moment. "There are several just in this area. There is one in Branson called the Branson Scenic Railway that travels through the Ozark foothills. Eureka Springs has one called The Eureka Springs and North Arkansas Railway. In Springdale they have a train called The Arkansas and Missouri Railroad that runs through the Boston Mountains."

"I had no idea there were so many trains in this area. I've never even ridden a train before."

"You would love it!" Jack went on excitedly, "The scenery is fantastic. Some of the railroads also have a dinner train that people can ride..."

The time just seemed to fly by as they continued to talk on into the afternoon sharing their hopes and dreams. Suddenly the boisterous bark of the auctioneer brought Veronica back to reality. "Oh, no!" she exclaimed. "I forgot about the apple pie awards." Veronica tried to stand, but her ankle had become more swollen as the hours had passed.

Jack picked her up. "You know if we are going to get married, I need to try out some of this cooking of yours," he teased. Veronica feigned surprise at Jack's remark, but in her heart she knew it was meant to be.

Jack carried her over to the makeshift aluminum bleachers near the auctioneer stand. The auctioneer started by announcing the third place winners in each age category followed by second place and then first place winners auctioning off the pies as he went. Veronica waited anxiously as the names were called out, hoping her name would be next. But it didn't happen. When the last of the prizes were awarded they began auctioning off the non-winning pies. Veronica tried not to look too disappointed.

"Don't worry," Jack whispered to her grinning from ear to ear. "I'll eat it no matter what it tastes like."

"Hey, I make great pies!" Veronica retorted.

They waited as pie after pie was auctioned off. Finally the last pie was lifted into the air for all to see. "And the grand prize, Top of the Crust Award, goes to...Veronica."

Veronica gasped. "I forgot about the grand prize! I can't believe it."

The auctioneer began the bidding. Jack raised his hand high in the air to place the first bid then quickly pulled it down again.

"What happened?" He turned toward Veronica. "I thought they started the bidding on the pies at ten dollars."

Veronica laughed. "Not the Top of the Crust Pie. The

bidding for it starts at one hundred dollars." The worried expression on Jack's face made her laugh. "Don't worry. I'll make a deal with you. You take me on that Branson dinner train you were telling me about and I'll make you your own pie."

Jack almost looked relieved. The bidding was now well over three hundred dollars and was still rising. He grabbed her hand and shook it. "It's a deal!"

It was a whirlwind romance and by Thanksgiving they were married. Veronica resigned her job at the nursery in order to move to Springfield. She and Jack bought a little three-bedroom rock house on North National Street with a huge backyard. Jack wanted to build a garden railroad, so a large backyard was essential. To their surprise and delight, the morning after they moved in, they discovered that the house also came with its own little kitten. A beautiful little yellow and white fur ball that sat at the front door pleading to come in out of the cold.

Before the years end they were expecting their first child. Veronica had planned to look for a job in Springfield after the move, but when she discovered she was with child she decided it might be better to wait.

She and Jack couldn't have been happier with the news. They both wanted children and this was a dream come true. They spent hour upon hour cuddled up in front of the fireplace petting their newly acquired kitten, Love, and talking about baby names for their future child. It was wonderful to just sit in the warmth of the fire and dream about their future family. She hoped for a boy, he hoped for a girl. Veronica's aunt, Sally, had even promised to help her learn how to crochet so that she could make her precious little one a baby afghan.

It was just last Thursday that Veronica and Sally had gone to the craft store and spent hours upon hours shopping for just the right yarns for the baby afghan. Veronica was a little overwhelmed by all the colors and yarn choices available. Her favorites were the new colors of baby yarns from Red Heart. Veronica had never particularly cared for pastels, but when Aunt Sally showed her Red Hearts new line of Soft Baby colors she thought they were just perfect; sky blue, lime, bright pink, and lilac would make beautiful baby blankets. She also purchased several skeins of new mint twinkle and white.

Veronica remembered Sally laughing at her as she tried to hold on to the numerous skeins of yarn in her arms. "You know you are purchasing way too much yarn," Sally remarked.

"I don't care." Veronica chuckled. "I want everything to be just perfect for my first child. Besides, the colors are beautiful and since I don't know if it will be a boy or a girl, I have to make a blanket for both sexes."

"Two blankets! But you don't even know how to crochet yet," Sally replied. "What if you don't like it?"

"Well, I can always use the yarn for knitting. Remember, Grandma taught me how to knit when I was a little girl. I haven't done it in a long time, but I think I still remember how. Don't worry, Auntie. The yarn will not go to waste. Come on. I want everything new and perfect. I still need lots of supplies."

"Well, first you had better get a cart!" Sally exclaimed, as Veronica began losing control of the skeins in her arms.

A set of Quicksilver in-line crochet hooks, a new pair of scissors, ruler, calculator, steel yarn needle, and even a diary to track her progress along with a new fancy purple ink pen were added to Veronica's shopping cart full of yarn.

Veronica looked down at the cart and noticed that the contents were brimming over the top. "Did I put all of that in the basket?"

Sally grinned sheepishly. "Well, most of it. When we were walking down the yarn aisle several skeins of Naturally

Caron Country yarn started screaming at me to take them home."

"Huh?"

"Forget it. Someday you will understand what I mean." Sally laughed.

Veronica didn't think she would ever understand that one, "yarn screaming"? She decided to change the subject. "Do they have special bags to put crochet things in?"

"Yes, and you are definitely going to need one."

Sally and Veronica headed down the bag aisle. There were bags of every kind, but Veronica knew she had found the perfect bag when she spotted the little kitten peering up at her from the face of a black canvas bag. Veronica thought it looked just like her kitten, Love, and was sold.

That very afternoon Veronica had her first crochet lesson. She carefully took her size "H" crochet hook out of its plastic wrapper.

"So, which color do you want to start with?" Sally had asked.

Veronica shifted through the colors, "I think I'll start with the lilac. That can be for a boy or a girl. Do you think that is a good idea?"

"I think that is a great idea," Sally replied. "But Veronica, you do realize you are not making a baby afghan today. This is just a lesson. I am going to show you how to make a chain and how to work single crochet stitches. The afghan will come later. Today we are just making a little square."

Veronica pouted. "I'm putting the cart before the horse again, huh, Auntie."

Sally leaned over and gave her a motherly hug then the lesson began.

She showed Veronica how to pull the tail out of the left end of the skein so that the yarn would pull smoothly out of the right end.

"The important thing to remember is to keep the yarn loose enough that you can work with it easily. Normally, I would start teaching someone to crochet using a worsted weight yarn. But, knowing you were interested in making a baby blanket, we'll try it with the baby yarn."

"What's the difference?" Veronica asked.

"It is just a difference in the thickness of the yarn. If you were using a worsted weight yarn you would use a larger hook, probably a size 'I' hook or a size 'J' hook. The larger hook and thicker yarn would make the project go faster." Veronica looked confused so Sally went on to explain. "It helps keep beginners from getting discouraged because they can see a finished project sooner. It is also helpful because one can see the stitches easier."

Veronica began fidgeting with the lilac yarn, for the first time realizing how thin it truly was. "Auntie, you are making me nervous. Should I take all this baby yarn back and start over?"

"No, no," Sally assured her. "You already know how to knit so you have worked with yarn before. I really don't think you will have any problem with this. But if it becomes a problem I'll bring some worsted weight yarn over next week for you to practice with."

Veronica's optimism was quickly returning. "Ok, what do I do first?"

"Since you are right handed, pick up the hook with your right hand. Hold it in whichever way feels comfortable to you. Some people hold it like a knife, some hold it like a pencil and some people even hold it like a chopstick. It really doesn't matter."

Veronica tried out the various positions. "I think I like holding it like a pencil."

"That's fine. Now hold the yarn in your left hand."

The lesson continued for over two hours. Veronica had a wonderful time. She learned to make a chain and then how to work rows of single crochet stitches. It was a little hard at first because she kept making the stitches too tight, but she quickly started to catch on and the more she practiced the more even her stitches became.

That night she had shown Jack the little practice square she had made. He was so proud of her. They had sat by the fireplace till two the next morning. It was just so unbelievable that they were soon to become parents.

But all their dreams had ended just a few short hours ago.

The miscarriage was totally unexpected. Veronica didn't want to think about the details. She couldn't remember half of them and what she could remember was just too painful. Jack had been at St. John's hospital with her for the past sixteen hours. She had finally convinced him to go home and get some rest. But she couldn't rest. She couldn't stop thinking about her baby, her little baby, just fourteen weeks old. How she wanted to stop thinking, wanted the pain to end. She would be leaving the hospital in just a few short hours. How could she face the newly decorated nursery? How could she face the next few days?

One

Two months had passed since the funeral. Veronica knew her little angel was in heaven. The thought of this made her feel slightly better, but there was still such emptiness inside. She needed to talk, needed someone other than Jack. Jack was wonderful, but he was going through the same pain she was. She needed someone who could...

Veronica's thoughts were suddenly interrupted by the loud music coming from her cell phone.

"Hello," Veronica spoke into the phone.

"Hi," Aunt Sally's cheerful voice came from the other end. "I have been thinking. I know you are going through a rough time right now. Listen, I know this might sound strange to you. But many people consider crochet very therapeutic. The repetitive motion of the crochet hook can be very relaxing, and I was just thinking, well, just wondering, if maybe you would like to continue with the crochet lessons?"

There was silence on the phone. Veronica loved her aunt, but this was ridiculous. How could she even think about learning to crochet after she had just lost her baby?

Sally continued, "I know what you are thinking, but I really think this would help you get through this time in your life. Remember the little crocheted baby blanket that the hospital gave you when you and Jack decided to have the funeral? That came from an organization called TLC for Angels. Crocheters from all over donate preemie afghans, bereavement gowns, caps, booties, and mittens for these precious little ones. You know, dear, the best way to help yourself is to help someone else."

"Yes, I know that is true, Auntie, but I just don't know."

"I'll tell you what, let's meet at Panera Bread around eight tomorrow morning. Bring your bag of supplies and if you don't feel like crocheting after you get there, we'll just talk and have some hot chocolate. Ok?"

Veronica was hesitant, but finally replied, "Ok, I'll see you then. Bye, Auntie."

Veronica slowly closed the cell phone. She still wasn't too sure about the crochet lesson, but she welcomed the opportunity to sit and talk with her aunt.

Jack dropped Veronica off at the bread shop the next morning. He sweetly kissed her goodbye then headed off to work.

Veronica could smell the espresso as she walked into the restaurant, crochet bag in tow. Aunt Sally, notoriously known for being early, was already seated at one of the solid wood, round, pub tables. Veronica thought she looked like a little kitten the way she was perched up on the bar stool. She never understood why someone as short as her aunt always wanted to sit at such a high table.

"Hi," Sally greeted her.

Veronica placed her bag on the table and sat down. "Hi. Sorry I'm late."

"No, no, you're right on time. I was early. Do you want to go ahead and get in line?"

"No. Let's wait awhile. The line is practically out the door," Veronica replied motioning toward the crowd of people.

"Well, that leaves talking or crocheting." Sally smiled.

"Believe it or not, I think I want to crochet. I've been thinking about what you said, and you are right. I need to get my mind off myself for a while and focus on someone else." Veronica took a deep breath. "Do you think you could teach me to crochet well enough that I could maybe someday donate some afghans to that charity you were telling me about?"

Sally placed her hand lovingly on top of Veronica's. "TLC for Angels?"

"Yes, TLC for Angels. That was so sweet of them to give me that little blanket for my baby. It meant so much to me. I'd really like to give back to someone else in return." Veronica's eyes began welling up as she spoke.

"Well, of course you can," Sally consoled her. "I'm not sure about the sizes for preemies or the requirements for donating, but I can get on the Internet this afternoon and look it up. I marked their home page in my favorites list so it will be easy to find out."

Veronica wiped her eyes with the back of her hand. "Thanks, Auntie, I really appreciate it."

"Now that we have that settled, let's go get in line for some of those bagels you are always telling me about. The smell is driving me crazy and I'm starving," Sally said as she began descending from her chair.

As they stood in line Veronica couldn't help but notice the floor tiles beneath her feet. "Auntie, isn't that a pretty checked pattern," Veronica said pointing to the floor. "I just love the simplicity of it."

Sally's focus shifted down to the floor, "Yes, it is beautiful."

"Do you think maybe I could make an afghan with that pattern? Would it..."

"Wait a minute," Sally interrupted. "You are starting to sound like a designer and you have only had one lesson!"

"I'm sorry, Auntie. I just thought it was pretty." Veronica turned away from her aunt.

"Hey," Sally said as she placed her hands on Veronica's shoulders, "I was just teasing you. Yes, that floor pattern could easily be made into an afghan. It is just a check pattern with solid blocks of alternating color, that are outlined by a third color."

Veronica turned back around. She wished she could stop being so emotional. Everyday life just seemed so hard since she lost the baby.

Sally continued, "What two colors do you think you would like to use?"

Veronica regained her composure. "I don't know for sure. When we get back to the table I'll take a better look at the yarns I brought. Maybe if I place the yarns on the table in that same floor pattern it will help me decide."

"Sounds like a great idea," Sally said cheerfully.

"Can I get anything for you Ma'am?" a male voice came from behind the counter.

They had finally reached the front of the line. Veronica was embarrassed. She and Sally had been so engrossed in their conversation that she had completely forgotten to look up at the menus hanging from the wall. Oh well, she thought, it didn't really matter. She always ordered basically the same thing every time she came anyway, bagels and cream cheese.

Veronica quickly glanced over the available bagels, Cinnamon Crunch, Asiago Cheese, French Toast, Blueberry, Cinnamon Raisin, Whole Grain, Sesame, Passion Fruit, Dutch Apple Raisin, Choc-o-nut, Plain and even one called Everything. "I'll have a Dutch apple raisin bagel with honey walnut cream cheese and a cup of hot chocolate."

"That sounds good," Sally spoke up. "I'll have the same."

They received and paid for their breakfast both agreeing that they would never tell anyone what they had consumed. After all, this was a girl's morning out. Forget the calories.

They took their pseudo woven, black, plastic trays and headed toward the toasters. Once the bagels were lightly browned they went back to the table to consume their feast, both rather surprised that the table was still available.

The bagel was warm and comforting. It was covered with clumps of brown sugar topping and full of raisins. The addition of the honey walnut cream cheese made it just perfect. The hot chocolate was frothy and delicious. It came with mounds of whipped cream piled on top and a drizzle of chocolate sauce.

The feast was consumed in silence, each enjoying the delicacies too much to talk.

"That was fantastic," Sally finally broke the silence as she gently patted the last of the hot chocolate off her lips.

"Yes. It was," Veronica replied as she finished up the last bite.

"Too stuffed to work?" Sally jested.

"Oh, no, the sugar just kicked in and I'm raring to go." Veronica began wiping the crumbs up off the table while Sally put up the trays.

When Sally returned she asked, "Did you decide on the colors you want to use for your floor tile afghan?"

Veronica grinned as she dumped her canvas kitten bag full of yarn onto the newly cleaned table. She carefully manipulated the colors placing them alternately on the table to match the color combination of the floor tiles. "I think I like sky blue and lime. What do you think, Auntie?"

"Hey, you're the designer here, not me." Sally grinned. "Now I have a big surprise for you."

"What's that?" Veronica asked.

"You already know how to make the afghan."

"Huh? I've only had one lesson and all I made was a little sample square."

"That's true." Sally went on to explain, "Veronica, look at the floor tiles again. Don't you see? They are just solid color squares that are attached together."

Veronica looked down at the floor a moment then looked back up at her aunt. "Yes, you're right, Auntie!" Veronica squealed with delight. "I never thought of that." Veronica looked back down at the floor. "But what about the black lines that connect them?"

"Well, after you get lots and lots of little squares

crocheted, you simply take a third color of yarn and attach them together. But the first thing you have to do is make the little squares."

"How many should I make?" Veronica asked enthusiastically as the excitement grew inside her.

"Since you are wanting to donate it to TLC for Angels, we'll need to find out what size they want the finished afghan to be."

"Hi," the baritone voice came from behind Veronica. Veronica turned around and smiled at Jack. "I'm on a coffee break. Thought I would come and join my two favorite girls."

"Guess what!" Veronica was so excited she could hardly contain her enthusiasm. "I'm designing a crocheted baby afghan."

"What?" Jack exclaimed as he sat down to drink his steaming coffee. "After two lessons?"

Veronica couldn't help giggling. "Well, actually, I've only had one lesson. We haven't got to the second one yet."

"Oh, yes, we have." Sally smiled then once again descended the chair. "That was your designing lesson. Listen, since Jack is on a break and can give you a lift home, I'm going to head back to Marionville and look up that information for you. I know you are anxious to get started and there is no point in your making a bunch of squares and then finding out they're the wrong size."

"Ok, Auntie. Thank you so much."

Sally leaned over, gave Veronica a hug and softly whispered in her ear, "It's so good to see you smile again. You are going to be just fine."

"Are you ready?" Jack asked as he swallowed the last of his coffee.

"Yes. Just let me gather all my supplies up." Veronica began stuffing the skeins of yarn back in her yarn bag then got down from the table. As she and Jack were headed out the door, Veronica noticed the walls. Such an interesting pattern she thought. She would have to ask her aunt about it the next time they came.

Veronica turned to Jack, "Do you have time to stop by the pet store? I think Love is in need of more kitten food."

"Of course, milady, you have time for anything you want when you own the store," Jack teased her.

Jack's dream, of owning his own train shop, had finally come true just a few short weeks earlier. The owner of the train shop had suddenly decided to retire. He had told Jack he was going to put the shop up for sale, but was offering Jack first option. Jack jumped at the chance. Train Land, as it was now called, sat on the corner of one of the main intersections in town. A perfect location, the store always seemed to have a steady flow of costumers. Jack was thankful that little boys never quite grew up.

Once at home, Veronica dumped the contents of her yarn bag out on the dining room table and sat down. She began studying the little square she had made in her first lesson, trying to remember how she did it. Love jumped up on the table to help. Before she could have time to remove him, the musical tones from her cell phone began to ring out.

Two

"Hello," Veronica spoke into the phone.

"Hi," came Sally's voice from the other end. "I tried to look up that size information for you, but I didn't really see anything on their Internet site. I guess they accept all sizes. So, I called St. John's hospital and asked what size blanket they prefer for a preemie baby. The nurse on the phone said that they usually liked them to be twelve to fifteen inches square for a preemie three pounds or less and twenty to twenty-five inches square for a preemie four pounds or more."

"I want to do the three pound or less size since that's what my little one was," Veronica explained.

"Well, that's kind of what I thought you would say. Do you still have that little sample square that you made?"

"Yes."

"Go get your sample square and ruler."

"Ok," Veronica said as she walked toward the table to retrieve the requested items. "I have them."

"Good. Take your ruler and measure how big your square is."

Veronica quickly did as she was told, then reported her results. "It's about three inches wide."

"Hmm, let's see. If you make each square two to two and a half inches wide by two and a half inches tall then you should come out about right. You made your sample square

26

with ten stitches. Get out your crochet diary and write this down."

Veronica opened her diary. "Ok, Auntie. I'm ready," she replied, pen poised in hand.

"Chain nine, single crochct in the back ridge of the second chain from the hook, like I showed you, then single crochet in the back ridge of each of the next seven chains. You will have eight single crochet stitches. Turn your work and chain one, then single crochet in each stitch back across. Keep working rows of single crochet stitches until your piece is two and a half inches tall."

"How many rows do you think that will be?" Veronica asked as she continued to write down the directions.

"Probably about nine rows. But don't worry about how many rows it takes. When you have two and a half inches, cut the yarn leaving about a six inch tail."

"How many of these squares should I make?"

"You will need twenty-five squares total. Make thirteen of one color and twelve with the other color. I'll tell you what, make thirteen squares with one color and then give me a call. We'll arrange to meet again so I can check your work and make sure everything is ok."

Veronica finished up her notes then set her pen down. "Sounds great, Auntie, I'll call you soon."

"I'm sure you will." Sally chuckled. "If you run into any problems let me know. Don't forget, count your stitches."

"I won't forget. Bye, Auntie." Veronica quickly hung up the phone. She couldn't wait to get started on her very first project. Veronica picked up the sky blue yarn, her size "H" crochet hook, diary, ruler and a pair of scissors then sat down on the loveseat to work. She began working the first square concentrating on every stitch. She soon had the square finished and quickly started the second square. As she worked she began to think about the baby she had lost and about the beautiful little blanket she had received from the TLC for Angels group.

Veronica began crying softly as she continued thinking about her child. She put her work down and went to get a wet cloth to wipe her face. As she patted her face with the dampened cloth another thought occurred to her. She was trying to make a preemie blanket for another precious little one, a little boy or girl, who hadn't even been born yet. The tears began to flow harder as the thoughts kept rushing through her head.

Love rubbed up against Veronica's legs. He always seemed to know when she was sad. She picked up the purring bundle and then began to ponder. If she didn't make the preemie blanket, then no preemie baby would be born. That was silly. Of course preemie infants would still be born. If she weren't working on a baby blanket she wouldn't be standing there crying and missing her own baby. That was even crazier. She would always miss her precious little one. A part of her heart would always ache for her child. Veronica continued to pet Love as the thoughts swirled through her head.

After a few more minutes, she carried Love into the bedroom and set him down on the bed. He immediately curled up on her pillow and went to sleep. She then went back to the loveseat and picked up her work. Veronica had made her decision. She didn't know if she would ever be able to crochet well enough to make preemie baby blankets, but if God granted her the ability to make them, she was going to do it.

Veronica began to crochet again, and as she did, she began to pray for the precious little one that would receive her gift.

A couple of hours later Veronica looked down at her pile of little squares and began to count them. There were thirteen of them. She couldn't believe it. Had she actually crocheted thirteen squares?

Veronica was so excited she immediately picked up the cell phone to call her aunt back.

Sally answered, "Hello."

"Hi, Auntie," Veronica said excitedly.

"Oh, hi, Veronica," Sally replied cheerfully. "Did you run into a problem with your crocheting?"

"No, Auntie. I just called to tell you I was finished." Veronica began stacking the squares in little groups as she spoke.

"Finished! Are you kidding? I knew you would catch on quickly, but I didn't think you would catch on that quickly. This is wonderful! I'll tell you what, you invite me over tonight for some of that world renowned cooking Jack is always bragging about and I'll check your squares."

"That's a deal, Auntie. See you about seven. Bye for now." Veronica closed her cell phone and placed it down on the table.

World-renowned cooking was really more of a family joke. Veronica couldn't cook. She was great at making pies and desserts, but had never learned how to cook real food. Veronica went into the kitchen to see what she could come up with. She turned on the oven to preheat then got out the flour and butter to make the dough for a piecrust. She carefully cut the butter into the flour then added just enough water to make a perfect crust.

After the dough was rolled out and placed in the pie pan she started preparing the filling. Tonight it was going to be pecan pie. She mixed sugar, melted butter, eggs, vanilla and light corn syrup together then carefully poured the mixture into the pie shell. Her secret for a perfect pecan pie was adding the pecans after the filling was already placed in the shell. Veronica opened the bag of pecan halves and placed them, one by one, with the pretty side of the pecan facing up, on top of the filling until there was a complete layer of pecans floating on top. She then gave each pecan a gentle push downward so that the sugary filling washed over the top of the pecans. Veronica placed her creation into the preheated oven then turned her attention to the rest of the meal.

She looked carefully through the pantry trying her best to come up with something that not only everyone would like, but also something that would be edible after she finished trying to cook it. After pondering the many possibilities she decided that a complete Chinese dinner would be just perfect; wonton soup, moo goo gai pan, chicken fried rice, sweet and sour chicken, stir fry vegetables, and egg rolls to top it off. One quick phone call later and Chinese delivery was on its way. Dinner completed.

Supper was delicious, but the pecan pie and coffee were the hit of the meal.

After consuming the last bite Sally teased Veronica, "You're really trying to bribe me, aren't you?"

"Well, you are my favorite aunt." Veronica pushed her chair back, stood up and began clearing the dishes.

"I'm your only aunt," Sally retorted as she too began clearing the table.

Veronica stopped what she was doing and looked at her aunt, then with complete sincerity replied, "You are still my favorite."

Once the dishes were washed Veronica and Sally sat down on the loveseat for a crocheting lesson. Jack quickly dismissed himself to go test out the new "N" gauge train set he had brought home from work. He headed toward his, at home, office with Love following close behind.

Veronica showed Sally the squares. "These are wonderful!" Sally exclaimed. "Do you want to make the lime squares exactly like them, or would you like to do a different stitch?"

"I'd like to try something different. I think I pretty well know the single crochet stitch."

"Well, this next stitch is actually still a single crochet stitch. The only difference is where it is worked. Go ahead and make your chain nine. Now, instead of working in the back ridge as before, turn it so that it looks like a chain on top." Veronica quickly did as she was instructed. "Great.

Now, for the first stitch, work your single crochet in the two loops of the second chain from the hook."

"Like this?" Veronica asked as she inserted the hook through the chain.

"Yes. Now, single crochet in the front loop of the next chain, then single crochet in the back loop of the next chain. Repeat those two stitches across the row till there is one chain left, then single crochet in both loops of the last chain and you will have your first row of eight stitches."

"Ok, now what?" Veronica asked when she finished her last stitch.

"Turn your work and chain one," Sally instructed. "Then work your first single crochet in both loops of the first stitch. Single crochet in the front loop of the next stitch, then single crochet in the back loop of the next stitch. Keep repeating that across the row, working in the front loop and then working in the back loop. When you get to the last stitch, single crochet in both loops."

"Is this right?" Veronica asked. She held up her work to show Sally the completed row.

"Yes, you have it!" Sally congratulated her. Veronica was absorbing the information as if she had been crocheting all her life. "Just keep repeating that row until your square is two and a half inches tall."

Veronica quickly finished her square then cut the yarn.

Sally continued the lesson, "Make eleven more lime squares just like that one. When you get finished, tuck in all your yarn ends like this." Sally picked up the newly purchased yarn needle and showed Veronica how to weave in the ends on the wrong side. "The important thing is not to weave them in a straight line. You need to weave the ends in as crooked a line as possible going in one direction, then turn and weave them in a crooked line going in the opposite direction. If you want to make sure they are extremely secure, you can turn and weave them in a crooked line going back in the original direction again."

"That will take forever!" Veronica exclaimed.

"Not forever, dear." Sally smiled.

Veronica's mind began to scramble for a simpler way out. "Couldn't I just tie the ends into a knot?"

"No." Sally shook her head. "This is very important. You should never put a knot in your crochet work. Over time the knot will inevitably work its way out and you will have a big hole in your project. You want to always weave the ends in."

"Ok," Veronica sighed. "But I still think it would be faster the other way."

"Faster isn't always better, my dear." Sally smiled at her niece then continued the lesson. "After you weave in all the yarn ends, you need to work the edging. Attach the white yarn in the top right corner of the square like this." Sally attached the yarn then handed the square back to Veronica. "Ok, Veronica, chain one, then single crochet in the corner. Work six more single crochet stitches evenly spaced across to the next corner. In that corner work a single crochet stitch, then chain one, then work another single crochet stitch all in the same space. You repeat that for each side, six single crochet stitches evenly spaced across and then a single crochet, chain one, single crochet in the corner, until you get back around to the first corner." Veronica diligently worked the stitches just as she was told.

"Now, work a single crochet stitch in the same space as the first white single crochet stitch you made and cut your yarn leaving a ten inch tail."

Veronica cut the yarn, but looked rather concerned. "There is a gap between the first and last stitch. Shouldn't they be connected in some kind of way?"

"Yes," Sally assured her. "You are going to connect them now. Pull the loop on the hook up until the tail pops through the top two loops of the last stitch. Now, thread the tail through your yarn needle. Do you see where the top two loops of the last stitch are?"

"Yes," Veronica replied.

"Ok, remember where they are. Run the yarn needle from front to back under the top two loops of the first white stitch made, then run the yarn needle from top to bottom between the top two loops of the last stitch. This creates the last corner, chain one, and connects the last stitch to the first stitch at the same time."

Veronica stared at her finished square. "That's amazing! I can't even tell where the edging was joined!"

Sally laughed. "That's the whole idea."

While Veronica scribbled down notes in her diary Sally crocheted the edging on another square then she continued. "Once you have the white edgings on all the squares, lay the squares out on the table in the order you want to sew them together. Hold two squares together with the right sides facing, take the tail and whip stitch the squares together like this." Sally quickly sewed the two squares together. "You will sew five sets of five squares together so that you have five columns. Then, using additional yarn, you will sew the five columns together in the same way. Then, you weave in all the new yarn ends."

Veronica's eyes were beginning to glaze over. "I think I am getting a little overwhelmed."

"Ok." Sally smiled. "We'll stop there. Just do as much as you can. If you have any problems, let me know. When you get all of this finished, I will show you how to add the final edging."

"You mean that's not the end?" Veronica was looking a little panicky.

"I'm sorry, Veronica, I didn't mean to scare you. Actually, all you do after you have all the squares sewn together, is simply work an edging around the entire blanket just like you did around the little squares."

Veronica looked completely perplexed. Sally leaned over and gave her a hug. "Don't worry, I have some time left, I'll sit here and watch you for awhile. You can do this. Look at how much you have done already."

Veronica breathed a sigh of relief. She and Sally worked and talked for a couple more hours. Veronica told Sally all about the upcoming neighborhood picnic and dance planned for Saturday evening in the park. She and Jack were both looking forward to the event. They had not met many of the neighbors and were excited about the possibility of making new friends. Veronica's only concern was what to bring. Everyone was supposed to bring a homemade something to contribute to the covered dish, picnic style meal.

Three

$\longrightarrow\!\blacklozenge\!\longleftarrow$

Early Saturday morning Jack went out to mow the grass. He returned a few minutes later holding a handful of purple berries. "Milady, your problem is solved."

"What are you talking about?" Veronica asked, looking up from the cookbook she was reading.

"These," he said showing her the berries. "When I went out to mow I discovered a patch of wild dewberries near the fence. They would make a great pie for the neighborhood picnic."

"Are they sweet?" Veronica asked, looking a little skeptical.

"Yes, they're wonderful! Try one." Veronica bit into the purple berry. Juicy and sweet, perfect for a pie. She happily set the cookbook aside and followed Jack out into the yard. They spent the next hour or so picking dewberries, more than enough for a couple of pies.

At five that afternoon they gathered up the freshly baked pies, a couple of lawn chairs and headed off to the park. Upon arrival they found that approximately twenty wooden picnic tables had been reserved for the occasion. One of the tables was already covered with fried chicken, potato salad, baked beans, coleslaw, deviled eggs and the makings for hamburgers and hotdogs, all in protective containers. Several of the men were busily preparing to cook meat on the park grills. Another table held containers of iced tea, coffee, bottled water and desserts.

Veronica took her pies to the dessert table then she and Jack headed over to one of the tables sitting under the large oak trees. It was a warm, humid day, but there was a nice breeze blowing and the trees provided just the right amount of shade from the sun. It was going to be a perfect picnic.

They had only been sitting for a few minutes when the music began. The Ozark Mountain Men, a group of seven musicians, five guitar players and two fiddle players, who played hillbilly style country music. The music was beautiful and definitely added a festive spirit to the occasion.

More people arrived and the various activities began. Several people had brought checkers, croquet sets, volleyballs, and a variety of other games. Some of the guests, to Veronica's surprise and delight had brought their crocheting, knitting, embroidery, needlepoint and various other crafts. Amongst all the activity, a precocious little curly haired boy, about six years old, was running about passing out numbers for door prizes.

Veronica turned to Jack, "I didn't know all of this would be going on. Would you mind if I went home and got my crochet work and joined the ladies?"

"You mean ladies and gentlemen, don't you?" Jack corrected.

Veronica looked back over at the group of crafters and quickly realized her mistake. There were as many men as there were women. She spotted one young man who was knitting, two who were doing needlepoint, one gentleman was weaving baskets, several were carving wood and a few were painting.

"Sure, go get your crochet." Jack grinned. "I was hoping to have a chance to play a little basketball anyway."

Jack loved playing basketball. Veronica enjoyed the game as well. She and Jack had even played a few times, but she really preferred watching more than playing. "It's a deal."

Veronica went to retrieve her crochet and Jack headed off to the basketball court.

It wasn't a long walk home and Veronica soon returned with her kitty cat bag in tow. She watched Jack make a few baskets then went toward the group of people working on crafts.

"Pull up a chair and join us," a slender young lady with shoulder length, mousy brown hair called out to her.

Veronica grabbed her burgundy colored, macramé lawn chair, with a picture of a little white squirrel woven into the back, and headed in the direction of the voice.

"Hi, I'm Katy. You're, Veronica, aren't you? I've seen you walking in the neighborhood." Katy pointed at Veronica's yarn bag, "Are you a crocheter or a knitter?"

"Hi, yes, I'm Veronica. I learned to knit when I was little, but I'm trying to learn how to crochet now. Which do you do?"

"Oh, I'm definitely a crocheter."

A tall red headed woman began to laugh, "Katy can't do anything that requires her to use two hands at the same time. Hi, I'm Audra. It's nice to have you join us." Audra reached out her hand to greet Veronica.

Katy interrupted, "If we are going to tell tales, do you want to explain why you crochet instead of doing embroidery work, or should I?"

Both women started to laugh again, then Audra began to confess, "I'm a nurse, but I can't stand needles. I admit it. Just don't tell my boss!"

"Audra does beautiful crochet work. She mainly works with thread. I work with yarn. What is your preference?" Katy asked.

"Well, I am just starting to learn how to crochet. The only thing I have used so far is baby yarn."

"You learned with baby yarn?" Katy asked. "That's impressive. Most people learn using worsted weight." Katy began adding stitches to the deep blue blanket in her lap, never looking down.

"Yes, I was told that, after I had already purchased a shopping cart full of baby yarn," Veronica admitted.

"So, what have you made so far?" Audra asked.

"I've been working on a preemie baby blanket. It's almost finished. I really don't know very much about crochet. I just learned to single crochet recently. This is my first project."

"Would you like us to show you some other stitches?" Audra asked.

"Oh, that would be wonderful!"

Katy and Audra helped Veronica with her stitches until everyone was called to eat. "Thank you so much! I really appreciate all of the help," Veronica said as she stood up.

"It was our pleasure," Katy replied gathering her supplies back into her yarn bag. "If you're interested, several of us meet on Thursday afternoons around four at the yarn shop in The Village. Sometimes we have a formal class with a teacher. Other times we just work on our own projects. But we always have a nice time."

"That would be wonderful. Thank you for telling me."

Veronica was so excited she practically floated back to the table. Not only had she learned some new stitches, she also felt like she had made some new friends. As she and Jack stood in line to get their food she told him all about it. He was excited as well. He had made several new friends and had a wonderful time playing basketball, of course being on the winning team certainly helped.

The food was delicious. After most were finished eating, a man stood up and announced that it was time for the door prizes. Veronica had been so excited about everything that she had forgotten all about the door prizes. She quickly retrieved her number from her pocket. Number 1596351134.

The man began calling out the numbers. Being a neighborhood picnic, all of the prizes were things people would use inside their homes or out in their yards. The prizes were quickly being handed out; rake, shovel, flower seed kit, electric blender, coffee maker, camera, houseplant. Then the number 1134 was called out.

"Hey, you won!" Jack exclaimed.

Veronica stood up with her winning ticket. The little boy who had been giving out numbers earlier ran up to her and handed her a package. "What did you win?" Jack asked.

"I don't know." Veronica quickly tore into the package. She looked up at Jack with a big smile on her face.

"Well, what is it? What did you win?" he asked inquisitively.

"A crochet kit!"

"You're kidding," he said in disbelief.

"No, look, it's a crochet kit. It has all the yarn, the hook, the instructions, everything needed to make this afghan in the photo!"

Jack gave her a hug. "That is wonderful! I am so happy for you."

After the last of the door prizes were handed out the musicians once again fired up their instruments and the dancing began. Veronica and Jack danced for several hours under the moonlight before heading back home.

Veronica finished her preemie baby afghan the following afternoon. It meant so much to her to be able to make the little afghan. The squares didn't quite lay flat like she thought they would, but she thought the puffiness gave the afghan a cute look. It also didn't form a perfect square. The afghan was longer than it was wide. She figured that would be ok though. Most blankets were not really square. She hoped the TLC for Angels' group would accept her contribution.

Veronica was anxious to get started on her next project. She quickly opened her crochet kit that she had won the night before. The yarn was beautiful. She grabbed the instructions and started trying to read them. They looked like they were written in some kind of foreign language; ch

4, dc in 4th ch from hook 7 times, join in 4th ch of beg ch 4. What was that supposed to mean? She decided to set that aside until her aunt or someone could translate it into English.

She thought about making another preemie baby afghan like the one she had just made, but although she loved the crocheting part, she didn't especially like sewing all the little squares together and she was especially not fond of all those yarn ends. Then another thought came to her, all she had to do was just make one giant square. She could even use some of the stitches that Katy and Audra had shown her the night before.

Veronica grabbed her hook and yarn and began to work.

Four

"Hi, Aunt Sally!" Veronica called out as she entered the bread shop. She had called Sally up the night before and had asked Sally to meet her at nine the next morning. There was no mention of the baby afghans on the phone. Veronica wanted it to be a surprise.

"Hi, how are you doing?" Sally returned the greeting. "Have you worked anymore on the baby afghan?"

Veronica was grinning from ear to ear as she joined her aunt at the pub table. Once she sat down, she carefully reached into her bag and pulled out not one but three baby blankets.

"What's this?" Sally asked.

"Well, you know that neighborhood picnic that I told you about? Well, when Jack and I went to it I met two very nice ladies, Audra and Katy. They showed me how to do some more stitches. After I finished the first blanket, I used some of the stitches they taught me and made two more blankets. What do you think?"

"They're beautiful!" Sally picked up the bright pink blanket and unfolded it. "I don't think I have ever seen this stitch before." She began to examine the stitch more closely. "Do you know what they called it?"

"Let me think. I did the new mint twinkle one in something called a shell stitch. I remember that one because I thought the new mint twinkle yarn looked kind of like the water and seashells. The bright pink one, the bright pink one, oh I remember, it was called slip stitch."

"Slip stitch? Are you sure?" Sally stretched the stitches slightly to get a better look at the details.

"Pretty sure, why?"

Sally continued stretching the stitches up and down then sideways. "I know how to do slip stitches and this just doesn't look like a slip stitch. Did you bring some of your yarn with you? Could you show me how you made it?"

"Sure." Veronica pulled a hook, and what was left of the bright pink skein of yarn, out of her kitty cat bag and began showing her aunt how to work the slip stitches.

"All you do is work chains until the piece is the length that you want the blanket to be, then you chain one more time." Veronica chained six to demonstrate. "You put the hook through the back ridge of the second chain from the hook. To work the stitch, you keep the hook facing down and wrap the yarn counterclockwise over the top of the hook and then underneath the hook so that you catch the yarn with the hook, then you pull the yarn through the stitch and the loop on the hook. Keep the hook facing you and turn it counterclockwise so that the hook is now facing up. Then you insert the hook in the back ridge of the next chain." Veronica worked slip stitches in each chain she had created then turned to do the next row. "On all the rest of the rows, you chain one to begin, then you work slip stitches just like on the beginning row except that you insert the hook through the back loop of the stitch, it's the loop that you see on the top."

Sally couldn't help laughing.

"Ok, tell me, what I'm doing wrong."

"You're doing the stitch backwards!"

"I am?"

"Yes. You have your yarn in the front of your work instead of in the back, and you are inserting the hook into the stitch from the back to the front instead of from the front to the back. You're supposed to make a slip stitch the exact same way you make a single crochet stitch."

"You are?"

"Yes." Sally took the hook and yarn from Veronica so that she could show her. "You keep your yarn in the back of your work. Insert the hook from the front to the back through the top loop, which going this direction is the front loop of the stitch. Wrap the yarn around the hook just like you did when you worked the single crochet stitch. Then, instead of just pulling through the stitch, you pull through the stitch and the loop on the hook like this." Veronica watched as Sally worked several rows of slip stitches. When Sally was finished, she handed the swatch back to Veronica.

Veronica carefully examined Sally's work noting the obvious differences between her aunt's work and hers. "You mean I did the whole thing wrong?"

"Not wrong, just different. Actually, I really like it." Sally picked the little pink blanket up and once again began admiring the uniqueness of the stitch. "It's unusual. It has a wonderful texture and is very stretchy. It seems to have a double thickness. It almost looks like the yarn has been woven or braided."

Veronica beamed. "Do you think TLC for Angels will accept it?"

"Yes. I think they will like all of them. Do you want me to send them off for you?" Sally asked as she carefully started folding the little blanket back up.

"Yes, please. I was going to do it myself, but if they turned them down... I don't know. I... I just didn't want to chance it."

Sally reached over and gave Veronica a comforting hug. "Don't worry," she whispered, "they are not going to turn them down. They are beautiful. You did a great job."

"Thank you," Veronica replied taking the words of comfort to heart. Veronica knew her emotions were still as fragile as eggshells and she decided, before she broke down crying in public, that she had better change the subject quickly.

Veronica pulled out of the hug then began speaking a little too excitedly. "Oh, I forgot to tell you, Auntie, I won a crochet kit at the picnic. It's for an afghan. And Katy and Audra said that on Thursday afternoons at four they meet at a yarn shop in The Village and crochet. I'm going to go this afternoon. Would you like to go? I was hoping to get some help deciphering the directions that came with the yarn kit. Did you know that crochet directions are written in some type of code?"

"Yes, I've heard that." Sally laughed. "And yes, I would love to go. You want to meet in front of the yarn shop say around three-thirty so that we can have time to look around before the class starts?"

"Yes, that would be wonderful!" Veronica replied. She had never been in a shop that exclusively sold yarn and yarn supplies before and was anxious to see it.

"Then it's a date," Sally said as she climbed down from her chair. "Now, let's go indulge in another one of those bagels that we had last time."

Five

It was a quaint little shop consisting of one large open room with a little room sectioned off in the back. When Veronica entered she couldn't believe her eyes. Colors came rushing from every direction overwhelming her senses. She had no idea where to look first. Even the furniture and fifties style music added to the picturesque scene.

Directly in front, hanging from the ceiling, was an old wood window frame. The glass had been removed and in its place hung little sample squares of various stitches. An antique looking green table just below the frame held a large display of pattern books. Tall black metal racks flanked the table on both ends. Off white, brown, rust, forest green, deep blue tweed and heather yarns were perfectly displayed on the racks as well as finished garments and craft bags.

To the left, colorful hanks of hand dyed wool yarns hung from wood pegs and bags of un-spun wool and bamboo sat in large wooden baskets. Crochet hooks, knitting needles, and various other supplies filled the wall.

To the right was a large aqua bookcase filled with rustic, multicolored wool yarns. To the side of the case sat an old kitchen chair that showed evidence of having been painted more than once. In its current state, sporting patches of aqua, yellow, red and a little white, it was as colorful as the shawl draped across its back.

Veronica and Sally stood by the door completely mesmerized.

"Hello, welcome to my shop," a friendly woman called from the back of the room as they entered. "Please feel free to look around and make yourself at home. There are drinks and cookies up against the wall to your left. Just help yourself."

They slowly began wandering around the room trying to take it all in. Veronica felt like she had stepped right out of summer and into autumn. Earthy colors were abundant in the shop; dark burgundy, brown, black, gray, green, blue, pumpkin, wheat, and sage were the primary colors to be found. Veronica whispered, "I love the colors, Auntie, autumn has always been my favorite time of year, but shouldn't they have bright summer colors out now?"

"It takes a lot of time to crochet a project. My guess is that they put the autumn colors out in the summer so that people can get started on their autumn sweaters and have them finished in time to wear."

"I hadn't thought of that. I guess people do need to get the yarn and work in advance of the season." Veronica set the burgundy ball that she was fondling down and reached for a hank of multicolored green. "Auntie, what is this?" she asked, handing the yarn to her aunt.

"Says Berroco, Jasper, fine merino wool."

"Auntie, I can read!" Veronica laughed. "I mean how do you crochet with it? It's all twisted up."

"Oh, I see. This is called a hank. You cut the thread holding it together. Then you untwist it so that you have a large ring of yarn. You put the ring on a device called a swift or over the back of a chair. Then you wind the yarn into a ball, either by hand or with a yarn winder." Sally handed the hank back to Veronica. "In old movies, sometimes you will see one person holding a ring of yarn around their two outstretched arms while a second person is winding the yarn into a ball."

"Yes, I've seen that!" Veronica exclaimed as she leaned over to pick up a hank of multicolored black.

"Watch out," Sally grabbed Veronica's arm.

"What's wrong?"

"You were about to fall over the basket."

Veronica looked down at her feet and saw the silver, wire basket piled high with cotton yarn. "This is incredible! How did she ever come up with so many ideas?"

"What do you mean?"

"Look around, haven't you noticed? She has yarn and books in old wash buckets, in an old green feed trough, in a white antique pie cabinet with mesh doors, in bookcases, piled in wicker, wire and apple baskets, in plant holders, in a large black canning pot, on a laundry stand, in sweater hangers, on a set of stairs that lead to nowhere, she even has yarn hung on wood sticks."

Sally looked around again, "I guess I was so absorbed with looking at the yarn I hadn't noticed. You're right. The décor is fascinating. I like the little rugs she has scattered around the room. They give the shop such a nice homey feeling."

Veronica put the hanks of yarn back and picked up a knubby ball of tweed. "I didn't realize there were so many different types and textures of yarn. This is fantastic!"

Veronica and Sally continued their tour of the shop touching everything in sight. Angora, mohair, alpaca, wool, cashmere and silk yarns, as well as yarns made from cotton, linen, milk fiber, bamboo, soy, crab shell, shrimp shell and corn were picked up and admired. "I didn't know they made yarn out of things like corn, bamboo and shrimp shells, did you, Auntie?"

"I've heard of it, but I've never seen it." Sally picked up a pink ball of corn yarn. "This is really amazing." She turned the ball over in her hand then began to laugh.

"What's so funny?" Veronica asked.

"It's called A-MAIZing! Manufactured by SWTC. Do you want to try crocheting with some?"

Veronica looked at Sally in disbelief, "Are you kidding, I want to try all of it!"

"Hi, Veronica, I'm glad you were able to come." Veronica

turned around and saw Katy coming across the room toward her. She and Sally placed the yarns they were holding back in the rack then headed in Katy's direction. "We will just be crocheting today," Katy announced when they met in the middle of the room. "No formal instruction. I just found out that Destiny, the lady who usually teaches the class, is going to be out of town for the next three or four weeks. Did you bring anything to work on?"

"Well, actually, I was hoping to get some help with the afghan kit I won at the picnic. I can't read the instructions."

Katy smiled. "Sure, I'll help you. A lot of people have trouble with the abbreviations at first. I'm sure you will catch on quickly though."

Veronica pointed toward her aunt. "Katy, this is my, Aunt Sally. She likes to crochet too."

Katy shook Sally's hand. "Welcome, Aunt Sally. I'm sure you will have fun also. We are a pretty informal group."

"Thank you," Sally replied. "This looks like it will be a lot of fun. I am so impressed already with all of these yarns!"

"Yes, Vashti always keeps a large variety of yarns in the shop. Did you see the new corn yarns?"

"Yes, we were just admiring those."

"We are about to begin ladies," Vashti's voice sang out. "If everyone will go ahead and take their seats, we will get started."

"Which table are we supposed to sit at?" Veronica asked, noticing the three separate wood tables.

"Follow me. You can sit anywhere, but crocheters generally sit together at the back table. People who knit and embroider generally use the other two tables." Veronica and Sally followed Katy toward the back of the shop. Audra, who was already seated, waved them over to the empty chairs beside her.

After everyone was introduced to one another, it was announced that class was going to be a question and answer session for anyone who was having problems.

Everyone quickly began digging into the crochet bags they had brought. Veronica watched as a dark haired lady, who had introduced herself as Jenny, pulled out a light blue cashmere sweater she was crocheting. Chrissy, who had been introduced as Jenny's little sister, pulled out a burgundy silk skirt.

Veronica was suddenly feeling very out of place. Katy gave her an understanding pat on the hand. "Don't worry. Everyone has to start at the beginning. We've all been there."

"Yes," Audra added, "and some of us still are!"

As the laughter began to die down, Veronica opened her crochet kit and handed the directions to Katy. Katy quickly read through them then began to explain to Veronica how to read the pattern. Audra, Jenny, Chrissy and Sally all contributed to the explanation and or the confusion, depending on one's point of view.

"This is crazy," Veronica complained, after spending an hour arduously trying to memorize abbreviations. "We'll be here forever. I don't understand why the directions are written in abbreviations. Wouldn't it be easier for people to follow if they just wrote double crochet instead of dc?" she asked.

"It might be a little easier for people to follow, but it would take too much room. All of the directions for that afghan are written on one piece of paper. If they didn't use abbreviations, it would take at least four," Katy answered.

"What's wrong with using four sheets of paper?" Veronica asked.

Jenny tried to offer an explanation in the form of a question. "Well, if you were buying a two hundred page hardback pattern book, would you want it to have eight hundred pages instead?"

Veronica quickly understood the ramifications of what she was asking. "I guess it does add up when you think of it that way, but this is impossible. How am I ever going to memorize all of this?"

Sally grinned. "Ladies, I think it's time we tell Veronica the truth."

"Oh, ok." Katie sighed. "If we have to."

Veronica looked around the table at all the smirking faces and knew her new friends were hiding something. "What truth?" she exclaimed.

Katy pointed her finger at the very bottom of the instruction sheet. "All of the abbreviations are written at the end of the pattern in alphabetical order. See, beg equals beginning, bet equals between, bpdc equals back post double crochet."

"You don't actually have to memorize anything," Chrissy happily chimed in.

Veronica looked at the long list of abbreviations Katy was pointing to, "Hey, they even tell what the brackets and parentheses mean!"

"After awhile you will have all the abbreviations memorized, but in the meantime, if you forget, just peek down at the bottom," Sally suggested.

"Excuse me, ladies, I hate to interrupt, but it's time to close up shop." Everyone looked up to see Vashti standing by the door, keys in hand.

"Oh, no, we've completely lost track of time again," Audra said in an excited voice as she noticed that everyone had left save the crocheters. "I was supposed to be home an hour ago. My in-laws are coming for dinner tonight."

As everyone scrambled to gather supplies, Veronica whispered to Sally, "Does this mean it's too late to buy yarn?"

"It's never too late to buy yarn!" Vashti declared as she walked back toward them dropping her keys down on the front table.

"Gee, she has good ears. Well, happy shopping, everyone!" Audra cried as she rushed out the door.

"What can I help you with?" Vashti asked when she reached the back table.

Veronica continued to gather her supplies as she explained, "When I came in I saw that you had yarn made from a lot of different types of materials. I just wanted to try crocheting with some of them."

"Were you interested in the animal fiber or the plant fiber?" Vashti asked picking up a sample of each from a nearby basket.

"I'm not sure." Veronica petted the two samples Vashti offered. "I don't know a whole lot about yarn yet. Which is best for crocheting with?"

"They are all suited for crocheting. It's just a matter of what you like. Most people, if they are not buying for a specific project, choose yarns by how they feel to the touch and by how pleasing the color is to the eye. Why don't you just go around the shop and feel the various yarns, pick out the yarn that feels best to you and then pick the color you like. It is really just a personal preference."

Veronica placed the last of her supplies in her kitty cat bag then headed over to the nearest bookcase, which was stuffed with yarn. She felt ball after ball after ball after ball of luxurious yarn while Vashti patiently waited. "This is impossible! I like all of them!" she exclaimed.

Vashti laughed. "Let's do it this way, tell me what your favorite colors are."

Veronica thought a minute. "I think I like the earthy colors best," she replied. "Especially the ones with the heather look."

"Ok, how about if I make up a sample box for you."

"Oh, that would be wonderful. Thank you!"

Sally spoke up, "Could you make a sample box for me too? I like the pink and off-white colors."

"Sure. Anyone else?"

"Well, now that you mention it, could you make one for me in blue and one for sis in burgundy?" Jenny asked.

"Hey, don't leave me out." Katy grabbed her bag off the table and joined the group. "I'd like one with shades of green.

This sounds like fun. I've always wanted to see how the different fibers compare to one another."

"Hmm, maybe I should add this to my inventory," Vashti thought out loud. "Ok, everyone who wants a box, go wait in the back section. I don't want any peeking."

"Are you kidding?" Katy asked.

"No, I'm not. This is going to be a surprise package. Now go on, all of you."

Vashti waited while the ladies walked, in disbelief, to the back of the shop. She retrieved several decorative bags from behind the counter then proceeded to fill them with an assorted array of yarn. When she finished she called out, "Ok ladies, you can come out now. I have the bags finished and they are sealed shut."

After the bags were purchased Sally asked, "Can we look now?"

"Not till you get home." Vashti laughed. "Don't worry. I'm sure you will like it, but if you don't, you are more than welcome to exchange it."

Six

————◆————

Jack and Veronica instinctively pulled the blanket over their ears, but the pounding sound continued to permeate even through the covers. "What is that?" Veronica asked.

Jack sat up wiping the sleep out of his eyes. "I think someone is at the door."

"Veronica, open up!" Sally called through the door.

"Something must be wrong." Jack jumped out of bed and ran to the door. Veronica grabbed her bathrobe and followed close behind. Jack quickly unlocked the door and swung it open. "Are you ok?"

Sally came bursting through the door completely out of breath. Veronica grabbed her arm and led her to the loveseat so that she could sit down. "Auntie, what's wrong!"

"Just let me catch my breath," Sally gasped.

Jack went into the kitchen to fetch a glass of water. He returned shortly and handed it to her. "Are you feeling any better?" he asked a few seconds later.

"Really, I'm ok. I just got a little overly excited."

"What happened?" Veronica asked.

"Here, read this," Sally said shoving a piece of paper toward Veronica.

Veronica read out loud so Jack could hear.

We at *Crochet Elite* magazine would like to thank you for submitting your design.

While we find the stitch quite intriguing, we would prefer that the stitch be used to make a ladies fashion scarf.

We would also like to change the yarn you selected to a brand new yarn from Moda Dea called Vision.

If you would be willing to make these changes, please let us know as soon as possible and we will request that the yarn be sent to you. We will also email you a copy of our writing and submission guidelines.

The finished model and written directions need to be in our office within one week from the date of this email.

We apologize for the short deadline. We are hoping to use this project as a fill-in, in our September issue, for another project that fell through.

Please keep in mind that when we purchase a design, we buy all rights to said design. The fee will be two hundred and fifty dollars.

Also, please keep in mind that all designs sold to us must be kept in the strictest confidence until after publication.

We look forward to seeing more designs from you in the future.

Sincerely,

Robert H. Howl
Editor
Crochet Elite magazine.

"I don't get it. What submission?" Veronica asked.

Sally took a deep breath. "Yesterday you asked me to send the three preemie blankets to TLC for Angels. I sent the little squares one and the shell one, but I kept the slip stitch one.

I thought it was so intriguing the way you had done the stitch backwards. I had never seen anything like it before, and I really liked the texture of it.

"Anyway, I thought, since I hadn't seen it before and since I thought it was interesting that maybe other people might be interested in seeing it too. So, yesterday after I got home from our breakfast, I emailed the editor of *Crochet Elite* magazine. I wrote to him about the stitch, which yarn you had used and the hook size. I also took a digital picture of the blanket and sent that to him, too."

Sally took another sip of water, then continued. "I got home so late from the crochet class last night that I didn't even think about checking my email. Then, about four this morning I woke up, couldn't go back to sleep, so I went to check my email and there it was. I was so excited. I made a copy and rushed right over."

"He wants me to make a scarf making the slip stitches the wrong way?" Veronica asked in disbelief.

"Not wrong, different!" Sally exclaimed.

Veronica thought a minute, "A scarf? Auntie, all I've made are three preemie baby blankets. I don't even know how to make a scarf."

"Sure you do." Sally laughed. "You just make a very, very, very, long, skinny, preemie blanket."

Veronica reread the letter. "Written directions? Auntie I..."

"Yes, I was there last night," Sally interrupted her. "Don't worry, I can help you with that part. The important thing is, do you want to do it?"

"Do you think I would have time? It says he has to have it in one week."

"Yes," Sally assured her. "As quickly as you made those three preemie blankets, I think you would have more than enough time. In fact, I would imagine you could crochet the whole thing in one day if you wanted to."

Veronica turned to Jack, "What do you think?"

"I think milady can do anything she sets her mind to. Besides, the two hundred and fifty dollars will just about pay for all that yarn you purchased last night," Jack teased.

"I didn't spend two hundred and fifty dollars!" Veronica teased back, "Just two hundred and forty-nine."

Sally started laughing. "So, do you want the job?"

Veronica read the letter for the third time. Still not quite believing that an editor would want her to send in a design, much less for him to write that he was interested in seeing more designs in the future. "Yes. I want the job." Veronica smiled. The shock was beginning to wear off and she was becoming more and more excited about the prospect. "Yes, I definitely want the job!"

Sally jumped up and handed the glass back to Jack. "Great! I'm going home right now and email him back. And say, you two look like you need to go back to bed," Sally yelled as she raced out the door.

"Drive slow," Jack called out to her. Then he turned to Veronica and grinned. "You know, your aunt gives great advice, let's go back to bed."

After the sun came up and Jack was off to work, Veronica decided to try looking up crochet on the Internet to see what she could learn. She was amazed at the amount of information to be found on the web. She found hundreds of free crochet patterns, sites where one could buy yarn and crochet books, and crochet instructions on how to do various stitches. She even found the history of crochet, the history of various stitches and a list of famous people who crochet at a site called crochetwithdee.com. But what fascinated her most were the crochet chat rooms and message boards, places where people who loved to crochet could come together.

She sat at the computer all morning. Love, who was perched on top of the monitor, purred softly while she investigated the various sites.

Before she realized it, the morning had passed as well as most of the afternoon. Her concentration was broken only by the sound of the cell phone.

"Hello," she spoke into the phone.

"Hi, Veronica. I just wanted to let you know that I emailed the editor back and told him that you would make the changes. I gave him your email address and your mailing address so that he can contact you directly. Anyway, I just received a response from him. He said that Coats and Clark is sending the yarn to you. You should have it first thing Monday morning. I'm sure he is emailing the same information to you. I just wanted to be sure you knew what was going on."

Veronica began checking her email. "That's great, Auntie. I'm starting to get really excited about this. I was playing around on the Internet this morning and I discovered that they have all kinds of message boards for crocheters." No email from the editor. Veronica stood up and stretched, then patted Love on the head while she continued talking. "They even have message boards set up for people who want to be designers. I joined several of them."

"Really?"

"Yes. One of the designer message boards is from a national organization called American Crochet And Knitting Association. It is abbreviated ACAKA. It says on their website that people who are interested in becoming professionals can send messages to their message board and they can also go into their chat room on Wednesdays and Thursdays and talk to people who are already designing for a living. They also offer mentors if people want one. It's a pretty big organization." Veronica sat back down in the brown leather computer chair. "They have a conference every summer and have speakers and classes and all kind of things."

"Yes, I think I have heard of ACAKA. Who are some of the designers in it?"

"Just a second." Veronica clicked on the website. "Let's see. I'll read a few names off to you; Keira, Noel, Alice, Emily, Margery, Destiny, Ellen, Sara, Cecilia, Mandy, Gloria, Deb..."

Sally interrupted, "Doesn't it give last names?"

Veronica looked again, "No. They only list first names."

"Some of the names sound familiar. I know Noel is a tapestry crochet designer. You should look her work up. It is beautiful. Margery has published designs of all kinds in just about every magazine there is. Ellen is known for her clothing designs and Cecilia is known for her Tunisian and double ended hook crochet. Gloria is probably the most famous one. She invents a lot of unique stitches and has authored several books. But I don't recognize a lot of those names. Are all those people crochet designers?"

"No. Some of them are knit designers." Veronica leaned back in her chair and, using her feet to push, slowly swirled around as she spoke.

"Oh, I see. Well, have you learned anything helpful?"

"Actually, quite a lot. The messages are archived and I've been going back and reading all the old messages." Veronica stopped the chair suddenly and sat up. "Did you know that when you show a photo of a design or talk about a design on the Internet that it is considered publishing the design?"

"I never would have thought about it, but I guess that makes sense. I mean if you post about a design on the Internet you are potentially telling the whole world about it."

Veronica picked Love up off of the monitor and held him in her lap. "I also read a lot of tips like you should always add a new ball of yarn at the beginning of a row, not in the middle of the row. And I learned a lot about yarn itself."

"Like what?" Sally asked.

Love began kneading Veronica's leg while she spoke. "Well, I learned that if you need to substitute one yarn for another that you should get a yarn that has the same weight per length."

"What do you mean?"

"Well, if the recommended yarn is fifty grams per one hundred and seventy-five meters and you want to substitute another yarn then you should find another yarn that is fifty grams per one hundred and seventy-five meters." Love began singing loudly while he continued to knead.

"Well, that certainly makes sense," Sally replied.

"I also found out lots of information on how to go about getting designs published. Apparently all the various magazines have editorial forecasts that they put out that say what type designs they are looking for and when to send the designs in." Veronica carried Love into the kitchen and set him down on the floor.

"Did you get a copy of the forecasts?"

"I emailed several of the crochet magazines and requested them. I'm sure they will send them. No one said anything on any of the message boards about having trouble getting them." Veronica poured left over coffee into a cup then reheated it in the microwave.

"It sounds like you are seriously thinking about trying to make designing a full time job."

"Well, the thought did cross my mind." Veronica opened the refrigerator. Love immediately jumped inside and started climbing to the top shelf where the milk was kept.

"I think that would be a wonderful career for you, but you do realize of course that you still have an awful lot to learn."

"Yes, I know, I'm getting ahead of myself again. But this just opens up a whole new world of possibilities for me. I just love the idea of it. Wouldn't it be fantastic if I could make a career out of crocheting?" Veronica got the milk out and poured a little in her coffee and a little in a saucer for Love.

"Yes, it would be fantastic. And I'm sure, if this is really what you want to do, that you will be very successful at it."

Veronica took a sip of her coffee. "Auntie, I want to thank you for sending that afghan in. I really appreciate it. I never would have thought of doing something like that."

"You're welcome, my dear. You know, I'm very proud of you and I'm sure you are going to do great."

"Thanks, Auntie. I am so excited. I can't wait for the yarn to get here!"

Seven

$\longrightarrow\!\blacklozenge\!\blacklozenge\!\longrightarrow$

Veronica woke up bright and early Monday morning with great anticipation. She and Jack had an early breakfast then they took their coffee outside and sat down on the front steps to wait for the yarn delivery. After about half an hour, Jack told her he was going to have to go on to work and kissed her goodbye.

Another hour passed. Veronica continued to sit and wait as the sun rose higher in the sky. Despite the increasing temperature she couldn't make herself go back in the house. The mixture of excitement and fear was steadily growing inside her with each passing minute.

Veronica realized she was feeling like a little schoolgirl on her first day at school, so many emotions and thoughts running through her head all at the same time. Would she be able to crochet a whole scarf in one day like her aunt said? Would she be able to write the directions? She had spent the weekend studying abbreviations, but she was still having trouble with some of them. If she did get the scarf finished, would they really want another design from her? Was it really a possibility that she could make a career out of crocheting? What would she design? The backward slip stitch was just an accident, or was it. Could this be something she was just meant to be doing? Veronica put her head down and covered her face with her hands. What had she gotten herself into?

"Sign here please."

Veronica looked up. She had been so deep in thought that she hadn't even heard the deliveryman pull up into the drive. She signed the paper she was being handed, took the box, then rushed inside to open it. She couldn't help thinking, as she opened the box, that she was quite possibly opening the box to her future.

Sedona, Veronica read as she looked at the yarn label. That's the name of a city in Arizona, she thought to herself. Veronica remembered the city from an old, late night movie she and Jack had sat up watching the week before. She looked at the rustic colors in the yarn and thought about the beautiful red rock formations she had seen in the movie. The color name was perfect.

Veronica continued to read the label. Recommended hook size five point five millimeter. She knew from crocheting the preemie blanket that with this stitch she would need to use a hook about two and a half millimeters larger than what was recommended on the label. She started digging through her kitty cat bag. She had purchased a complete set of hooks, but the largest was only six and a half millimeters.

She picked up the hook and made a chain, four and a half inches long, then began working her backward slip stitches. She was upset that the hook was smaller than what she thought she needed and tense from the stress of trying to crochet her first design. The consequences of which were small tight stitches. Stitches so tight that she could barely get her hook through the loops. She tried to loosen them, but the more she tried the tighter they got. After a few hours of what seemed like hard labor she set it aside frustrated with the whole thing. Love jumped in her lap and began to sing. Veronica smiled. "You always know when I need you don't you, baby." She pulled Love closer to her, feeling the warmth of his body, as the pent-up tears began to flow.

Jack arrived home late that evening. He greeted her with a kiss then asked, "How is your new career coming along?" Veronica gave him a dirty look. "What's wrong?" he asked.

"I hate it. They changed the yarn I was using to a yarn that is a lot thicker. I'm using the biggest hook I have, but the stitches are so tight it looks awful."

"Oh, come on, it can't be that bad. Here, let me have a look." Veronica picked up the partially made scarf and handed it to him. "Well, the scarf is stiffer than the baby blanket you made, but it isn't that bad."

"I just don't like it. The yarn is beautiful, but I hate the way the stitches look."

"Well, why don't you get a bigger hook?" Jack asked, handing the scarf back to her.

"There isn't one," Veronica cried. "I bought every size hook they make."

"That doesn't sound right. Why don't you call your aunt or that lady at the yarn store and see if they can help you?"

"I can't call Vashti," Veronica said as a tear trickled down her check. "The email from the editor said I wasn't supposed to tell anyone."

Jack wrapped his arms around his wife trying to console her. "Well, your aunt already knows about it and they know your aunt knows about it. She submitted the design in the first place."

"That's true," Veronica said as she began to calm down a little. "But it's too late tonight. I'll try calling tomorrow."

"Good. That's settled." Jack grinned. "Now, what's for supper?"

Sally couldn't stop laughing as Veronica lamented her frustrations of the day before.

"Quit laughing at me!" Veronica shouted into the phone.

"I'm sorry, Veronica," Sally said as she tried to stop laughing. "No, really, I am. I just don't understand why you didn't call me yesterday. It is a basic fact, when people get upset they crochet tighter. You have to relax when you crochet. And as far as the hook goes, I've seen hooks all the way up to nineteen millimeters and they probably make them even bigger than that. What size did you say you needed?"

Veronica tried to compose herself before answering. "Well, to make the stitches look like they did on the baby blanket I think I would need an eight millimeter size."

"Let's see." Sally thought for a moment. "That means you need an 'L' hook. I was already planning on going to Springfield today to do a little shopping. Would you like me to pick you up? We could get the hook and then get another one of those bagels."

Veronica tried to sound as seriously concerned as possible. "Auntie, you are becoming a bagelaholic. You need help!"

Sally laughed. "Yes, I know, I know. But if you buy me a bagel, I'll come over to the house this afternoon and help you get the directions written up."

Veronica breathed a sigh of relief. "It's a deal!"

"Gorgeous, it's absolutely gorgeous! Auntie, look."

Veronica and Sally had spent the entire morning shopping and were now back at the house. Veronica had insisted on purchasing every size hook she could find from the very tiniest point zero-four millimeter hook all the way up to the giant nineteen millimeter one. "I'm never going to be without the correct tools again!" she had declared vehemently.

When they got back to the house the first thing Sally showed Veronica how to do was frog the work she had done the day before. Then Veronica had set to work using her brand new eight millimeter hook while Sally made coffee in the kitchen.

Sally now walked over to where Veronica was sitting. "You're right, that is gorgeous," Sally agreed when she saw

Veronica's work. "I love the way the colors seem to change with every row and the texture is fabulous. This Vision yarn is really fantastic. I've never seen anything like it."

Veronica admired her work again. "I love it too. I guess you were right, Auntie. It is definitely a lot easier to crochet when you're relaxed. And when you have an eight millimeter hook!" she added.

Sally smiled. "Well, now that you are nice and relaxed and have all the proper tools, what do you say we go ahead and get the pattern typed up?"

"Sounds good." Veronica took her supplies over to the computer desk, sat down and began typing.

"How many stitches are you doing on each row?" Sally asked.

Veronica turned toward her aunt. "I chained thirteen to start so there are twelve stitches, but before I start typing the pattern I have to type all this information about the yarn and hook and gauge." Veronica handed her aunt the copy of writing guidelines that Robert had sent via email, pointing to the section about materials used.

Sally began to read. "It says to tell how many stitches are in four inches and how many rows are in four inches for gauge. Have you measured that?"

"No. I need to do that." Veronica picked up the ruler and carefully measured a four inch section of the scarf. Meanwhile, Love jumped on top of the monitor, purring loudly. Veronica gave him a quick pet before turning back to the computer, to type in the information.

Backward Slip Stitch Scarf
tttttttttttttttʃʃʃʃʃʃʃʃʃʃʃʃʃʃʃʃʃʃʃʃʃʃʃʃʃʃʃʃʃʃʃʃʃbvvvhg/
(»»»»»»»»...,mmmmmmmmmmmmmmmmmmmmmmmmmmm

"What happened?" Veronica exclaimed, when she saw the screen.

Sally laughed. "I think your precious baby kitty, whom you love dearly, decided to help you with the pattern."

Veronica stood up, gave Love a kiss then spoke softly in his ear, "Thanks, Love, but I think I better do this myself." She sat back down and began printing the page.

"What are you doing?" Sally asked inquisitively.

"It's Love's first paper. I'm printing it so I can hang it on the refrigerator."

After Love's paper was printed and prominently displayed Veronica began her pattern again, carefully following the writing guidelines. Sally stayed the rest of the afternoon to help out with the abbreviations. When they were finished they both looked quite pleased with themselves. "That didn't take long at all," Veronica said in surprise.

"No, it really didn't. You're doing a great job." Sally began gathering up her possessions. "I'm going to head on home now so you can finish crocheting the scarf. It would probably be a good idea for you to go ahead and send it in tomorrow."

"Thank you, Auntie. I really appreciate all of your help," Veronica said as she hugged her aunt.

"It was my pleasure. And thank you for the bagel!"

Veronica and Jack sat on the loveseat that evening. They watched the late movie followed by the late, late, movie while Veronica fervently worked on the scarf. As the orchestra music played the finale and the credits rolled across the screen Veronica excitedly held up her finished scarf for Jack to see.

Sound asleep. Veronica smiled. That was ok. She knew he would be just as pleased with the scarf as she was. The accolades could wait till morning. Veronica picked up the remote, turned off the television then snuggled up in his arms.

Eight

—◆◆—

"Hi, Auntie," Veronica called out when Sally answered the phone the next morning.

"Hi, Veronica. Did you get the scarf finished?"

"Yes. I finished it last night." Veronica whirled around still brimming with excitement.

"That's wonderful!"

"I sent it to the editor first thing this morning. I still can't believe I sold a design to a national magazine! Anyway, I wanted to ask you, are you going to the crochet group in The Village tomorrow afternoon?" Veronica slumped down in the computer chair.

"Yes. I was planning on it. I had a great time last week."

"I did too. I'm really looking forward to it." Love, hearing the commotion, ran into the room and jumped on top of the monitor.

"So, Veronica, what are you your plans for today?"

"I think I'm going to spend some more time on the Internet." Love began to purr loudly. "See what I can learn about designing."

"Ok, well I'll see you tomorrow then. Let's meet about three-thirty again."

"Sounds great."

Veronica turned on the computer and entered the ACAKA chat room.

Keira: Welcome to the group, Veronica. I don't think I've seen you here before. My name is Keira and I'm the moderator of the group.

Veronica: This is my first time.

Margery: Hi, Veronica.

Gloria: Hi, Veronica. Are you a crochet designer or a knit designer?

Veronica: I learned how to knit when I was little, but I haven't knitted anything since then. I want to learn about being a crochet designer.

Gloria: Good. Crocheting is a lot better than knitting.

Margery: There she goes knocking knitting again.

Gloria: I'm just saying there isn't anything you can do with knitting that you can't also do with crochet.

Keira: Let's play nice ladies.

—Mandy has just joined the group—

Keira: Hi, Mandy. Welcome to the group.

Gloria: Hi, Mandy.

Sara: Hi, Mandy.

Mandy: Hi, what is everyone talking about?

Margery: Gloria is trashing knitting again.

Gloria: I just don't see the point of knitting when it is so much easier to get the exact same results with crochet.

Margery: Oh, come on Gloria, you don't get the exact same results.

Gloria: Well, close enough. Plus, there are so many more things you can do with crochet that you can't do with knitting.

Margery: Like what?

Sara: Gloria is right. I knit beautiful granny squares. You can't crochet those.

Mandy: Sara, don't you have that a little backwards ☺

Keira: Please ladies. Let's drop this topic. We have a new person in the room and she wants to learn about crochet designing.

Margery: What would you like to know?

Veronica: I got the forecasts from the crochet magazines. Most of them say that you are supposed to send in a sketch and swatch and they give the date that they want them by. What exactly is a sketch and a swatch?

Gloria: A sketch is a drawing of what your finished design will look like. If it is a clothing item it should include sizing information, at least four different sizes.

Sara: At least.

Margery: A swatch is a six by six inch crocheted sample of the stitch that you plan to use.

Mandy: Be sure and include what the edging will look like on your swatch.

Veronica: I'm not very good at drawing.

Keira: That's ok. I'm not very good at it either. They just need it to look enough like the item you want to crochet that they can get an idea of what the finished design will look like.

Veronica: Can you send the same design to several editors at the same time to better your chances of someone wanting it?

Sara: Yes.

Gloria: No! You can only send to one editor at a time.

Sara: Oops, sorry, I meant to type "No".

Mandy: If an editor turns it down you can send it to another editor, but definitely not at the same time.

—Ellen has joined the group—

Margery: Are you a yarnie or a threadie?

Gloria: I have to go now.

Mandy: Bye, Gloria.

Sara: Me too.

Keira: Bye, Gloria. Bye, Sara.

—Gloria has left the group—

—Sara has left the group—

Veronica: I haven't been crocheting very long. I've only used yarn so far.

Keira: Hi, Ellen, welcome to the group.

Margery: I'm glad Gloria left. Why does she always have to insult knitters?

Mandy: I don't know, but she always does it. It's like she has some kind of vendetta against them.

Margery: Hi, Ellen.

Keira: It is best to just try to ignore it.

Ellen: Hi, everyone.

Margery: You just missed another grand performance by Gloria. I know she is a great crochet designer. Probably one of the best there is. But I get so tired of her attitude.

Mandy: Margery, I agree. But why do you get so upset? You don't knit.

Margery: It's the principle of the thing.

Keira: Let's get back on topic, ladies. Veronica, do you have any other questions?

Veronica: Do you have any tips you could give me?

Ellen: Don't design with extremely dark colors. They don't photograph well.

Mandy: Play with the yarn. Try out different stitches. Use the stitch that looks best with the yarn.

Keira: Yes. Always use the stitch that looks best with the yarn. I always try to think of designing as an advertisement for yarn. I design something, people see the design then they go buy yarn to make the design.

—Deb has joined the group—

Keira: Hi, Deb, welcome to the group.

Veronica: Do you start with the yarn and come up with a design or do you start with the design and then try to come up with a yarn?

Margery: Hi, Deb.

Mandy: I can do both. But my favorite thing is to get a ball of yarn and just play with it. It always turns into something. I try to let the yarn speak to me.

Margery: I prefer the other way around. I'll get a vision of a design in my mind. Then I find a yarn to make the vision become a reality.

Keira: I go to the park or someplace nice for inspiration. I like looking at all the colors and geometric shapes. That's where I get my ideas for my designs. So, I guess I start with the design.

Deb: Hi, everyone. I start with the design also. Before I begin knitting anything, I always look at fashion magazines and the forecasts for style and color. I try to keep up with the latest trends and what trends will be here in the future.

Ellen: Veronica, everyone goes about designing in his or her own way. There is no right or wrong way to do it.

Keira: Ellen is right. You just have to figure out what works best for you.

Veronica continued to chat with her new friends the rest of that day as well as the following day. Designers would come in the room, some for only a few minutes, others stayed a few hours, but she learned something new from each and every one of them.

When she finally shut down the computer her head was swimming with everything she had learned. She was so excited she could hardly wait to get to the yarn shop that afternoon to share the news with her aunt.

Nine

———◆◆———

"Are you going to share your good news at the meeting?" Sally asked as she and Veronica walked toward the door of the yarn shop.

"No, not about the design. The email Robert sent said that no one could know about the design until after it was published. But I might tell them I'm interested in the possibilities of designing. They might be able to give me some helpful hints. I've learned a whole lot in the last two days on the designer chat line, but there is always more to learn." Veronica swung the shop door open.

"Hello, welcome back," Vashti greeted them from behind the register as they entered the shop. "What did you think of your surprise boxes?"

"They were wonderful," Sally replied as she pulled out a little teddy bear sweater from her crochet bag. "I crocheted this using the pink corn yarn I found in the box. I love the feel of it. And I want to thank you for putting more than one of each of the yarns in the box so that I could actually do a project."

"You're welcome. That is beautiful! You did a wonderful job," Vashti said as she admired Sally's work. "What about you, Veronica, did you like the yarn I put in your box?"

The question took Veronica completely off guard. When she arrived home last Thursday she had set the yarn aside so that she and Jack could spend some time together. Sally had surprised her the next morning with the letter from the editor and she had spent the rest of the week reading web sites, working on the scarf and chatting on the designer chat line. She had forgotten all about the surprise box. She hadn't even opened the bag.

Sally saw the look on Veronica's face and immediately realized the problem. "Veronica spent the week job hunting," she blurted out. "She hasn't had a chance to work with the yarn yet."

Veronica smiled at her aunt. It wasn't really a lie. She had been, in a way, job hunting.

"What kind of job are you looking for?" Katy asked as she walked briskly around a basket of yarn toward them. "I might be able to help. I probably forgot to mention it, but I work with a job placement service."

"Oh, hi, I didn't see you," Veronica replied stalling for time. "I... I was kind of looking for an at home job. Maybe a job that has something to do with crochet?"

Katy started talking a mile a minute. "Oh, there are lots of crochet jobs you could do at home. You could crochet things and sell them on the Internet or place them in boutique stores. You could be a model maker and crochet patterns that designers have designed to make sure the patterns are correct. You could teach other people how to crochet. You could learn to design things yourself and try to sell them to the crochet publications. You could learn to be a technical editor and correct patterns. Say, now I know it doesn't pay anything, but if you would like to try your hand at teaching, we could really use your help this weekend."

"This weekend?" Veronica looked puzzled.

"Yes, at the Ozark Empire Fair." Katy continued at her mile a minute pace, "We have an exhibit every year on Friday, Saturday and Sunday. We show people samples of finished crochet and knit pieces as well as the different types of tools that we use. We demonstrate the crafts and also teach people how to do them. There are games and contests too. We have a fastest crocheter and fastest knitter contest. We have a raffle for an afghan and give away several door prizes. We basically try to keep activities going the whole time."

"It sounds wonderful, but I only know a few stitches," Veronica reminded her.

"That doesn't matter," Audra spoke.

"Where did you come from?" Katy asked, looking around in surprise.

Audra laughed. "I was standing behind the pie cabinet looking for some lace weight alpaca for a shawl I want to make. There are a lot of things to hide behind in this store. Better watch what you say," Audra teased.

Katy tried to ignore the teasing. "Well, anyway, she's right. Most people who come by are people who have never crocheted before." Katie went on to explain, "We just show them how to do the chain and the single crochet stitch. You are good at both of those and it would give you some teaching experience."

Teaching. Veronica hadn't thought about that before. "Thanks," she replied. "I think I would like that. Jack and I were already planning on being at the fair this weekend anyway. He started a train club at work and some of the men decided to have an exhibit."

"Hey, that works out great! You could help us while he is at the train exhibit." Katie turned toward Sally who had wandered off a ways to admire yarn. "What about you Sally?" she called out. "Would you be able to come and help out?"

"Thank you for asking, but I volunteer at the library on the weekends. I…"

"It's four o'clock," Vashti interrupted. She walked out from behind the counter. "If everyone can go ahead and find their seats we will begin."

Everyone sat down and began working on their projects while continuing to converse about the fair. Veronica reached into her kitty cat bag and pulled out the surprise bag of yarn she had purchased the week before. She began playing with the yarns marveling over the various textures that were produced by the different types of fibers. She thought about Mandy playing with the yarn and letting it speak to her. Veronica wondered if the yarn would speak to her as well. If she played with the yarn long enough, would it actually turn into a unique design?

Veronica picked up her "I" crochet hook and the ball of Bamboo Wool yarn from Moda Dea. She liked the soft feel of the bamboo and wool mixture, the celery color was a bonus. She chained eleven then began working rows of single crochet stitches. As she made the stitches a thought occurred to her. If a backwards slip stitch was something new, could a backwards single crochet stitch be something new as well?

Veronica placed the yarn in front then inserted her hook from the back to the front of the stitch. With the hook facing her, she wrapped the yarn around the hook counterclockwise and pulled it through the stitch turning her hook clockwise then wrapped the yarn around the hook counterclockwise again and pulled it through both of the loops on her hook, again turning her hook clockwise. She repeated the backwards single crochet stitch all the way across the row then worked several more rows of them.

"Hey, Veronica, you haven't said hardly anything. What are you working on?" Katy asked.

"I was just playing around. Wondered what would happen if I worked my single crochet stitches by inserting my hook from the back to the front instead of from the front to the back."

"So, what happened?" Audra asked.

"Nothing really. My stitches slant to the right now instead of slanting to the left."

"Here let me see," Jenny said. As Jenny began to examine Veronica's stitches a look of amazement came over her face. "Your stitches look like mine now!"

"What do you mean?" Veronica asked.

"I'm left handed. When you did your stitch, working across the row from right to left, inserting your hook from the back to the front, you must have done exactly what a left handed person does when they work from the left to the right and insert the hook from the front to the back." Jenny handed the cashmere sweater she was working on to Veronica. "Look at my stitches," she said pointing to the perfectly formed stitches on her sweater. "My stitches all slant to the right."

Veronica was intrigued. "So, does that mean if a left handed person inserted their hook from the back to the front, that their stitches would slant to the left just like a right handed persons?"

"That's an interesting question," Chrissy piped up. "Why don't you try it Sis?"

Jenny placed the yarn in front then inserted her hook through the stitch from the back to the front. With the hook facing her, she wrapped the yarn around the hook clockwise and pulled it through the stitch turning her hook counterclockwise, then wrapped the yarn around the hook clockwise again and pulled it through both of the loops on her hook, again turning her hook counterclockwise. She repeated the stitch for several rows then examined her work.

"It did! That is fascinating. I didn't know I could make left slanted stitches that looked just like a right handed persons," Jenny said in amazement.

"Hey!" Chrissy exclaimed. "That means you and I could actually crochet on the same project and the stitches wouldn't get turned around. I could crochet from the back to the front to have right slanted stitches to help you, and you could crochet from the back to the front to have left slanted stitches like me! Thanks, Veronica. This is great!"

Jenny looked at Chrissy and the enormous skirt project she was working on. "Yeah, Veronica. Thanks a lot," she replied sarcastically.

As the laughter died down Veronica went back to her work. Something was bothering her. If right hand single crochet stitches worked from the back to the front looked like left hand single crochet stitches worked from the front to the back, why didn't her slip stitches that she had worked from the back to the front look like left hand slip stitches?

With her right hand she made a couple of rows of slip stitches inserting her hook through the loop on top. She then put the hook in her left hand and made a couple more rows. The only difference was that the stitches were going in different directions. The left hand slip stitches didn't look like her backward slip stitches at all. She put the hook back in her right hand and did a couple rows of backward slip stitches. There was a definite difference, but why?

Suddenly, she could see it all clearly. It was as if someone had just turned the light on. It was all in the way she was turning the hook. To make right hand single crochet stitches she was wrapping the yarn counterclockwise and turning the hook clockwise whether she was inserting the hook from the front to the back or from the back to the front. To make left hand single crochet stitches she was doing just the opposite. However, when she was making the backward slip stitches she was not only wrapping the yarn counterclockwise, but also turning the hook counterclockwise.

If her calculations were correct, if she used her left hand and worked the slip stitches from the front to the back, she should be wrapping the yarn and also turning the hook clockwise to get the same ridge effect.

She quickly put the hook back in her left hand to give it a try. It worked like a charm.

She switched the hook back to her right hand. Since that was true, if she worked slip stitches from the front to the back with her right hand, all she would have to do is wrap the yarn counterclockwise and turn the hook counterclockwise and she would have her ridges. Veronica quickly worked a few rows to prove her theory.

She studied the stitches. They didn't quite look the same. There were ridges, but the stitch looked different somehow. Suddenly Veronica blurted out loud, "Of course, they're slanting in the opposite direction."

"What?" Audra asked.

"Sorry I..."

"It's time to stop working, ladies," Vashti declared in a loud voice.

"Hey, we still have five more minutes," Katy complained.

"Nope, I remember what happened last time. You now have five minutes left to shop." Vashti smiled at the thought of her own ingenuity.

"Was there anything you wanted?" Sally asked Veronica as they started gathering up their supplies.

"Yes. I want one of those coffee mugs. I thought I would take it with me this weekend to the fair."

"Coffee mugs?"

"Yes, didn't you see them? She has yellow ones and tan ones, and they have crochet hooks, and balls of yarn, printed on them." Veronica grabbed her kitty cat bag off the table then led Sally over to the display of mugs on the wall. "I'm going to get a yellow one."

Sally took a mug from the wall. "Oh, these are cute! No, I hadn't seen them before. I think I'll splurge and get the tan one."

Veronica and Sally took their mugs to the register to check out, but Veronica's mind kept going back to her stitches. There were so many possibilities. What if she worked the single crochet stitch by putting the yarn in front and inserted the hook from the front to the back, or if she put the yarn in back and inserted the hook from the back to the front? What if she tried working the double crochet stitch backwards? What if she...

"Veronica. Earth to, Veronica!" Vashti tried again.

"Oh, I'm sorry. My mind was somewhere else," Veronica said handing Vashti the money for her new crochet coffee mug.

"I hope it was on all the crochet activities that will be going on at the fair tomorrow," Katy said as she walked up to the register to pay for her purchases.

"Yes, crochet, it was definitely on crochet. I'll see you at the fair tomorrow afternoon."

Ten

---◆---

Veronica could smell the candied apples, funnel cake and cotton candy as she and Jack walked through the fairground toward the Eplex building Friday afternoon. Barkers called out to them, as they walked by, to test their skills at tossing rings over bottles. The tinkling sounds of carnival music could be heard in the distance along with the screams of teenagers as rides turned them upside down then right side up again. Veronica always enjoyed the atmosphere of carnivals. But there was no time for that now. Jack was running late getting to his train exhibit.

They located the Eplex and went inside taking just a few moments to let the cool comfort of air conditioning envelope them. As Jack headed off toward the far left wall where the train display had been set up the night before, Veronica went in search of the crochet group.

She stopped every few steps, as she walked down the aisle, admiring the beautiful crochet work that had been judged earlier that morning. Veronica thought she had never seen so many blue first place ribbons before.

A little blue and white cowboy sweater and a pink and white flower sweater were hanging on one wall. Inside a glass display case she could see delicate lacy doilies and collars. Along the aisle she saw every type of crochet imaginable; crocheted pillows, pillowcases, placemats, dishtowels, handkerchiefs, scarves, bookmarks, picture frames, stuffed animals, afghans and adult sweaters. Another case held bed dolls, purse dolls and teen dolls.

At the end of the aisle she spotted the crochet and knitting group. Several people were already gathered around them watching and trying to learn. Veronica walked over to the display tables that surrounded the group on three sides. They had been artistically set up to show the various types of crochet hooks, knitting needles, yarns and craft books. There were sampler squares of various stitches and full size garments on display as well. A beautiful, full size, off white, thread tablecloth was draped across one of the tables. Veronica guessed that Audra had probably made it. She admired the finished pieces and the hand carved wood crochet hooks for a few moments before taking a chair and joining the group.

"Hi, everyone," she greeted them.

"Oh, hi," Chrissy, who was trying to help several people at the same time, said as she looked up. "Could you help Andrea with her single crochet stitches?"

Veronica looked at the petite little girl Chrissy was pointing at. "Sure, I'd be happy to." Veronica smiled encouragingly at the little girl who was being steered toward her.

Over the next couple of hours Veronica worked with Andrea as well as several others who wanted to learn the art of crochet. Everyone who stopped by received a free ball of yarn and crochet hook. And at the end of each lesson an invitation was extended to the Thursday afternoon crochet meeting in The Village.

By days end, Veronica was having such a wonderful time teaching, that she vowed to come back earlier on Saturday.

"Just a dollar a ball, ladies and gentlemen! Come test your skills at basketball! All you have to do is get the ball in the hoop to win a prize!"

"Come on, we're early, let's play a little," Jack said as he and Veronica were walking through the throngs of people early Saturday morning toward the Eplex.

"How about you, young man!" the barker called out to Jack. "Show the little lady your skills! Get one ball in and you win a prize!"

They walked over to the booth. Jack handed the man a dollar and took the orange ball.

"Get the ball in and you win a prize!"

Jack gave the ball a gentle toss sending it straight into the basket.

"Why, you must be a professional basketball player! Try another ball and you can trade up for a better prize!"

Jack handed the man another dollar. He picked up the ball and shot it toward the basket, but the ball hit the rim and bounced off.

"Just an unfortunate accident, sir! Why a man of your talent could easily have sunk that ball! Give it another try, just a dollar a ball! Win the little lady a prize!"

Jack smiled at Veronica. "Just one more time."

Jack eyed the basket, bounced the ball a few times on the concrete below then took careful aim before making his throw. Veronica started clapping. "That's wonderful!" she exclaimed.

"Professional, professional all the way! Why if the Missouri State Bears knew about you you'd be living on easy street! Try another ball! Let's see what you can do!"

Jack couldn't help laughing. "Thanks, but since the Bears haven't called yet, I think I had better get back to work. What did I win?"

The barker looked a little disappointed that he had lost his mark as he handed Jack an orange and yellow furry monkey, but the disappointment didn't last long. He was calling new customers before they could even get away from the booth.

Jack kissed Veronica on the forehead and handed her the monkey. "A present for Love."

Veronica laughed. Love would love it. Using the hook-and-loop fasteners that were on the bottom of the monkey's hands and feet, she attached the monkey's long arms and legs around the handle of her kitty cat crochet bag.

"Ready to get to work?" Jack asked.

"Ready," Veronica replied as she and Jack once again headed toward the Eplex.

Veronica was immediately put to work teaching people how to do the single crochet stitch. She worked all morning and right through the lunch hour.

"I'm going to get something to eat, can I bring anyone else something?" Chrissy asked around two that afternoon.

"I forgot all about lunch," Veronica said as she looked up. Veronica had been working with a young girl named, Summer, for the last half hour on her crochet stitches. "I'd love one of those smoked turkey legs. They smelled fantastic."

"Things are slowing down a little right now, why don't the two of you go ahead and enjoy your lunch. I can help Summer," Jenny volunteered.

"Thanks, Sis! We'll be right back," Chrissy called out as she grabbed Veronica's hand and rushed her out the door.

"What's your hurry? Are you that hungry?" Veronica asked when they got outside.

Chrissy laughed. "No. I was afraid she might change her mind!"

"Where have you been?" Audra asked as she rushed up to Veronica.

"Ladies and Gentlemen," Vashti's voice rang out over the fairground loud speakers, "this is the final call. If you wish to be in the Fastest Crochet Contest or in the Fastest Knit Contest, please go to the registration desk at this time to sign up. The contests will begin in fifteen minutes."

Audra grabbed Veronica's arm, "Come on, let's get in line."

"Are you kidding?" Veronica began to protest as Audra dragged her along. "I haven't been crocheting long enough to be in a contest."

"No, I'm not kidding." Audra began to present her case. "I've seen you crochet! Anyway, it's just for fun, everyone participates. Besides, I need your help."

Veronica gave in. She could never turn down a plea for help. "What do you need me to do?"

"They follow the national rules. Using a 'J', six millimeter, hook, and worsted weight yarn, you chain twenty-three, then you double crochet in the fourth chain from the hook. You work a double crochet in each chain across so that when you are finished you have twenty double crochet stitches plus your beginning chain three. Then you chain three to turn. That is when the contest begins. They time you for three minutes while you crochet as many rows of double crochet stitches as you can. Then they count how many stitches you did. They don't care about neatness so just work as fast as you can."

"But, Audra, you don't crochet with yarn do you?" Veronica asked as they continued to hurry toward the growing line of participants.

"They have a second crochet contest using thread. That is the one I'm going to enter and that is the reason I need your help." Audra and Veronica finally reached the end of the line and took their place.

Veronica turned to Audra. "How can I help you?" she asked, not quite understanding.

"They allow you to have someone feed the yarn to you so that it doesn't get tangled during the contest. Since we will be in different contests, I can feed yarn to you and you can feed thread to me."

It was obvious from her tone that Audra had worked out all the details and left no room for argument. So, Veronica didn't even try. But as they stood in line Veronica began to feel more and more anxious. She was a competitive person by nature, but the only contests she had entered before were the apple pie contests back in Marionville. Speed was not a factor. As she waited, Veronica nervously pulled a ball of yarn and a hook out of the kitty cat bag she had slung over her shoulder and began practicing.

"Try to stay calm. Focus only on your stitches. If you make a mistake, just keep going. I hear they don't care what the stitches look like," Jack, who had walked up behind Veronica, put his arms around her as he spoke soothingly in her ear.

"How did you know?" Veronica turned around in surprise.

"Loud speaker. Crochet. Contest. Milady. It didn't take much detective work," Jack teased.

"Thank you, Sherlock," Veronica said as she started to relax. "I'm glad you're here."

"We will begin the crochet yarn contest in one minute. All non-participants need to step back out of the competition area," Vashti announced.

Jack gave Veronica a kiss for luck then went to stand with the other observers.

As the final seconds ticked by, Veronica sat poised in her chair, crochet hook in her right hand, first row of twenty double crochet in her left. Audra was busily pulling just the right amount of yarn out of the ball; enough to easily crochet with, but not so much that it might become tangled during the contest.

"Crocheters, on your mark, get set, go," Vashti sang out as she hit the clock, prominently displayed on the table in front of her, to begin the three-minute countdown.

Veronica began crocheting as fast as she could, trying not to think about the fifteen other people who were doing the same. She finished the first row then started the second and then the third. Two stitches in one hole, a stitch catching only the back loop, a couple of stitches in between two double crochet of the previous row, she wondered if they meant what they said about neatness not counting.

"One minute left," Vashti called out.

Concentrate, I have to concentrate, Veronica kept saying to herself over and over. Her hands were beginning to shake and her heart was racing as she neared the end of the third row then turned to begin the fourth.

The buzzer sounded. "Put your hooks down," Vashti announced.

A tall blonde judge walked over to Veronica and began counting her stitches. Veronica rubbed her shaking hands on her pant legs in hopes of trying to make the shaking stop. She wondered if the other contestants were experiencing the same adrenalin rush.

"Seventy-six stitches," the judge announced.

"That's great!" Veronica heard Audra's voice say through all the commotion.

"Ninety stitches."

"Fifty-three stitches."

"Seventy-two stitches." Three more judges called out as the counting continued.

Vashti's voice came over the loud speaker once again. "Ladies and Gentlemen, the winners will be announced and will receive their awards after all the contests are over. If you are going to be in the knitting contest remain in your seat, if not, please move to the observation area at this time. The crochet thread contest will be held immediately following the knitting competition."

Veronica happily joined Jack in the observation area. She was amazed at the number of people who stayed in their seats. "I couldn't do that," she whispered to Jack.

"What are you talking about? You did great! You haven't been crocheting as long as the others," he tried to console her.

"No," she explained, "I mean be in more than one contest. My hands are still shaking from the last one."

Jack lovingly held Veronica's hands in his. The knitting competition soon began, but his mind was elsewhere. Due to work at the train shop, the fair and the newly formed train club he and Veronica had spent very little time together lately. They needed a day, one very special day.

Eleven

—◆—

Monday morning Veronica was awakened by a heavy weight on her chest followed by a big wet kiss. She opened her eyes in surprise. Two beautiful green eyes were staring at her. "Good morning, Love." Love began to purr.

Veronica started to get up, but then heard the water running in the shower. Love cuddled up closer to her, his purring getting louder by the minute. "Ok, I take it I am supposed to stay in bed all day and pet you?"

Love gave a sweet little mew in response then slowly began working his way under the covers in preparation for his early morning nap.

A few minutes later Jack walked into the room still wet from his shower. "Good morning," he said as he bent over and gave Veronica a kiss. "I was just thinking, we both worked all weekend, what do you say we take a break and go to Silver Dollar City today."

"Oh, that would be wonderful! I haven't been there since I was a little girl. But, don't you have to work?"

"No. I called Jim and he's going to fill in for me. What do you say, just the two of us. Let's go right now." Jack sat down on the side of the bed and put his arms around Veronica.

"Umm, do you mind if I get dressed first?"

"Only if you let me help you," he mumbled as he kissed her again.

Two hours later Veronica and Jack were dressed and ready to go. "What do you say we take the scenic route," Jack suggested, as they were about to walk out the door.

Veronica smiled. Jack never seemed to appreciate the high speed of the super highways. "Sounds great," she replied. "Would you mind if I take my crochet along to play with in the car?"

"Not a bit."

Veronica grabbed her kitty cat bag off the loveseat and flung it over her shoulder. She and Jack said goodbye to Love then headed out to the car.

As they drove toward Highway 256, a rather misleading name since it was just a two lane road, Veronica began working on her crochet, picking up where she had left off at the yarn shop. She was thoroughly enjoying experimenting with the different crochet stitches, but once they reached Highway 256, she had to put the crochet down.

Driving along the winding mountainous road in the Ozarks, generally at speeds of no more than twenty miles per hour on the numerous curves, made the trip much longer than necessary. But it was such a picturesque route that most people didn't complain. Lush green trees covered the mountains and colorful summer wildflowers dotted the hillsides and road edge. The scenery was just too beautiful to miss.

Silver Dollar City wasn't really a city. It was a theme park, set in the 1880's, which had been built on top of a cave. All employees dressed in appropriate costumes of the time and various crafts were demonstrated throughout the park; glass blowers, blacksmiths, bakers, candy makers, silversmiths, basket weavers, potters, glass cutters, candle makers. The list of craftsmen was endless. Several different festivals were held each year depending on the season. The park also boasted live shows, thrilling rides and a cave tour.

Jack pulled into the parking lot then he and Veronica

walked toward the tram that would take them into the park. As they stood in line, next to a young woman holding a newborn baby girl, Veronica couldn't help feeling a little depressed. Jack put his arms around her, "Do you want to leave? If you do, it's ok. I'm sorry. I didn't realize it was National Kid's Festival this month."

"No. I'll be ok. Just give me a minute," Veronica replied as she tried to compose herself.

The tram pulled up and everyone quickly boarded, except the young mother. "Would you hold my baby for me while I climb on?" the young woman asked, holding out her child for Veronica to take.

Veronica hesitated, but then reached down and took the small infant while the mother climbed onto the tram. "Thank you so much," she said gathering her infant back into her arms. "I really appreciate the help."

Jack pulled Veronica toward him and whispered in her ear, "I love you."

"I love you too," she whispered back.

With everyone safely seated, the tram sped toward the front entrance of the park. Veronica volunteered to help the young woman get back off the tram then she and Jack headed into the park.

Stepping into the park was like stepping into another world. It wasn't just the costumes that the workers wore. It was a combination of all the sights, sounds and smells throughout the park. Beautiful music was coming from every direction. Entertainers were performing on the park's streets. The smell of fresh baked bread drifted from the bakery. Everywhere one looked there were smiles and laughter coming from people of all ages.

Jack purchased two Silver Dollar City mugs, filled to the brim with fresh squeezed lemonade, from one of the vendors. Then they sat down, on a bench in front of the Gazebo, and watched as cloggers performed to the bluegrass music playing in the background.

As they watched the young girls dance, Veronica spotted a row of colorful giant pinwheels blowing in the breeze off to the right. She loved to play with pinwheels as a child. Veronica began to study the color combinations on the wheels, red, pink, orange, yellow, blue, green and purple. "Jack, do you have a pen and a piece of paper?" she asked when the performance ended.

"Yes. Is something wrong?"

"No, no problem. I just wanted to write down that color combination," Veronica said as she pointed at the pinwheels.

Jack looked around, "Aren't those just the colors of the rainbow?"

"Close. Rainbow colors are red, orange, yellow, green, cyan, blue and purple. The pinwheels have some of those colors, but the arrangement is different." Veronica quickly scribbled down the color sequence then she and Jack strolled over to the booths on the right. "Look, they have pompon marionettes!" Veronica exclaimed, as she spotted the little tufts of yarn. Veronica picked up a fluffy gray and white elephant.

"Let me show you," the sales lady offered. She placed the marionette on the ground then, holding the T-shaped wood frame in her hand, demonstrated how to move the control to make the elephant walk. "Here, you try."

Veronica took the control and the elephant began to wobble back and forth. "This is so cute!" she exclaimed.

Jack picked up a clown marionette and began to play as well.

Gunshots loudly rang out. "What was that?" Veronica asked.

"I don't know. It came from over by the ice cream parlor," Jack replied as more gunfire was heard exploding into the air. "Come on!"

"Get the Marshal! Get the Marshal!" a man's voice yelled.

Jack and Veronica followed the crowd as they headed toward the back of the gazebo. A tall, thin man was aiming a gun up in the air. Another man, who appeared to be the Marshal, was shouting something about shooting being against the law.

Veronica looked around and spotted a short rock wall that was being used to line the flowerbeds. She and Jack sat down on the rocks to watch the rest of the street show.

That was really amusing," Jack said as the show ended. "I was thoroughly entertained."

"Me too," Veronica replied as she stood up and dusted herself off. "Oh, look, aren't those cute?"

"What?" Jack asked turning around.

"The little flowers growing in the wheelbarrow. Look, purple ones, pink ones, white ones, red ones…"

"Yea, I know," Jack interrupted her. "You want to write down more colors."

Veronica jokingly punched him in the arm. "I was just admiring," she replied. "Say, where do you want to go next?"

Jack referred to his park map. "I want to check out the swinging bridge." He folded the map back up then hand in hand they walked down the hill.

Veronica stepped onto the wooden planks. "Let's see how much we can make it swing."

"Are you sure?" Jack asked in disbelief.

"Of course!"

Jack pushed his body weight to one side of the bridge and then to the other in quick succession. The bridge creaked then slowly began to sway back and forth. Two teenaged boys walked onto the bridge and decided to join in on the action. More boys followed suit and the bridge began to sway faster and faster.

Veronica was beginning to find it hard to keep her balance. She grabbed onto the ropes along the sides of the bridge and held on for what seemed like an eternity. After awhile most of the boys lost interest, or got tired, she wasn't sure which. In either case, the bridge began to slow down. When the swaying reached a point where she could walk again, she hurried across to the other side and got off. Jack followed close behind.

"What did you think?"

"I think I better be more careful of what I ask for in the future!" Veronica grinned.

Jack gave her a quick hug. "Come on, let's go watch the candy makers," he said when the sweet smell of sugar wafting down the street caught his attention. "It will be a lot cooler inside."

They entered the candy factory and began watching two women in long white aprons prepare peanut brittle whilst joking with the audience. After the demonstration the brittle was broken into little pieces and everyone was invited to have a sample. Veronica and Jack took their piece then followed the rest of the audience into the candy shop where every kind of old-fashioned candy imaginable could be found. Rock candy that looked like real rocks, sugar crystals shaped like stalactites, taffy, brittle, fudge, it was all there.

A large wood barrel filled with ice and bottles of water caught Veronica's attention. The air-conditioned building felt wonderful, but Veronica knew they would soon be headed back out into the summer sun and their lemonades were long gone. She grabbed two bottles then went to the check out stand. Jack spotted a tray of succulent looking, chocolate covered strawberries sitting on the counter by the register and added two giant sized ones to the water purchase.

"These strawberries are delicious!" Jack exclaimed, as he consumed the last bite.

Veronica smiled and licked the last of the juice off her fingers in reply.

They began walking downhill going deeper into the park.

Suddenly they heard the sound of horses galloping toward them. Veronica instinctively moved to the side of the bridge they had stepped onto to get out of the way. The horses galloped past them, but were never seen. "What was that?"

Jack read the sign nailed to the side of the rustic red bridge. "They must have been ghost horses." He smiled. "You want to watch the glass blowers?"

"Of course."

They walked into the open building and began watching the craftsman as he demonstrated the fine art of glass blowing. There were three furnaces behind him each set at over two thousand degrees. Veronica tried to imagine the passion he must feel for his craft to be willing to work in that kind of heat.

The man picked up a four and a half foot pipe and dipped it into a reservoir of liquid glass. He then began to describe the process of glass blowing as he shaped the orange glowing mass into a ball. Once it was shaped, he blew into the end of the long pipe creating an air bubble in the ball of glass. He continued shaping the ball for several more minutes. Veronica stood mesmerized as the glowing shape was transformed into a beautiful vase.

"Come on!" Jack urged as he tugged on her arm.

"What's wrong?" Veronica asked as she turned around. Then she heard it, the sound of the train whistle coming from farther down the hill.

"Come on! We're going to miss it."

Jack took off down the hill, answering the call of the train whistle. Veronica reluctantly left the glass shop and followed close behind. A few minutes later they arrived at the depot. And there it sat. Train number seventy-six, the Frisco Silver Dollar City Line steam engine and three open passenger cars. The cars had been freshly painted red with yellow trim. Jack and Veronica took a seat on one of the wood benches in the center car just seconds before the train was ready to leave the station.

It was a beautiful ride through the Ozarks. Jack began telling her the individual history of each car that made up the train they were riding on. "Is the train slowing down?" Veronica interrupted.

"This is a train robbery!" a loud voice bellowed.

Veronica looked out the window. A man in torn coveralls was yelling and waving a gun around. "I want all your women and your money."

Veronica continued to watch as the robbery unfolded. When the robber came up to her she handed him a penny then several others began handing him pennies as well. Veronica was impressed with how the actors could change the story up to accommodate the audience response.

When the drama came to its inevitable conclusion the train whistle blew and once again they were on their way.

"I'm starving," Jack proclaimed as they stepped off the train. "Let's see what we can find to munch on."

As they headed back up the hill Veronica saw some words etched on the side of a piece of wood. "Big Skillet Vittles Just Ahead," she read out loud.

"Sounds good to me," Jack replied.

When they reached the top of the hill they found a shack with two five foot black skillets inside. Something called Family Feud was cooking in one while a concoction called Harvest Skillet cooked in the other.

"Let's try one of each then we can share," Jack suggested as he eyed the food hungrily.

They purchased their bowls then headed toward the picnic tables, which were artistically arranged under the oak shade trees behind the shack. Despite the summer sun, the park was filling up rapidly and they soon discovered there were no empty tables to be had. A young woman saw them looking for a place to sit down and gestured them over. "You're welcome to join us if you like," she offered.

"Thank you!" Veronica replied. "This is awfully nice of you." Gratefully she and Jack sat down on the wood bench being offered them. "We appreciate your sharing your table with us. I'm Veronica and this is my husband, Jack."

"It's nice to meet you. My name is Laura and these are my children, Paul, Ethan and Ken. Ken is the baby," she said pointing to the stroller.

Veronica looked in the stroller at the sleeping infant. "He is so cute! How old is he?"

"Four weeks," she replied as she gently rolled the stroller to and fro.

"I love the little romper he is wearing. Did you make it?"

"Why, thank you! Yes, I did." Laura beamed with pride. "I learned how to crochet when I was expecting Paul. I've made clothes for all of them. Just finished crocheting that outfit last night. I found the pattern in a magazine called *Crochet For All*. Do you crochet?"

"Yes." Veronica placed her hand across Ken's belly. "I started recently and I'm really enjoying learning the craft. What kind of yarn is this? It feels so soft."

"It's called Luster Sheen. It's a size fine yarn and comes in a wide variety of colors. I think it's perfect for baby clothes. Worsted weight just seems too heavy to me, especially in the summer."

Ethan dropped a piece of chicken on the ground and dived under the table to retrieve it. Laura grabbed him just in time. "We don't eat off the ground, that's dirty," she said as she picked him up and set him back down on the bench.

Jack watched the goings on in amusement. "You have quite a handful. Are you here by yourself?" he asked.

"Yes. I thought it would be a nice outing for the kids. We live nearby. Where are you from?"

"We're from this area also. Live in Springfield," Jack responded.

"We rode the roller coaster!" Paul exclaimed as he bounced up and down on the bench; fork in hand.

"You did? Was it fun?" Jack asked, sharing the little boy's enthusiasm.

"We rode fast!" Ethan interrupted.

"And we're going to the dog show!" Paul added excitedly.

Laura looked down at her watch. "Oh, I almost forgot about the dog show. We better get going. It was nice meeting you both." Laura quickly cleared the white plastic food bowls off the table then ushered the boys down the hill toward the show.

"That sounds like fun, do you want to go?" Jack asked.

Veronica swallowed her last bite of Family Feud. "Sure, I love animals, but before we start walking in the sun again let's refill our mugs."

Veronica and Jack hurried down the hill toward the dog show. About halfway down they were asked to wait as a crossing gate swung across the road. "How did you manage to arrange this?" Veronica teased.

"Ah, anything to impress, milady!"

As they stood behind the crossing gate waiting for the train to pass Veronica watched a cute little girl with brown pigtails as she tried to eat a large dish of ice cream.

"Is everything ok?" Jack asked, noticing how quiet Veronica had become all of a sudden.

Veronica looked up at him, "Jack, are you ready to try again?"

"Try again?" Jack looked a little confused.

Veronica pointed toward the toddler.

"Are you?" he asked.

"Yes."

"Are you sure?" he asked again, a little concerned.

Veronica thought for a second. "Yes, I am. I really am."

"Then your wish is my command, milady!" Jack said as he jokingly bowed forward waving his hat in front of him.

The train whistle blew as the black and red steam engine passed by the crossing gate. "And I suppose the train whistle seals the deal?" Veronica laughed.

"Certainly. Well, at least until we can get home." Jack winked.

The crossing gate swung back open and they continued on their way. Concerned about the time lost at the gate Veronica looked down at her watch. "I think we've missed the beginning of the show."

"That's ok," Jack said cheerfully. "There are a lot of things to do here." Suddenly, he stopped in the middle of the road and pointed toward a wood fence railing. A little baby squirrel was sitting perfectly poised on top of the post.

"Is he eating popcorn?" Veronica whispered.

Jack carefully took a few steps closer to get a better look. "Yes," he whispered back. The squirrel slowly finished the treat, obviously enjoying his lunch, then climbed down off the post. They watched as he quickly scurried through the grass toward a red building a few feet away then disappeared. The sign above read, Kettle Corn. "I guess he's going back for seconds." Jack laughed.

"Oh, look!" Veronica practically squealed. "There's a toy store. Let's go buy the baby a present!"

"The baby?"

"Sure, he'll be here in only nine months." Veronica linked her arm with Jack's. "Come on!"

Veronica led Jack into the toy store. "Wow, it's air-conditioned in here!" he exclaimed. "You may shop till your hearts content, milady." Jack removed his hat then made himself at home on the customer courtesy bench by the door.

"And, if it wasn't air-conditioned?" Veronica asked.

"Well, we won't talk about that." Jack laughed.

Veronica began looking around at the massive array of toys on display. She picked up a soft, cuddly, stuffed animal then a little rattle and a squishy ball. As she was looking at the various items a thought occurred to her. "Jack, let's go," she said, a slight urgency in her voice.

Jack grabbed his hat and jumped up. "Are you ok?"

Veronica shook her head yes. Jack gave her a funny look, not understanding the urgent tone. "No, really. I'm ok. I just want to go. I'll explain later."

"Ok," he said as they left the little toy shop.

Once outside, he gently turned Veronica toward him. "If this is too soon, I understand."

Veronica looked at the concern on his face. "Oh, no, it's nothing like that. I was just thinking. I could crochet those toys. It would make it so special. I know I can do it. I've already crocheted several preemie blankets. I just need to crochet a bigger one. I think I could even crochet a little ball and a rattle. And I was looking at one of the stuffed bears in there. It is just tubes for the arms and legs, a large round ball for the body and a smaller round ball for the head. Then all I would need to do is crochet some ears. I could embroider the face."

"That sounds wonderful. You know, it wasn't that long ago when parents used to make everything for their children. I think it would be great." Jack patted his wallet. "And our bank account thinks it would be great too."

Veronica laughed. "Come on. Let's go ride a roller coaster while I still can."

Veronica and Jack started walking toward Wildfire, a multi-looping roller coaster. "You know, it doesn't seem as warm as it was earlier," Jack observed.

Veronica looked up in surprise. "The sun has gone down. I didn't know it was that late. What time is it anyway?"

Jack checked his watch, "It's just five o'clock. There should be plenty of daylight left. I wonder if we are..."

Jack never got to finish his sentence. The sky opened up and the floods came down. A rolling thunder could be heard in the distance. Lightening lit up the sky. Little children were screaming as parents rushed to get them under some kind of shelter. Jack grabbed Veronica's hand. "Let's try to make it to the Hospitality House. We can take the short cut through the middle of the park," he called out to her.

They began running as fast as they could up the hill toward the entrance of the park. "Hey, let's go in here," he yelled spotting a large white house to his right.

They entered the house, both dripping wet.

"Where are we?" Veronica asked once they were safely inside.

"I don't know," Jack replied as they began walking up a ramp.

A giant music box, to the right of the ramp banister, was tinkling out the tune, "There's No Place Like Home". Flickering lights, coming from the candelabra above, gave everything kind of an eerie effect. Veronica watched the revolving characters inside the music case for a few moments, enjoying the reprieve from the rain.

"It's odd," Jack whispered.

"What is?"

"The place is deserted. I don't even see any employees. Come on, let's look around."

They walked to the top of the ramp and turned right. A large living room, with what looked like a bridge going across it, was before them. As they began to cross the bridge the room began to sway to the left and then to the right. Veronica started to laugh. "We must be in some kind of haunted house."

They turned left into a hallway then took another left into a room where everything was upside down: candelabra on the floor, rocking chair on the ceiling. Taking another left led them to a flight of stairs, stairs descending into darkness. Carefully they began walking down the stairs in total silence. Veronica subconsciously began counting to herself: one, two, three...twenty-two, twenty-three. When they reached the bottom they took another left and started up a short ramp. Veronica noticed that it was becoming more and more difficult to walk. Jack spotted a billiard table and watched as the billiard balls began to play a game of pool all by themselves.

"Let's sit down over there," Veronica said pointing at a green porch swing that was hanging in a bedroom. They began awkwardly walking toward the swing holding onto the walls to help keep their balance.

"Look at this place! Are you sure you want to sit on that thing?" Jack teased.

Veronica looked around. "Well, um, after you test it out." She smiled.

"Anything for you, milady," Jack said as he carefully sat down on the crooked swing. He bounced up and down a few times. "Perfectly safe for, milady." Jack gallantly stood up to tip his hat and take a bow, but lost his balance and went tumbling across the room.

"Are you ok?"

"No," Jack said surveying the damage. "I've broken me pride." He tried to stand back up, but once again went sprawling on the floor.

"Here, let me help you," Veronica offered.

"Nope, I have to conquer this floor by myself," he declared. "No son of mine is going to think his old man is a quitter. Go ahead and sit down," he said softly. "I'll be there in a minute."

Veronica carefully sat down on the swing thinking about Jack's words, "No son of mine..." A baby. They were really going to try to have a baby. And she was going to design crocheted toys and blankets and clothes and...

Jack, slightly out of breath, climbed back onto the swing, put his arm around Veronica and whispered in her ear, "What do you say we stay here awhile."

"Sounds wonderful," Veronica replied as she snuggled up in his arms. They cuddled together on the swing for the next two hours, listening as the thunder clashed outside, dreaming about the future...

Twelve

———◆———

Veronica had been working on swatches all morning. She had decided that she was going to try to make at least half a dozen, six inch, swatches all with different types of stitches. Then she would send them to the editor at *Crochet Elite* magazine. If he didn't want them she would send them to *Crochet For All* magazine.

As she made each swatch she carefully labeled it with her name, address, email address and phone number then she placed an identifiable number on it. She typed up the directions explaining exactly how she made the stitch. She added a listing of all the materials she used and wrote down the gauge for the swatch. Then she placed a corresponding number on the directions.

The rhythmic repetition of crocheting the swatches created the perfect atmosphere for daydreaming. Daydreaming about her future baby and what she could crochet for her little one. Daydreaming about the wonderful time she and Jack had the day before, Jack and his silly hat flailing across the floor.

A hat. Her baby needed a hat! She looked down at the swatch she was working on, how could she turn a swatch into a hat? She could roll it up and sew the sides together to form a tube. No, she hated sewing. Then it dawned on her, if she could make the swatch in the round, she wouldn't have to sew it. The more she contemplated the idea the more she liked it. Only problem was, how does one work in the round? But she would worry about that later. Right now she had more important things to do. She had to pick out just the right yarn and color for her baby.

Veronica read the label on the yarn she was using to make the swatches. Hand wash only. That would never do for a baby. She needed a washable yarn. She tried to remember the name of the yarn Laura had told her about at Silver Dollar City. It was a beautiful yarn and looked so cute on Laura's baby. Luster something.

Making swatches for magazines temporarily forgotten, Veronica began searching for her car keys. A few minutes later she was dashing out the door to do a little detective work. There was a missing yarn to be found. Her only clue, a first name...Luster.

A few hours later Veronica was back at home with a skein of turquoise Luster Sheen yarn. Mission accomplished.

Veronica read the label and discovered that the recommended hook was a size "F". She removed the hook from her bag then, yarn at the ready, called her aunt for directions.

Although her aunt made it sound like a great question, Veronica felt a little silly. The answer was so simple. To work in the round all she had to do was make a row of chain stitches then, being careful not to twist the chain, work her first single crochet stitch in the first chain she made thereby creating a ring of stitches. Oh well, she thought after she hung up, at least she was learning.

Veronica began trying out the various stitches she had "invented" earlier that day. She remembered Mandy and Keira telling her to always use the stitch that looked best with the yarn. After trying out several stitches she made her decision.

Veronica worked a chain fourteen inches long, a total of forty-seven chains, then single crocheted in the back ridge of the first chain to form her ring. She worked two rounds of single crochet stitches then began the new stitch.

Veronica inserted the hook in the next stitch, wrapped the yarn around the hook and pulled it through the stitch, wrapped the yarn around the hook again, inserted the hook in the stitch directly below the stitch that she had just inserted the hook into, wrapped the yarn around the hook and pulled it through the stitch and up even with the row. Then she wrapped the yarn around the hook one last time and pulled it through all four loops on the hook.

She alternated her new stitch and the single crochet stitch back and forth creating a cute little hat. She even added a topknot to finish it off.

Veronica placed the finished hat on the table then took a step back to admire her work. She liked it, but for some reason she felt a little sad.

Veronica picked up the hat and sat back down on the loveseat. She wished Jack were home so that she could get his opinion. She also wished it was Wednesday so that she could talk to the designers in the ACAKA chat group. She had so many questions to ask them. She didn't know how to decrease to make the top of the hat smaller so she had skipped stitches. Was that the right thing to do? It left little holes in the top of the hat. Was that bad?

Veronica liked the idea of potentially being a crochet designer and she was having a lot of fun. But she just wasn't used to working at home, alone. She needed feedback. She needed someone to talk to.

Suddenly Love jumped up on the back of the loveseat and mewed loudly. Veronica gave him a pet. "I'm sorry, Love. I forgot. I'm not really alone am I? Tell me, what do you think, will the baby like it?" Veronica asked as she waved the little hat in front of him. She quickly realized her mistake, but it was too late. Love crouched down, clicked a few hunting sounds, twitched his tail then lunged at the hat turning a flip in midair. He then proudly trotted off with his prize.

Veronica smiled. I guess that means yes, she thought to herself. Veronica started to go after him, but knew the futility of such a pursuit.

She quietly got up, went into the kitchen and opened the refrigerator door. Love peered around the corner right on cue, hat still dangling from mouth. A few minutes later, a mutual agreement was struck—one hat for one saucer of milk.

Thirteen

Keira: Hi, Veronica. Welcome back.

Veronica: Hi.

Cecilia: Hi, Veronica. I don't think I have met you.

Margery: Hi, Veronica.

Mandy: Veronica came to ACAKA for the first time last week.

Keira: You were asking about swatches. Were you able to get some made?

Veronica: Yes. I made six. I sent them off this morning.

Ellen: That's wonderful.

Sara: Congratulations.

Keira: Did you have any more questions?

—Gloria has just joined the group—

Veronica: I was wondering how you decide which yarn you want to make something out of. There are so many to choose from.

—Gloria has left the group—

Margery: That was fast.

Cecilia: Guess she decided not to stay.

Sara: I hope she comes back.

Keira: Most of the time I just use the newest yarns that are available on the market. Publishers want you to use the latest yarns.

Veronica: How do you know what the latest yarns are?

Cecilia: Contact the yarn companies that you are interested in. Tell them that you are a designer and ask them if they will send you an information sheet telling about their newest yarns.

Margery: Ask them which yarns are discontinued also. You can't design with a discontinued yarn.

Cecilia: Yes. You want the people reading the magazine to be able to make the exact same design that you have made. If the yarn is discontinued, they can't.

Keira: Sometimes even if a yarn is available it will be discontinued before the magazine is published. It usually takes at least six months from the time you send in a design to the time it is published.

Margery: Sorry, I worded that badly. You should ask the yarn company if the yarn is "going to be" discontinued. Not if it "is" discontinued.

Ellen: I sent in a crocheted sweater that was published in *Crochet With Flair* magazine just a few days ago. The yarn was good when I crocheted the sweater, but discontinued before it made it to print. Hopefully there will be enough yarn left in shops that people will be able to make the sweater.

Keira: Sometimes it happens that way. Of course people can generally substitute a yarn of equal weight and size. But it's still frustrating.

Mandy: Oh, I saw that sweater. It was beautiful. I have a cardigan in that same issue, but it is nowhere near as nice as your sweater. How do you think up such wonderful designs?

Ellen: Thank you. I'm glad you liked it.

—Gloria has just joined the group—

Cecilia: I haven't seen that issue. Is there a photo on their website showing the sweater?

—Gloria has left the group—

Margery: What is with that girl today?

Keira: She's probably just having trouble getting in.

Ellen: I guess I should be going too. Bye, everyone.

—Ellen has left the group—

Margery: People sure are coming and going quickly today.

Mandy: Well, since we are designers, I guess we really should be designing and not just sitting here all day chatting ☺. But I am really enjoying the break.

Veronica: How many hours a day do you usually spend designing?

Mandy: Depends on if I have a deadline or not. I generally work at least eight hours a day.

Keira: Deadlines are great. I love overnight jobs.

Margery: You've got to be kidding. I hate deadlines. I have enough pressure trying to teach and design without having editors rush me.

Veronica: Overnight jobs?

Keira: Sometimes an editor or yarn company will call you and ask you to do an overnight job. They have the yarn sent to you overnight, you have a day or two to design and make the model, then you overnight the model back to them. You generally get paid more than the going rate because of the fast deadline.

—Gloria has joined the group—

Keira: Welcome to the group Gloria. Were you having trouble getting in today?

Sara: Hi, Gloria.

Gloria: Yes, trouble getting in. What is everyone talking about?

Cecilia: How many hours we work and the fact that we should probably all be working right now instead of sitting here chatting ☺

Gloria: Twenty-four hours a day. It's a never-ending job. I even design in my sleep.

Margery: Really. And what did you design last night?

Gloria: You think I'm joking, but I really do design in my sleep. I keep a pad of paper, a pen and a flashlight beside my bed so I can jot down pattern ideas in the middle of the night when they come to me.

Cecilia: That's interesting. I do the same thing. If I am having a problem with a design, I go upstairs and get in bed and the solution just comes to me.

Keira: I've actually fallen asleep while knitting, when I wake up...well enough said.

Mandy: Flashlight? Gloria, you're not married. Why don't you just turn on the light?

Gloria: I don't want to disturb my sleeping partner.

Margery: What? You haven't told us anything about this.

Keira: Yes, Gloria, do tell!

Gloria: Relax, ladies. He's a cockatiel. If I turn on the light, he squawks the rest of the night.

Sara: I didn't know you had a cockatiel. When did you get him?

Gloria: It's my brother's bird. I'm just babysitting him while John is out of town on business. He will be back next week and pick him up. I have no intentions of taking a noisy, squawking bird to the ACAKA conference.

Sara: I love birds.

Keira: Do you have your speech ready?

Gloria: Yes. Of course, I'm ready.

Sara: What is your speech about?

Gloria: The wonders of crochet! How versatile crochet is compared to other yarn crafts. How many more uses it has. How crochet can actually mimic other crafts and therefore is really the only craft one needs.

Keira: Gloria, this is a crochet and KNIT conference. You're not going to get up there and insult half your audience are you?

Gloria: I was chosen to speak because I am the best in the field and I fully intend to tell the truth. Are you actually asking me to lie?

Keira: Look, I know you are well known in your field and you were asked to give the keynote speech at the conference in large part due to the celebrity status that you have managed to obtain, but that doesn't mean that the rest of us are dirt underneath your feet. There are famous knit designers also. And I dare say some are more famous than you are.

Mandy: Keira, remember your famous saying, "Let's play nice ladies!" Maybe we better change the subject.

Cecilia: I'm looking forward to the conference. I just about have all my classes prepared that I am teaching. There are some last minute things to do, but I will not be able to do them until the day before the conference.

Mandy: What are you teaching?

Gloria: I have six classes. Check out the ACAKA website and you can read about them.

Sara: I signed up for all of your classes Gloria.

Cecilia: I'm teaching a class on double ended hook techniques and a class on Tunisian crochet. I also have a couple of professional classes. One is on how to design in crochet and the other is on how to write out a pattern.

—Alice has joined the group—

Gloria: If you can't make it with a real crochet hook, you shouldn't be calling it crochet.

Sara: I always use real crochet needles.

Keira: Welcome to the group, Alice.

Cecilia: Stop being such a purist. Tunisian hooks and double ended hooks ARE real hooks.

Alice: Hi, everyone. Sara, I am a knitter. I use needles. You are a crocheter. You use hooks ☺

Keira: Veronica, are you going to the ACAKA conference?

Margery: Hi, Alice.

Veronica: I don't know. I hadn't really considered it. What do you do at the conference?

Keira: Have a lot of fun mainly. There are all kinds of classes you can take. And they have an open market so you can buy just about any type of crochet or knit product you want.

Alice: Last year I purchased buffalo yarn. They have a lot of unusual things there.

Margery: Oh did you get some of the buffalo yarn? I was going to, but decided to get one of the hand carved crochet hooks instead.

Cecilia: Which one did you get?

Margery: It has a carved elephant on the end. It's really pretty.

Keira: Crocheters and knitters from all over the United States come to it. It is a great way to meet other addicts ☺

Gloria: They have guest speakers also. I am the featured speaker this year.

Mandy: They have a lot of door prizes and freebies too. Last year I got a whole suitcase full of yarn to bring home. And they have a gift exchange for anyone who wants to participate.

Alice: There is a fashion show on Saturday night. That is always my favorite event.

Gloria: Yes, I am modeling this year. My design will be a showstopper.

Keira: Really?

Gloria: You can count on it. I will be presenting a new stitch that I invented, but that is the only hint I'm going to give.

Cecilia: They have Designer and Teacher Growth Day also.

Veronica: What's that?

Cecilia: It's a day specifically for people who make a living or who want to make a living with crochet or knitting. They have speakers and classes. A lot of the editors and yarn company representatives go to it also. It is a good way to meet people in the industry.

Veronica: Editors and yarn company representatives go to this also?

Alice: Of course they do. Editors like to knit and crochet too ☺. It's a great opportunity to do a little networking.

Veronica: Where is the conference going to be?

Mandy: They have it in a different place every year. This year it is going to be in Marshall, Texas.

Keira: Veronica, if you are interested in going, be sure and make your plans soon. Classes fill up very quickly.

Gloria: Five of mine are already filled.

Veronica: I'll think about it. I better get going now.

Keira: Bye, Veronica.

Cecilia: Bye.

Veronica thought about the ACAKA conference the rest of the day. Texas was a long way away...how would she get there...she had never flown before and wasn't looking forward to the prospect of doing so...she could drive, but it would take at least nine hours to drive and it would be over mountainous roads...the bus?

What about Jack...he had been really sweet and supportive...hadn't even complained about all the yarn strewn about the house...not even the money she had invested.

The money...it would cost a fortune to go to Texas...money for hotel and food...and what about the expense of taking the classes. If she was closer to the conference...if she was already making a little money...she hadn't even received the check for the scarf yet...they said it would be forty-five days.

Did she really want to go...she and Jack had been married less than a year...did she really want to go away by herself for a week...they were still on their honeymoon.

And editors...Cecilia said there would be editors there...could she carry on a conversation with an editor...she had learned a lot, but she was still new at crochet...would they think she was totally out of her league...would she give them a permanent bad impression of herself and her abilities to work in the crochet world?

On the other hand, it would be fun...it would be extremely educational...her knowledge of crochet and the crochet industry would be expanded dramatically...it would be a great opportunity to meet people in the crochet industry...it would be exciting to talk with so many people all of whom were interested in crochet...

So many people! She was generally on the bashful side...how could she strike up a conversation with people she had never met?

Should she discuss the pros and cons with her friends in The Village the next afternoon? No. By the time the sun began to fade from the sky Veronica knew this trip was definitely not for her.

That evening, she and Jack had a lovely dinner, talked about everything but crochet, then fell asleep in each other's arms.

Fourteen

"Hi, Veronica," Sally said as she walked up behind her niece in the parking lot.

Veronica turned around to greet her aunt. "Oh, hi!" she exclaimed. "I didn't see you."

Sally shifted the heavily loaded crochet bag she was carrying on her shoulder. "I just got here," she replied. "Say, this is the first time you have beat me to The Village. You must be anxious to get started."

Veronica laughed. "No, my watch is fast. I actually thought I was running late."

"Are you going to the ACAKA conference?" Sally asked as they walked toward the shop entrance.

"What?" Veronica asked in surprise.

"The ACAKA conference," Sally said a little louder.

Veronica pulled the door to the shop open. "How did you know about the conference?"

"You told me about it the day you found ACAKA on the Internet," Sally reminded her as they entered the shop. "Plus, you were finding so much useful crochet information on the Internet, I decided to do a little research myself."

"Good afternoon ladies," Vashti called out from the back of the shop. "Just make yourselves at home. You know where everything is."

"Well, since we are so early I guess we should do a little shopping," Sally teased.

"Too late for that, I already know what I want," Veronica said as she began walking straight toward the center of the shop.

Sally followed wondering what Veronica was up to. "Really? What did you find?" she asked. Veronica reached her destination and pointed up at the ceiling. An old wood ladder, which had been strung to the ceiling so that it could be used as a shelf, was supporting five large baskets. "Those look like rice baskets," Sally observed.

"They are," Audra confirmed as she popped up behind Sally.

"Audra, you've got to stop sneaking up on people," Sally said as she turned around in surprise.

"But it's so much fun and so easy to do in here." Audra laughed. "Actually I was just looking at some of the silk threads down on the bottom shelf. I didn't really mean to scare you."

"Sure you didn't," Katy joshed as she walked up. "So, what's the topic?"

"I was just admiring the rice baskets," Veronica replied.

"Beautiful aren't they? But, what would you use it for?" Katy asked.

Use it for? Veronica hadn't really thought about that. The uniqueness of the design just appealed to her. She thought for a second. "I umm...I want to put my yarns in it and make kind of a display to go in the living room."

"Oh, that would be gorgeous!" Audra agreed.

Sally laughed. "Yes, Love will certainly think so!"

"It's four o'clock ladies," Vashti announced. "Oh, by the way, I heard from Destiny this afternoon. She said that her cousin was feeling better and she would be back in Springfield on Saturday. Of course there are no classes next week since everyone is going to the ACAKA meeting in Texas, but classes will begin again a week from next Thursday."

"Everyone is going?" Veronica asked in surprise.

Katy laughed. "When Vashti goes, everyone goes."

"Huh?"

"The shop is closed next week," Chrissy began explaining as everyone worked their way toward the back table and sat down. "Vashti is one of the vendors in the open market. She has a booth every year."

"I didn't know she went to ACAKA," Veronica pulled a ball of hunter green, silk yarn out of her bag as she spoke.

"Of course. We all try to go every year," Jenny replied. Veronica watched as Jenny began working on a black sequined shell.

"Yes, I was just asking Veronica outside if she was planning on going this year," Sally remarked. She pulled a skein of pink yarn out of her bag then added, "I'm not going to be able to go myself, but I thought Veronica would have a nice time."

"So, are you going?" Audra asked.

"I don't know." Veronica began running her fingers through the soft yarn. "Texas is so far and I haven't discussed it with Jack."

"Oh, I bet he would have a nice time," Katy countered.

"He? You mean husbands go to this also?" Veronica asked in surprise. In all her debating, the possibility of Jack going with her was not an aspect that she had considered.

"Well, most don't," Katy admitted. Katy was crocheting the forest green yarn in front of her so fast that her fingers were almost a blur. Her hands slowed only slightly as she winked at Audra. Veronica assumed the gesture meant Audra's husband was one of the abstainers. "But a few of the women bring their husbands. Some even bring their kids. And of course there are a few men who bring their wives also," she continued, never missing a stitch.

Audra added, as she began putting the finishing touches on the alpaca lace shawl she was working on, "Robert, he is the editor of *Crochet Elite* magazine, he always brings his wife along. She doesn't crochet, but he has been crocheting ever since he was a child. Wrote several crochet books before he became the editor of *Crochet Elite*. Very nice man, you'd like him."

"What do the people do that don't crochet?" Veronica asked, concerned that Jack would have nothing to do.

"Just use the time for a vacation I guess," Chrissy suggested.

"I know some take the hook carving class. They learn how to carve a crochet hook out of a piece of wood," Audra replied.

"Of course, they spend time with their spouses also," Katy added, fingers still flying.

"Are all of you going?" Veronica asked as she wound the yarn around her hook.

"I am," Jenny said holding up her sequined yarn. "I'm wearing this Yang top in the fashion show, well, presuming I can get it finished in time." She laughed.

"Oh, you'll have it finished," Chrissy assured her. "I'm the one having the problem. I'm supposed to wear this silk skirt I have been working on for the last two weeks. It takes forever to crochet with lace weight yarn, but I love the feel of it."

"Yang?" Veronica asked.

"That's the name of the yarn. It's made by South West Trading Company," Jenny explained. "I love the little sequins in it."

"Audra and I are going also. We're not going to be in the fashion show, but we'll be watching. It's always a lot of fun." Katy put her work down on the table then began digging through her crochet bag from which she retrieved several sheets of white paper. "And, of course, we'll be taking classes. I'm taking a class on how to crochet socks and also one on fair isle single crochet," she said placing the class papers in front of Veronica.

"So, I guess that leaves you," Sally teased.

"I don't know." Veronica quickly read through the two classes that Katy was taking. "It sounds like a lot of fun. I just don't know if Jack would want to do something like that or if he could even get away from work." She paused a moment. "When are you all leaving?"

"It starts on Thursday so we'll fly down Wednesday night," Chrissy replied.

"They have a Designer and Teacher Growth Day on Wednesday, but we don't go to that. None of us are interested in being in the business. Well, except Destiny, of course. She is a professional teacher in the ACAKA," Jenny explained as she busily maneuvered her hook through the sequined yarn.

Katy placed her papers back in her crochet bag. "Say that would be a good thing for you to go to. You said you were interested in the idea of an at home job in the crochet field. I bet you could learn a lot of valuable information if you went."

"Have you pursued that any further?" Audra asked as she cut her thread.

"I made a few swatches and sent them to *Crochet Elite* magazine on Wednesday." Veronica looked down at the silk yarn in her hands and realized she had been mindlessly crocheting, but what, she wasn't quite sure.

"That's wonderful! You should definitely go to Growth Day then," Jenny agreed.

Veronica stared at her work. It was pretty, but what exactly had she done? "I just don't know," she replied. "It sounds like an extremely expensive trip for someone who isn't earning an income at the moment."

"Can't help you there." Katy laughed.

Veronica analytically began frogging her work, one stitch at a time, trying to discern how she had created it. Maybe she would talk to Jack. Maybe...

Fifteen

$\longrightarrow\!\blacklozenge\!\blacklozenge\!\longleftarrow$

"Honey! Sweetheart! Wake up!" Jack called from the bedroom door.

"What's wrong?" Veronica asked as she sleepily opened one eye.

"Get your digital camera and get dressed."

Veronica reluctantly crawled out of bed. "What's going on?"

"Just grab your clothes and I'll explain on the way," Jack said as he ran out of the house.

Veronica pulled on her clothes as fast as she could. Something must be terribly wrong…makeup and hair would have to wait. She went to the desk, grabbed her camera then ran outside.

"What's wrong?" she asked again as she jumped in the car.

"I woke up early this morning and decided to go jogging," Jack began explaining as he backed out of the driveway. "When I got to the railroad crossing I found a brass rail observation car sitting on a siding. I asked the engineer and he said it would be there for about half an hour. I've got to have some photos! That's not something you see every day!"

"You mean you woke me up from a sound sleep to photograph a train sitting in the weeds?" Veronica asked in disbelief.

"Yes! It's going to be fun isn't it?" Jack exclaimed excitedly.

Veronica smiled. Little boys definitely never grew up, she thought.

They pulled up to the siding a few minutes later. "Don't get on the tracks, but get as close as you can. Try to get some of the railing in the picture, along with the car," Jack instructed as Veronica began tromping through the knee-high weeds.

Veronica took several pictures before Jack announced he wanted to drive over the crossing to the other side of the tracks, so that he could have photos from all angles.

A dozen photos later Veronica realized, despite being awakened so abruptly, she was actually beginning to enjoy herself. The morning breeze almost made it seem cool outside. And tromping through the weeds early in the morning was kind of an adventure. Definitely not what she would have pictured herself doing the night before, but all the same, it was a nice adventure.

"Thanks, I appreciate your taking the photos for me," Jack said when she turned to go back to the car. "I'm not too great with a camera. Would you like to go get some breakfast?"

"Yes. Coffee would be wonderful."

What are your plans today?" Jack asked while they were awaiting their breakfast orders.

"I wanted to talk to you about something. I was going to wait until you got home from work tonight, but I guess now is as good a time as any." Veronica stirred sugar and cream in her coffee, obviously stalling.

"What's wrong, sweetheart?"

"Nothing's wrong." She picked up a fork then put it back down again. Jack patiently waited. A minute later, speaking a little too fast, she began. "I was just thinking. There's a crochet show in Marshall, Texas next week. They have a designer meeting that starts at eight Wednesday morning then they have crochet classes that people can take Thursday through Sunday. They have a fashion show, gift exchange, auction, door prizes, guest speakers, and all kinds of things. I was even told that the editor I sent the scarf to will be there. I know it's a long way away and you would miss a whole week of work, but I was just wondering if maybe you would be interested in going?"

"Yes!" Jack replied enthusiastically as he pulled out his cell phone and began dialing.

"Who are you calling?"

"Amtrak, of course! We can catch the train just a few towns down the road from here. The train goes straight to Marshall."

"How do you know this?"

"Marshall is a big railroad town. They just remodeled the depot a few years back. Put in a museum. I was hoping to get a chance to see it, but I figured you would think it was a boring trip, so I never brought it up." Jack spoke into the phone, "Agent." Then he looked playfully at Veronica. "When did you say you needed to be there?"

Monday, how would she ever get ready by Monday? Just three days away. The plan was to drive to the train station Monday afternoon and board the train around midnight. They would ride all night long and get to Marshall around eight the next morning. Check into the hotel and sleep so that she would be rested and ready for the conference on Wednesday.

Veronica called all her yarn shop friends to let them know she was going to the conference and arrangements were made to meet on Thursday morning.

Now what to do, she wondered. Love jumped into her lap and began purring. "Ok, you're next," she said as she picked up the cell phone and began dialing her aunt.

"Hello?"

"Hi, Auntie. I talked to Jack. I still can't believe it. He wants to go!"

"Really?"

"Well, I doubt he wants to go to the crochet show, we didn't actually discuss that part." Love, deciding it must be naptime, began kneading her leg. "But he wants to ride the train to Marshall."

"That's wonderful!"

Veronica scratched Love under the chin. "Love wants to know if his favorite, Great Aunt, would be willing to kitty sit while we're gone."

"Sure, I'd be happy to. Actually it will help me out also because I need to be in Springfield all next week. The library is holding a training seminar for the volunteers and I promised I would attend and help out. That's the reason I couldn't go to the crochet conference with you. Tell Love, his, Great Aunt, will spoil him rotten."

"I think you're a little too late for that." Veronica laughed. "Thanks, Auntie. I really appreciate your doing this," she said as she hung up the phone.

"Well, Love, you have a kitty sitter. Now march over to the computer and help me make reservations." Love obediently leapt on top of the computer monitor, turned around a few times then sat down, with his right paw dangling in front of the screen. Veronica turned on the computer then went to the ACAKA site to see what she could learn about the conference.

Gloria was right. Most of the classes were full. And, she discovered to her dismay, there was no room in the inn, literally. When she called she was told that rooms were booked at least six months in advance. She had no idea the conference was so huge. Over seven hundred rooms had been reserved for the conference and they were all taken.

It was also too late to enter the fashion show. Not that she would have had enough guts to get up on the stage, but it was just surprising to her that everything was done so far in advance of the actual conference date.

She had been on an emotional rollercoaster for the last few days for nothing. Veronica decided not to disturb Jack at work. She would let him know when he got home that it was too late to get accommodations.

Veronica continued to peruse the site. She clicked on a button labeled, Teachers, and was delighted to discover that it was a list of all the teachers who would be at the conference. It gave each teacher's biography and a little photo. Veronica began reading the information. It was wonderful to be able to see the faces of the designers she had been conversing with on the chat line.

She looked up Gloria's name first. Veronica was surprised at how tiny Gloria appeared in the photo. In her mind she had pictured her to be a much larger person. An avid crocheter since the age of fourteen...had her first design published while still a teenager...over fifteen years teaching experience...has written ten crochet books, all best sellers...published in every crochet magazine as well as in some non-crochet magazines...produced and starred in a DVD on crochet technique...designs sweaters for famous television spokesman Phillip LeBlanc...travels extensively on lecture tours sharing her love of crochet...has her own line of clothing...native born Texan.

"Good grief, Love, no wonder she acts the way she does on the chat line. I don't see how she even has time to go into a chat room with all she is doing," Veronica spoke softly to Love as she stroked his long soft fur. "I didn't know she was that famous! I guess that's why everyone seems so jealous of her and why people act so defensive around her. What do you say we look up Keira?"

Keira...master knitter...began knitting in college...went on to study art and design in Paris...teaching for the last twelve years...has written nine books on various aspects of fashion design...prolific knitter for magazines...runs ACAKA chat line on Wednesdays and Thursdays.

"Oh, Love, I am way out of my league! I never dreamed they had all those credentials. They must think I'm an idiot with all my childish questions. If I'd known all this, I never would have gone in that chat room." Veronica picked Love up and went and sat on the sofa. Love curled up on her chest and began to purr. Now he was certain it was naptime. Veronica continued to speak softly, "Of course, they have all been nice to me. Keira keeps asking if I have more questions and Ellen congratulated me when I said I had sent in some swatches. Hey, let's go read about Ellen." Veronica went back to the computer with Love following close behind. He was giving her one of his, would you please make up your mind looks as he jumped back up on the monitor.

Veronica clicked a few buttons. "Ellen must not be teaching. I don't see her name," Veronica informed him. "I'll try Margery." Love, who was getting quite bored with the conversation, gave a big yarn and went to sleep.

Veronica began to read to herself. Margery...master crocheter...

Veronica's reading was suddenly interrupted by an email notification.

Good Afternoon Veronica,

We received your swatch submissions this morning and are very impressed with your work. Your insight into crochet is amazing for someone who is just starting out. Several people on our staff have gone over your swatches and all have been equally impressed with your unique ability to create new stitches out of old ones.

I don't know if you are familiar with the American Crochet and Knitting Association. They hold a conference once a year so that people can get together and learn more about the fiber arts. This year the conference will be held in Marshall, Texas.

The conference begins on Wednesday with Designer and Teacher Growth Day. Fiber classes are taught Thursday through Sunday. It is basically five days of intense learning.

Crochet Elite magazine, since we are always in search of new talent, sponsors one person who shows a large amount of potential each year.

About six months ago we chose Dave, a young man from Washington. He emailed us yesterday that, due to family obligations, he will not be able to attend.

We would like to offer you his place at the show.

We will pay all travel expenses for you and one traveling companion. Overnight accommodations and food for two will also be covered. If you decide to accept our offer, you will have the room that was previously booked. It is a nice room with a king size bed, refrigerator, microwave, cable television and Internet hook up, conveniently located in the same inn as the conference. Although your class fees will be covered, we do not pay for classes for your companion.

It is probably too late to sign up for the classes of your choice, but all of the previous recipient's selections are available to you. If you are interested let us know and I will send you a list of the classes Dave had chosen. Also, if you see a class still open that you would rather take, you can change to the class you prefer. We just know from experience that it is hard to find a class that is still open at this late date.

We do expect you to attend Designer and

Teacher Growth Day. We also request that you be available to us outside of class time for whatever meetings might come up.

Please let us know ASAP if you will be able to attend.

Sincerely,

Robert H. Howl
Editor
Crochet Elite magazine

Veronica couldn't believe her eyes. She read the email again. Still not quite believing what she was reading, she hit the reply button and began typing her response.

Sixteen

Darkness filled the sky. Veronica could barely see the outline of the moon as it hid behind a cloud. She and Jack walked carefully toward the depot rolling suitcases behind them. The depot was locked. Jack circled around to the side and signaled Veronica to follow. There were six cast iron benches lined up about six feet away from two rows of tracks. A mother, father and little boy were seated on the fourth bench. Veronica followed Jack to the fifth one and sat down. Despite the warmth of the evening the seat felt cool.

Policemen were patrolling the area, driving up and down the pathway to the depot. An occasional siren was heard from one of the cars.

Jack, too excited to sit, said he was going to look at the depot and a yellow baggage cart he had spotted. Veronica looked around. It was so dark she could barely even make out the building, which loomed behind them.

Watching the night sky, looking at the tracks, suddenly Veronica began to feel very peaceful. She noticed that the tracks in front of her looked fluid, almost like water, as the light from the streetlamps across the way shown down on them.

"The train is late," Jack announced when he returned. He sat back down beside Veronica. "It could have left Chicago late or it might have been held up in St. Louis."

The moon came out from behind the cloud and Veronica

began counting the stars in the sky. A few minutes later Jack began regaling her with stories: tales of trains, remodeling projects, mail trains, depots, boxcar graffiti, ghosts of people from the past riding the train.

The minutes ticked by, still no train.

"I'm glad we decided to come the night before," Veronica remarked. "I wouldn't want to be late for the conference."

"They'll probably make up some of the lost time in route. But I'm glad we came a day early also. We probably won't sleep much on the train. That is, if it ever gets here. I think I'll walk around a little more."

Veronica continued sitting on the bench listening to the soothing sounds of the diesel locomotive idling on the siding. The lull of the engines had just about put her to sleep when suddenly she saw four bright lights headed straight toward her. A banging sound was heard as the freight train crossed the junction. Within seconds the train was whizzing by less than six feet in front of her. She heard the little bell ringing followed by a blast from the whistle, felt the breeze from the cars on her face and listened to the rumbling, clacking sounds as the flanged wheels rolled along the ribbon rail. This was going to be more fun than she expected, she thought.

"That freight must be what was holding up our train," Jack said as he walked up behind her.

More time passed, still no train.

A baggage clerk, who had arrived a few minutes earlier, walked up to Jack and began talking about railroading.

A second freight train rumbled by, followed by a third.

Jack and the baggage clerk continued conversing.

Several minutes later, a man drove up and got out of his car. He was busily talking on his cell phone. When he hung up he announced that his wife, who was on the south bound train, told him that the train left St. Louis an hour and a half late, but should be there shortly.

"Here it comes," the baggage clerk announced. "I hear the

whistle. I'm sorry I monopolized all of your husband's time," he said turning toward Veronica. "I guess I was just born with the gift of gab."

The whistle got louder as Train 21 approached the depot. Veronica could hear the squeal of breaks as the train came to a stop. She and Jack grabbed their luggage and headed toward the open door of the coach. Jack showed the conductor their identification and handed him the tickets, then they stepped aboard.

Veronica found herself on the lower level of a double-decker car. "Go to the left then climb up the stairs on your right," Jack instructed. They slowly climbed up the ten narrow winding stairs dragging their luggage behind them. "Where do you want to sit?" Jack whispered.

Veronica looked down the aisle. A row of blue chairs, with randomly scattered green triangles on them, flanked both sides. "It doesn't matter," she whispered back. "They all look the same."

Jack quietly led her past the water station toward the front of the car. Trying not to awaken the other passengers, he stowed their luggage in the rack above seats numbered sixty-one and sixty-two, then they sat down.

Veronica began playing with the buttons on the chair. The silver round button on the arm of the chair lowered the back of the seat while the black round knob lowered the leg rest. The rectangular knob on the seat in front of her lowered a tray and the square knob raised a footrest. The buttons above her head worked the lights and air-conditioning and called the steward. She also found a black mesh bag that she could stow things in.

"I take it you are having fun?" Jack asked as he watched her explore her surroundings.

"Here are your pillows," the steward said as he handed each of them a small white pillow, then walked away.

"Do you want to go see the observation car or do you want to try to get some sleep?" Jack asked.

Veronica knew there was no way Jack was going to sleep, which meant she wasn't either. "Sure, let's go."

Just as she stood up, the train pulled out from the station, and she fell back into her seat. "Hold onto the seat until you get your balance. When you walk, walk with feet between twelve and eighteen inches apart. It will help you maintain your balance," Jack explained as the train began to rock back and forth.

"I'll be ok. I just wasn't expecting that." Veronica stood up again. Following Jack's advice, she walked to the vestibule then stopped. "How do you open the door?" she asked.

"Press the top black rectangle with your hand or press the bottom one with your foot," he replied. "The door will open automatically. Be careful once you are inside the vestibule that you don't step on the opening between the two cars. Always step over it. You never know when the train is going to jostle. You can hang onto the red and white striped, vertical bars to help keep your balance."

Veronica pressed the top rectangle. A loud whooshing sound could be heard as the door slid open. Veronica discovered that the rumbling of the train was much louder when standing on the vestibule. She quickly pushed the rectangle on the next door so they could enter the observation car.

"This is really nice," Veronica said as she looked around. "You can see out in every direction." Veronica looked up, "I can even see the stars through the top of the car."

"Yes, this is my favorite car. Come on, I'll show you the downstairs lounge and snack bar."

Veronica followed Jack down the stairs. On one end, several people were seated at tables. Some were playing cards while others were playing checkers. On the other end was a closed snack bar.

"It's a little crowded down here. Let's go back upstairs and look out the windows," Veronica suggested.

They climbed back up the stairs and took a double seat

facing the west. The train whistle blew and Veronica began waving at the people in their automobiles waiting for the train to get past the crossing. A few minutes later they were out in the country. Jack put his arms around Veronica and kissed her sweetly on the lips. "You're right," Veronica whispered. "Trains are wonderful."

A couple hours later Jack decided he was going to try to get some sleep and headed back to the coach. Veronica opted to stay and enjoy the view a little longer. She did, however, go back with him long enough to fetch her kitty cat yarn bag.

As she sat crocheting swatches she began dreaming about the conference. Dreaming and praying that she wouldn't make a fool out of herself in front of all those editors.

The door of the car rattled open and the whooshing sound once again filled the air. A petite woman with shoulder length blonde hair walked in followed by a slightly taller, slightly older woman. "Ah, I knew we would find a yarnie in here," the petite woman announced as she walked toward Veronica. "You must be going to the conference. We are too. My name is Keira."

"Keira? Are you the, Keira, on the ACAKA chat line?" Veronica asked.

"One and the same." Keira smiled sweetly. "And what is your name?"

"I'm Veronica. I started going into the chat room a couple of weeks ago."

"Of course! Veronica. It's nice to meet you in person. This is Margery," she said pointing to the brunette standing beside her. "I believe the two of you have talked on the chat line also. So, you decided to go to the conference. That's wonderful." Keira and Margery sat down in chairs next to Veronica and began digging through their bags. "I'm working on a multicolored Mobius shawl for the class I'm teaching on Sunday," Keira explained.

Margery pulled out a partially finished, turquoise colored, alpaca sweater. "I only have until Friday morning." She laughed. "Oh, what messes I get myself into. I should have started crocheting this weeks ago."

"Well, at least it's a top down sweater. You could always make it a crop top if you have to," Keira suggested.

"Oh, I'll have it finished in time. Might have to stay up all night, but I'll get it done. I have to have it for class on Friday and it's already in the lineup for the fashion show Saturday night."

"So, Veronica, what are your plans for the conference? Were you able to get into any of the classes?" Keira asked as she began working on her shawl.

"Yes. After I talked to you in the chat room I received an email from Robert at *Crochet Elite* magazine. He said that the designer they were sponsoring this year couldn't make it at the last minute and offered to give me his place. I ended up with a full schedule of classes," Veronica answered jubilantly.

"Oh, you poor little thing," Margery said sympathetically, clucking her tongue.

Veronica was so surprised at the melancholy tone of Margery's voice that she dropped her crochet hook. "What do you mean?"

"I'm sorry, I didn't mean to scare you." Margery retrieved Veronica's hook from under the seat and handed it to her. "I guess we should have warned you. Taking more than four classes in a weekend sends most people into crochet overload. You are learning so much so fast that your mind just can't keep up with it. A full load is twenty-four hours of class time and that doesn't count the homework time or the time at the fashion show."

Keira jumped in, "It also doesn't include the time you will be spending networking with editors, shopping in the market, going to the speed contest, helping teach the beginners, working in the Doctor Is In booth, going to the auction, or any of the business meetings."

Veronica was dubious. Crochet overload? Were they kidding or sincerely trying to give her much needed advice. She looked at Margery then Keira then Margery again trying to read their faces.

Margery worked on her sweater a few more minutes before happily continuing. "Veronica, you need to give yourself some time to absorb what you have learned. To let it all sink in. Girl, you are going to be in crochet overload! I can see it coming." Margery began chuckling and shaking her head, obviously enjoying Veronica's predicament.

Veronica realized, kidding or not, Margery was making a good point. She hadn't really thought this trip through. Everything had happened so fast. "I didn't think about needing down time," she confessed.

"Oh, and the Designer's Contest, we left that one out!" Margery continued to tease.

Veronica wanted to ignore the teasing, but the word contest intrigued her. "What is the Designer's Contest?" she asked a little too excitedly.

Keira looked up from her knitting, "Ah, now we have her captive."

"Yep, I believe she's caught!" Margery replied thoroughly amused by Veronica's exuberant naiveté. When the laughter finally died down Margery explained. "Every year all of the designers go into a private room. They take turns picking a closed sealed box. When the bell rings, they open their box. They have four hours to create whatever they want to out of the contents of their box. The completed designs are put on display and everyone votes on their favorite. The two winners are reigned Crocheter of the Year and Knitter of the Year.

"Afterwards, all of the designs are published in a book and the proceeds go to charity. No one is paid, not even the publishers. It's all done for charity. The book has been a huge success every year and has benefited several worthy organizations."

"That sounds exciting! Do all of the crochet designers participate?" Veronica asked, noting that, despite all of the conversing she was doing, Margery's sweater had grown several inches.

"Not Gloria, she never participates," Margery replied sarcastically. "Personally, I don't think she could take it if she lost. She is so competitive. I guess she figures it is best not to enter than to take the chance."

"You don't seem to like her very much," Veronica observed.

"I just don't care for her personality," Margery explained. "She has let the fact that she is a, quote unquote, 'celebrity designer' go to her head. She thinks she is better than everyone else. Struts around acting like some kind of prima donna."

"She is pretty hard on the knitters also," Keira added. Her needles clicked out a steady rhythm as she spoke. "I'm glad she likes to crochet. I think that's wonderful. But there is nothing wrong with the fact that I like to knit."

The train slowly came to a stop. Veronica watched out the window while a dozen or so passengers climbed on board.

Margery added, "I'm a crocheter. Keira is a knitter. We get along great together. The two crafts are completely different in the way they are produced, but they both use the same yarns and they both are used to make fashion designs. That's why the ACAKA organization combines them. But for some reason Gloria just doesn't seem to want the knitters around. It's ridiculous. Plus, she is making a lot of enemies along the way."

"Enemies?" Veronica asked. The whistle blew and once again they were on their way.

"Yes, in the fiber field." Margery began crocheting a sleeve onto the sweater as she spoke. "Editors are starting to work with her less and less. She has basically just become too much trouble. I've heard rumors that she has sunk so low she has actually started flirting with people in position of power." Margery stopped crocheting and looked at Veronica. "She's a great designer, but some editors are beginning to feel that the problems are not worth the result. That's why she has had fewer designs published the last couple of years."

Keira nodded in agreement. "That probably scares her too. Maybe that's why she seems to be lashing out at knitters more and more. I mean she is almost violent toward us sometimes."

"Changing the subject, I've crocheted a whole ball of yarn and I don't feel like winding anymore," Margery placed the sweater she was working on back in her bag as she spoke. "Veronica, would you like me to show you a few crochet techniques and stitches?"

Margery, Veronica and Keira sat in the observation car talking, laughing and working on stitches until the wee hours of the morning.

Veronica yawned. "I hate to leave, but I can hardly keep my eyes open. I think I need to go to the coach and get some sleep." Veronica gathered her supplies then slowly stood up. "It's been great meeting both of you."

"It's been great meeting you also. I'm sure we'll see you running around the conference. Don't forget to breathe once in awhile," Margery joked as Veronica started toward the vestibule.

"Yes, I'll be the one with the jogging shoes on," Veronica replied as she yawned again. She pushed the black rectangle on the door and as the door slid open the car was once again filled with the sounds of the train rolling down the track.

"Where are we?" Veronica asked as she pulled herself up in the seat.

"We just made it to Texarkana," Jack said. He pulled back the dark blue curtains so that Veronica could see the chalky green and off-white depot.

Veronica watched as several more people boarded the train. "What time is it?" she asked.

"Six-thirty. We're about half an hour late right now. They'll probably make up some time between here and Marshall. Do you want to go to the dining car and have some breakfast?"

"Sure, sounds good to me," Veronica said as she began to stretch.

Jack stood up. "Did you get any sleep last night?"

"Not much. I stayed in the observation car most of the night. Oh I got to meet Keira and Margery. They are two of the designers I have been chatting with on the Internet. They are both really nice ladies!" Veronica stood up, steadied herself then stepped out into the aisle, feet eighteen inches apart.

"Ah, milady learns fast!" Jack grinned.

Veronica and Jack walked into the dining car and waited to be seated. Men in uniform were busily serving breakfast. The tables were covered with white linen tablecloths and were set with dishes and silverware sporting the Amtrak emblem. Each table also held a vase of colorful flowers.

Veronica held onto the wall as she tried to maintain her balance. "How do they manage to carry hot coffee without dumping it on everyone?" she asked as one of the waiters walked by with a tray full of hot beverages.

"Years of practice," another waiter said as he walked up to them. "Right this way please." He pointed to a table where two people were already sitting. "We have communal seating on the train," he explained.

Veronica slid into the booth followed by Jack.

"Hello," said one of the two ladies already at the table.

"Hello," Jack replied as the menus were placed in front of them. "Railroad French toast, turkey sausage and coffee please," he said as he handed his menu back to the waiter.

"I'll have the same. That sounds delicious."

The waiter filled out their order sheet then left. Jack once again greeted their breakfast companions. "My wife is going to the fiber conference in Marshall. Is that where the two of you are headed?"

"Yes, we are," replied the one sitting closest to the aisle. "I look forward to this conference every year. I'm one of the charter members." The waiter brought the coffee back. Veronica loaded her coffee down with cream and sugar as the woman continued to speak, "I'm a crocheter and my friend here is a knitter. Which are you?"

"I learned to knit when I was little. I am trying crochet now." Veronica tasted the coffee. Perfection. She carefully placed the sloshing liquid back on the table. "This is going to be interesting eating."

"I imagine we're speeding up since we're late and I have the feeling we're sitting on a wheel, which always makes it a little rougher." Jack looked reassuringly at Veronica as the train suddenly jerked to the right. "But this is good, you get the complete train dining experience!"

"That's wonderful that you do both," the woman continued. "Several people at the conference both crochet and knit."

"Oh, look, the sun must be coming up! I can see some orange streaks in the sky," the woman by the window said as she glanced out.

"Feels like the train is stopping, are we coming to another town?" Veronica quickly took several sips from her cup, taking advantage of the gentler rocking motion.

Jack leaned over and looked out the window. "I think we're heading onto a siding. A freight train must be coming. Freights are always given the right of way," he explained.

The train came to a complete stop. Veronica looked out at the woodland scene surrounding her. It was a beautiful morning. She watched as a flock of birds flew across the sky. "Are both of you designers?" she asked as she turned back to the table.

"No. Just crochet and knit fanatics," the woman by the

aisle answered. Then she went on to explain, "We won't actually be at the conference until late Wednesday. We're taking the train on to Dallas to do a little shopping. We'll spend the night there and then catch the train back to Marshall Wednesday afternoon. Are you a designer?"

"More like a designer wannabe." Veronica smiled.

"Ah, our food's here," Jack said as the waiter began presenting plates filled with breakfast delicacies.

Silence quickly fell over the table as everyone began to eat.

"That was a wonderful meal," Veronica said as they sat in the lounge car looking out at the scenery.

"I thought you would like it," Jack replied.

The train rolled out of the woods then past an old cemetery. Veronica looked at the tall monuments, most of which were in need of repair. Then she saw the little angel, a perfect little angel sitting atop a tall pedestal looking down over the dead as if it were protecting everyone in their abode. Veronica said a little prayer. Time would pass, life would go on, but she would never forget.

Veronica took out her crochet swatches and began working on them. One by one passengers came up to her to see what she was crocheting. Before long there was a whole crowd of people excitedly chattering away in crochet lingo. "Excuse me, ladies and gentlemen," Jack said as he stood up to leave. "I think the conductor is calling me. You just go right on doing what you are doing. I'm sure it is nothing serious. Don't pay any attention to me. The train is probably just being hijacked or something and he needs my assistance."

No one heard a word he said. They were all too deep in their own little world of crochet.

"Next stop, Marshall, Texas. Five minutes ladies and gentlemen. Marshall, Texas," the voice from the loud speaker announced.

Veronica looked around as the crowd dispersed, for the first time realizing Jack was gone. She hurried back to the coach car and found him sitting in the seat looking out the window. "I thought you were in the observation car with me. I didn't know you had left."

"You were slightly on the busy side." He laughed. "But that's ok. Now I know how you must feel when I get together with my train buddies. Come on, let's go downstairs and wait." Jack grabbed the luggage off the rack then they headed toward the back of the car and down the winding stairs. Through the downstairs door window, they watched as Train 21 slowly pulled into the station.

When the train came to a complete stop, the conductor opened the door and placed a step stool on the payment. He then courteously helped the passengers down one at a time. As Veronica stepped off the train, she felt her very first wave of true Texas heat.

The depot was a large, multilevel, red brick building with elaborate white trimming. It looked very distinguished with its manicured lawn, black wrought iron gates and park like atmosphere.

Veronica and Jack walked through the gate toward the depot, down a flight of stairs and into a large tunnel lit by sunlight that entered from both ends. Once through the tunnel they began climbing another flight of stairs. Veronica looked down at the steps as they ascended them, *The Texas T & P Pacific Railway*, was imprinted on each stair along with a large letter "*S*". "I wonder what the 'S' stands for."

"Smith Steel Casting, it's the monogram of the company that did the repair work on the stairs."

"How do you know these things?" Veronica exclaimed.

Veronica sat down on one of the benches, which lined the depot and called her aunt to let her know they had arrived safely while Jack went exploring. Robert had emailed earlier that his plane was landing at seven fifty-five. He was going to rent a car at the airport then he and his wife would drive out to the train station and pick them up around ten. As she sat and waited she could hear Train 21 in the distance departing the station.

Seventeen

———◆◆———

"Hello. You must be Veronica," a gray haired man of around fifty said as he stepped out of a light blue Buick Sedan.

Veronica stood up, "Yes, and you're, Robert?"

"Yes, I'm Robert and this is my wife, Clara." Robert motioned toward his wife, a robust woman who seemed to radiate happiness. Clara hurried over to Veronica, gave her a gushing hello and a warm welcoming hug.

"It's nice to meet both of you," Veronica returned the greeting. "I want to thank you for giving us this trip. I really appreciate it."

"No, we thank you. You have more than earned it. The whole staff has been very impressed with your creativity." Robert gestured toward the building behind her. "Is your husband in the museum?"

"Yes. He should be out any second now."

"Well, let's go ahead and get your luggage loaded into the car."

Robert bent over to pick up a bag, but Veronica stopped him. "I wanted to ask you, I'm a little concerned, I talked to Margery on the train and she said that signing up for eight classes was a mistake. She said..."

"Don't worry about it," Robert interrupted her. "We want you to attend the Growth Day on Wednesday and be available for meetings. Other than that, take the classes that you would enjoy." He picked up a few suitcases and headed toward the car. Veronica grabbed the rest and followed. "You may end up taking all of them or might only take four or five. We understand that you didn't pick the classes, the previous recipient did. Just take the ones you are interested in." Robert popped the trunk open then began stowing away the luggage.

"Thank you. There were several I thought would be interesting," Veronica replied just as Jack walked out of the museum. Jack joined the group then Veronica made the introductions.

"Nice to meet both of you," Jack greeted them.

"We have your luggage in the car so if you are ready to go we will head on down to the Marshall Inn," Robert said as he opened the car door.

"Thank you," Jack replied. "I've been thinking about it, and if it wouldn't be too far out of your way, would you mind taking us to a rental shop?" Jack opened the car door for Veronica then continued, "I'd like to have a means of transportation while we are here. I thought I could come back and look at the museum some more and maybe visit a few other places in this area while Veronica is at the conference."

"Oh, sweetie, that's no problem at all!" Clara smiled happily. "In fact, there is a place just down the road from the Inn."

"It's beautiful!" Veronica exclaimed as they turned off Highway 59 into the inn's parking lot. Jack pulled into a parking place then began unloading the car.

Veronica stepped out into the blistering heat, instinctively raising her hand to shield her eyes. "I love all the flowers," she said as they walked toward the entrance. "Oh, look at the elephant ears! They are huge! I've never seen elephant ears that big before. I love it!" Veronica placed her luggage on a nearby bench then squatted down on the sidewalk. "They're so cute!"

Jack was confused. "Elephant ears are cute? Veronica, they're just giant green leaves."

"No, the lizards are cute! Look!" Veronica pointed toward the ground. "There are dozens of them running around in the flowerbeds." Veronica picked up one of the little lizards, gave it a quick hug then began petting it.

"Well, before you fall too much in love, let's get checked in and see what the rooms look like. We're not sleeping in the flower beds," Jack teased.

Veronica returned the lizard to his home. Then with luggage in hand, she and Jack walked under the awning into the inn. It was just as lovely inside as out. Decorated in an African motif from top to bottom; ceiling fan blades shaped like giant leaves, carved leaves on lamps, ornate elephant statues artistically placed around the lobby, large wood chests, safari paintings on the walls, foliage lining the mezzanine and along the walls, tall trees in every corner, colors of green, brown, burgundy and orange, all contributed to the atmosphere.

"Hello," Robert greeted them as they walked in. "You will be in room 203 on the mezzanine. Here are your entry cards. Did everything work out ok at the car rental?"

"Yes. Thank you. Everything went very well." Jack handed one card to Veronica and placed the other in his pocket.

"Good, good. Clara and I are going to eat downtown this evening, would the two of you care to join us?"

Veronica looked at Jack then turned back to Robert. "That would be very nice. Thank you," she replied.

"Good. We'll see you about six-thirty."

Veronica and Jack slept most of the afternoon, then dressed for dinner. Veronica shuddered as they stepped out into the hallway.

"Are you nervous or just freezing?" Jack asked.

"Both. I just don't want to make any mistakes tonight. The more I think about it the more I want to be a professional designer. I mean I play with the yarn and it just feels right somehow. Like something I am meant to be doing. I just don't want to blow it tonight."

Jack jiggled the door to make sure it was locked. "Sweetheart, you're going to dinner, not a job interview. They already like your work. They paid for you to come to this conference. Just relax and be yourself. They'll love you." Jack leaned over and kissed her on the lips. "I know I do."

"Good evening," Robert greeted them as they stepped off the elevator. "You both look nice and rested."

"Yes. The nap was wonderful," Veronica replied. "I hope we didn't keep you waiting."

Clara put the paper down she was reading and stood up. "No, no, sweetie, I was just reading in the paper about the conference." She walked over to Veronica. "That *Marshall News Messenger* makes it sound so exciting! Almost makes me wish I knew how to crochet. Say, you're going to love the restaurant we're going to. It's right downtown. I hear they have fabulous..."

While Clara and Veronica continued to chat, or rather, while Clara continued to chat, Jack turned to Robert. "Would you mind if we took our car? I'd like to get to know the layout of the town a little better."

"Not at all," Robert replied. "Actually neither I nor my wife care to drive at night anymore so that works out great."

As they walked toward the car Veronica couldn't help noticing that the heat had intensified through the course of the day. The humidity was almost stifling. "Is it always this hot and muggy in the summer?" she asked.

"I couldn't really say. We've only been here a couple of times. But my guess is, being this far south, that it probably is," Robert replied.

They climbed into the rental car, turned the air-conditioner on full blast, and headed north toward the downtown square. Clara conversed cheerfully with Veronica the whole trip about the beautiful, Victorian style, two story homes they passed along the way while Robert gave Jack directions to the restaurant.

"Oh, look, sweetie, the streets are made out of bricks!" Clara exclaimed, as they drove onto the downtown square. "I had forgotten about that."

"That is interesting," Veronica agreed. "I wonder if other streets in town are brick also."

"Oh, there's the OS² Pub on the right," Robert said as he pointed toward the restaurant.

Jack pulled into a parking space and everyone, once again, stepped out into the sweltering heat. "Listen," Veronica whispered when she heard the melodious tones ringing out. "I wonder where it's coming from."

Clara pointed to the courthouse across the street from the restaurant. "I think it's coming from over there, sweetie."

"I love the sound." Everyone gathered under the shade of the awning, quietly listening to the tranquil bongs, before peacefully going inside.

A young waitress directed them to one of the semi circle, purple velvet, booths that lined the walls in the dimly lit restaurant. "This is nice and cozy," Clara observed as they all scooted around the table. The waitress passed out the menus then took their drink orders.

"When did you start designing?" Veronica asked.

Robert put his menu down. "My mom taught me how to crochet when I was a little boy. I used to watch her all the time. I thought it was fascinating the way she could take a ball of yarn and turn it into anything she wanted it to be. After a few weeks of pestering her, she gave me my own ball of yarn and a hook and showed me how to do the stitches. I immediately fell in love with it. Just the idea of it still excites me, to be able to wield a stick with a hook on the end around a strand of yarn, and turn it into anything I desire. I've just never gotten over that feeling."

"Sweetie, Veronica asked when you started designing, not when you started crocheting," Clara jokingly scolded.

"Yea, I know. But I like the story about my mom." Robert laughed. "Clara is right though, designing and crocheting are not the same thing. I started designing when our children were babies."

"He designed sweaters for all of our children. Created some beautiful pieces," Clara added.

"How many children do you have?" Jack asked.

"Oh, sweetie, we have six, two boys and four girls. Three of them are still living at home," Clara replied.

The waitress brought their drink orders and set them on the table. "Have you decided or do you need a few more minutes?"

"A few more minutes please," Robert responded picking his menu back up.

"Do your children crochet?" Veronica asked.

"The oldest boy does and three of the girls," Clara replied. "I just can't seem to get the hang of it myself. Besides, five crocheters in the family are enough." Clara chuckled. "If we had any more yarn in the house there wouldn't be any room for us!"

"Now Clara," Robert said, putting his menu down again, "you know one's stash can never be too large!"

"Yes, sweetie, that's what I've been told," Clara mockingly agreed.

"Oh, look!" Veronica exclaimed, looking up at the ceiling. "Wouldn't those colors make an interesting afghan?" Veronica began studying the alignment of the vibrant green, brown, and blue jewel toned tiles.

Robert immediately looked up. "You're right, they would," he said as he too studied the color arrangement of the tiles. "Actually, I need an afghan for our January issue. Would you be interested in submitting a swatch showing the stitch you think would work best for the design?"

Veronica's heart began to race. "I would love to! Thank you!" she squealed.

Robert continued in a business tone, but couldn't help getting caught up in her enthusiasm. He remembered the glorious excitement he felt when he received his first commissioned jobs. A feeling he would never forget. A feeling he loved bestowing on others. "I would need the afghan before the end of next month," he continued. "Would that be a problem? I could offer six hundred dollars for the design."

Veronica tried to catch her breath. "Oh, that would be great!" she gasped.

"Careful, sweetie, he will work you to death if you don't watch out," Clara teased.

Jack sighed heavily, going along with the teasing, "She's too far gone to care."

"Ok, ok, our spouses are making fun of us. It's time to put business away." Robert winked at Veronica. "Besides, I'm hungry, I want to order some of that delicious looking food," he said as he saw a plate of Tilapia Veracruz go by.

Eighteen

Veronica woke up bright and early the next morning. Conference registration was at eight and she wanted to get something to eat before the meeting began. A free hot breakfast downstairs was not something she planned to miss out on.

The aroma of coffee drifted up to the mezzanine, from the breakfast room below, as Veronica and Jack headed toward the elevator.

While in route, Veronica kept staring at all the wonderful crochet designs she saw people wearing; cashmere sweaters, silk tops, mohair wraps, wool socks, alpaca lace shawls. Just about everyone she saw was wearing or carrying crochet.

"Now I know why they are keeping this building so cold!" Jack exclaimed as they walked into the breakfast room. They quickly gathered their breakfast from the buffet bar then sat down at one of the empty tables. "Excited?" Jack asked.

"I don't know when I have felt so many emotions all at the same time before. I don't even know how to sort them out; excited, scared, nervous, hopeful, just everything all rolled up into one," Veronica said as she gulped down eggs, sausage, waffles, orange juice and coffee all at the same time.

"You left out hungry!" Jack laughed.

Veronica stood in line to register her presence and pick up her badge. She watched as a forty something year old woman, at the head of the line, removed her identification from a beautiful tapestry crochet bag. The design was of cats marching along the top of a fence. Veronica wondered if the woman was Noel. The woman picked up her badge and began walking away. Veronica took a quick peek, Noel, the badge read. Veronica smiled to herself. She wondered if she would be able to recognize other people by their work as well.

"Oh, there you are," Robert said as he walked up to Veronica. "Since you're our guest we have your badge, you don't need to be in line."

"Oh, thank you. I didn't know," Veronica replied as she stepped out of the line.

Robert continued, "The Designer and Teacher Growth Day is being held in conference room 'A', just follow me."

Robert led Veronica to the conference room. As they entered they were handed a morning program along with a stack of papers explaining the afternoon sessions. There were several round tables set up in the room, each with eight folding chairs placed around. All of the tables were decorated with crochet hooks, knitting needles, rulers, scissors, yarn needles, and a colorful variety of numerous balls and skeins of yarn. Robert pointed to a table toward the front of the room and they went and sat down.

"Hello, I'm Ann and this is, Judy, Melissa, Ellen, Sara, and Duke," a young woman said as she pointed to each person already seated at the table.

"Hello, I'm Robert, and this is Veronica. It's nice to meet all of you."

"Hi, Ellen," Veronica greeted the somewhat athletic looking woman. "I think we have met in the ACAKA chat room." Veronica reached over to shake Ellen's hand. Ellen accepted the gesture, but seemed rather reticent. "It's nice to meet you in person."

"Yes," Ellen replied as she looked down at her feet. "If you'll excuse me a moment, I...I forgot my program." Ellen quickly got up and left the table.

"Did I say something wrong?" Veronica asked, a little concerned.

Melissa, a woman who was probably older than she actually looked, gave Veronica a motherly smile. "You'll have to forgive Ellen. You didn't say anything wrong. She is just extremely shy when she first meets people in person. Talk to her a few more times. She will warm up to you."

"Has anyone seen Gloria?" Sara asked looking around the room. "I...I was going to talk to her about knitting."

"Don't you mean crochet?" Ann asked.

"I haven't seen Gloria, but I saw her car parked by the exit door," Judy offered. "She lives near here. Must have driven in this morning."

"Yes, she and her brother both live in this area," Sara said wistfully.

"Sara, I've met you in the chat room also haven't I?" Veronica asked.

"Probably, I hang out there a lot," Sara responded straining her neck to get a better look around the room.

"Duke? That is an unusual name," Robert remarked.

Duke smiled. "It isn't my real name, just a childhood nickname. About twenty-five or so years ago, back when I was in elementary school, mom crocheted my sis and I hats with little earflaps on them. They were supposed to keep our ears warm, but being a boy I would take the strings and tie the earflaps on top of my head." Duke laughed remembering his childhood antics. "Anyway, due to the abuse, I guess, the strings broke. I didn't want to tell mom I broke the hat so I just kept wearing it. But after that, every time I would run and play, the earflaps would bounce up and down. My teacher called me Duke. Said I looked like a cute little puppy dog."

"Didn't that make you mad?" Robert asked, surprised that he had kept the name.

"No. It was all good fun. And of course now it reminds me of mom, of all the time she spent crocheting for me, of the love she had for me." Duke sighed. "I'll always remember that little blue hat fondly. Plus," he said more cheerfully, "it's great for designing purposes, I mean, people tend to remember a name like, Duke."

"I guess you're right. I imagine you are the only person here named after a crocheted hat! So, can I presume from this little story that you are a crochet designer?" Robert asked.

"Yes. I started designing..."

Veronica began reading the papers she was handed as the two men got more acquainted. There would be a panel discussion in the morning followed by classes in the afternoon. The morning session was to be a discussion amongst professional designers telling how they got started in the business, the pros and cons of being a designer and...

Veronica's reading was interrupted by the thunderous sound of applause. A tall, thin, feisty woman with shoulder length strawberry blonde hair, who looked like she had just stepped off the front cover of a fashion magazine, was walking up to the podium. Ellen quietly slipped back into her seat. "Good morning, ladies and gentlemen. My name is Tammy. As your new president I want to welcome each and every one of you to the ACAKA conference." Cheers broke out from the audience as she spoke.

"First order of business, the yarn you see before you is not for decorative purposes. While you are listening to the discussion this morning, we would like to ask each of you to crochet or knit a snuggle. *Snuggles*, for those of you who are not familiar with them, are small blankets for animals in animal shelters. It is just a little something soft and cuddly for them to curl up with to help eliminate some of the stress and fright they feel. We would like to ask each of you to create a snuggle fourteen inches wide by fourteen or so inches long, which will be donated to the organization, Hugs for Homeless Animals. The snuggle can be larger if you are a fast crocheter and or knitter."

Veronica watched in amazement as a feeding frenzy began to unfold right before her eyes. Everyone standing up and digging through balls and skeins of yarn all at the same time, hurriedly trying to pick out the perfect yarn and color for the snuggle they wished to make. People from other tables coming over to their table to fast talk a trade.

Veronica saw a skein of Red Heart Easy Tweed in the color bright teal off to the left of the pile. She carefully reached out her hand and grabbed it. Then she started thinking a darker color might be better with animal hair, so she grabbed a ball of black, Easy Tweed, as well. She quickly sat back down hoping to herself that designers were not the violent type when it came to getting the yarn they wanted.

"Second," Tammy continued after the noise died down, "the morning session will be broke up into two parts. Our first panel will consist of crochet designers—Gloria, Margery, and Noel & knit designers—Keira, Deb, and Emily."

As she called out their names, the panelists walked to the front of the room.

"Oh...isn't she wonderful!" Sara exclaimed.

Veronica watched as Gloria strutted across the room. She was dressed in a cool, peach colored, spaghetti strapped, crocheted dress. Her ensemble also included a large, crocheted, peach and white, floppy summer hat and matching gloves. Although the others were decked out in crochet and knit garb as well, none compared to Gloria, not even Tammy. Gloria was definitely dressed to kill.

After the panelists sat down behind the long white table at the front of the room Tammy continued. "Our panelists will speak about their own personal designing experiences and the pros and cons of being a professional designer. We will have a thirty-minute break, then we will reconvene and listen as book and magazine editors as well as editorial and publicity directors from the various yarn companies, explain how to go about submitting designs to them. They will also share with you information about the type of designs, stitches, colors and styles they will be looking at for upcoming publications. When they are finished the floor will be opened up for questions and answers. Lunch will be served promptly at noon. The afternoon sessions will begin at one o'clock. There are several options for afternoon sessions and you will be able to choose three of them."

Veronica picked up a "K" crochet hook and began making a chain with the black yarn. Then it occurred to her that the thicker she could make the blanket the better it would be. She began frogging her chain. Veronica smiled to herself. *Rippit rippit.* She didn't know who came up with the idea that when one rips out their crochet work that it should be called frogging, but ever since her aunt told her about frogging, ripping out her crochet work always brought a smile to her face, despite seeing all her hard work coming unraveled.

"At this time, I will turn the mike over to Gloria so that we can begin." Tammy sat down beside the designers who were to speak.

Veronica held a strand of black and a strand of bright teal together. She picked up a ten-millimeter crochet hook then began remaking her chain stitches.

"Good morning everyone, my name is Gloria. I was raised in a little east Texas town not too far from here called Elysian Fields and I still live in the ArkLaTex area today. I started crocheting in the summer of my fourteenth year and fell in love with the craft. My grandmother taught me the art of crochet and I will always be grateful to her for bestowing her knowledge on me. Memaw said crochet would give me an outlet to express my creativity and she was absolutely right. The versatility of crochet is just amazing. It far out weights all other crafts..."

Veronica watched as Ellen nervously began working her stitches. "That is very pretty," Veronica whispered.

Ellen looked up at Veronica's smiling face then slowly began to return the smile. "It's the half double crochet stitch," Ellen whispered back as she showed Veronica how to make the stitch.

"...I began designing clothes for myself and friends at school. I was receiving so many accolades for my work that I decided to send some of the designs off for publication. All of the designs were accepted of course..."

Twenty-six chains looked to be about right. Veronica worked a half double crochet in the back ridge of the second chain from the hook then she worked half double crochets in each of the remaining back ridges across, so that she had twenty-five stitches.

"...I have had designs published through every possible avenue. On top of which, I have also been commissioned to design for some of the top actors and actresses in the world today..."

Veronica turned her work then chained one to begin the next row, but she noticed that instead of two loops there appeared to be three loops going across the top. She got Ellen's attention and pointed to the three loops. "The first one is called the front bar. It was created when you wrapped the yarn around the hook before inserting it in the stitch. The second loop is called the front loop and the last one is called the back loop. When you work your half double crochets back across, insert the hook through the front and back loop. Just pretend the front bar isn't there," she whispered softly.

"...And I am currently in close contact with several television executives about possibly having my own crochet show next season. As for pros and cons I think crochet designing is what you make of it. It is hard work and ridiculous hours. But if you have a lot of genuine creativity inside you and you want to be a professional designer, it is definitely worth going after. I was able to install an in-ground swimming pool and hot tub with the proceeds from my first book. And I just purchased my latest vehicle, a sunburst colored Element, with the proceeds from my last book. I love the color. It is a color that only a designer could love and it's just unusual enough that I can always find my car! Of course I always park right by the door, which helps also." Everyone began laughing. Gloria took a bow then handed the mike to Margery.

Veronica glanced around to see what the others were working on. She noticed that Sara was trying to crochet using a knitting needle.

"Hello, everyone, my name is Margery. I began designing professionally about fifteen years ago. A friend of mine gave birth to a preemie girl. I wanted to crochet a little dress for her, but I couldn't find a pattern. I decided to just create one. It was a cute little dress with blue hearts on it. My friend was so excited when I gave it to her, and her little girl looked just precious in it..."

After she had completed a few rows, Veronica stopped to examine her work. It was definitely thicker, but the half double crochet stitches looked a little flat and boring in the dark color. Veronica began studying the stitch while Margery continued.

"...I started thinking, if I couldn't find a pattern for a preemie dress maybe others couldn't either. Maybe others would be interested in the pattern I had created. So, I sent the pattern in to one of the magazines..."

Veronica wondered what would happen if she worked a half double crochet stitch in the front bar of the first stitch, in the front loop of the next stitch, in the back loop of the next stitch then in the front loop of the next stitch and just kept repeating the sequence all the way across. She quickly worked a row.

"...I got a call a few days later saying that they loved the dress and would purchase it if I made the dress in a full term baby size..."

Working in the various loops gave it kind of a wavy look.

Her last stitch on the row was worked in a front bar. Veronica turned her work and chained one to begin. Since the work was turned, the last stitch on the last row was now in the back. She began the next row by working a half double crochet stitch in the back loop then she worked a half double crochet in the front loop of the next stitch, in the front bar of the next stitch and in the front loop of the next stitch and repeated the sequence across. A definite wavy material was forming.

Veronica loved the look, but noticed that the waves were making the material less than the required fourteen inches. She picked up a ruler and measured her piece, then calculated that to have fourteen inches of waves she would have to start with thirty chains, so that she could have twenty-nine stitches. Once again, Veronica began frogging her work.

"...Making the dress in a full term size kind of defeated the original purpose of the dress, but I was so flattered that they liked my work that it didn't matter to me. Actually, that is one of the most important things I have learned about this business. One has to be extremely flexible. If you want your design to be brown and the editor wants the design to be blue, you have to be willing to make it in blue. If you want to make a top with short sleeves and the editor wants long sleeves you have to be willing to make the changes. If you are not willing to make adjustments, if you are not flexible, you will not last very long in this industry..."

Veronica chained thirty and worked her first row of twenty-nine half double crochet stitches. Then she began working row after row of her new wave half double crochet stitch pattern.

"...You can't take changes personally."

Gloria stood up. "Yes, and I want to add to this," she said as she stole the mike from Margery. "Designs are not your baby! A design is a design. Most companies buy all rights to a design anyway. I know, I know, some companies will pay for first rights, but they are few and far between. So understand, if you sell all your rights, the design no longer belongs to you. The company can change it anyway they want to. They don't even have to give you credit for creating it if they don't want to. The best thing for you to do is forget about it. It's gone. You are a creative person. Go on and create another design..."

"Sure, if you don't care," Ann sarcastically whispered to her table companions. Veronica looked up from her work as Ann continued. "I worked six weeks on my last project. I put my heart and sole into my work. Work out every single detail. I know my design inside and out. It becomes a part of me. Yes, it is my baby!"

Gloria's voice rose louder, "...If you are a real designer, you always have another design or two or three in the back of your mind to create. Real designers are creative people. They don't need to dwell on what they have already sold and more importantly they don't need or even want to steal other people's patterns. Real designers would never douse their own creativity by copying someone else's work. I get so disgusted when people ask me how much of a pattern needs to be changed in order for them to call it their own creation. The answer is ALL OF IT!"

Veronica watched as Ann slowly went back to crocheting, apparently agreeing with Gloria's last comment.

"No, you can't simply change the color or size and say it is your design. That is ridiculous. You also can't take several sweater patterns and copy the sleeves from one pattern and place them on the front and back of another pattern. The truth is, if you have to look at any part of someone else's pattern in order to design, you are not designing, you are copying."

Veronica listened intently as the speakers shared from their experiences. She learned of their trials and tribulations as well as their successes with, submitting designs to publishers, self-publishing, contracts, agents, model makers, schematics, pattern writing, and more. She soon became so engrossed in what they had to say that she forgot all about measuring for length. When she suddenly realized she had run out of yarn her snuggle was nineteen inches long.

Nineteen

Tammy stood up when the last speaker finished. "It is almost ten o'clock. Refreshments have been provided compliments of the inn. You will find coffee, hot tea, fresh fruit and bagels on the tables by the entrance. We will begin the second part of our morning session promptly at ten-thirty."

People gradually began to stand up and meander toward the refreshment table. Duke announced that he was going to go sneak a peek at the snuggles others had made while their creators were not around. Ann, Sara, Judy & Melissa followed suit. Robert excused himself so that he could call his wife. While he was gone, Veronica showed Ellen what she had created with the half double crochet stitch, that Ellen had shown her how to make. "That is beautiful!" Ellen said as she examined the work. "I love the texture. You are very creative."

Veronica couldn't believe what she was hearing. Ellen was complimenting her! "Thank you so much! That really means a lot coming from you."

Having just returned to the table, Robert apologetically interrupted. "Excuse me, Veronica, I just wanted to let you know that I was back. I'm going to go get something to eat now." Robert eyed the morning treats. "Did you want to come?"

"Yes, thank you. Ellen, would you like to go with us?" Veronica asked as she stood up.

Ellen looked down at her snuggle. "I...I think I'll work on my snuggle a little longer. I'm almost finished."

Robert and Veronica went to the end of the refreshment line where Melissa and Judy were already waiting. "I like the pattern you created for the snuggle," Robert complimented Veronica. "I'm looking forward to seeing what you come up with for the ceiling afghan."

Veronica looked at him in surprise. "Thank you. I didn't realize you had noticed."

"Oh, I notice everything. That's my job. I am always on the lookout for creative designers like you."

Veronica felt her face begin to blush and decided to change the topic. "Speaking of noticing everything, is that Sara over there with Gloria?" she asked pointing toward the front of the room.

Robert looked over the crowd of people to where Veronica was pointing. "Yes, I believe it is."

"I was just wondering does she always confuse crocheting with knitting?"

"Yes, the poor dear," Melissa answered shaking her head. She and Judy had turned around in line eager to express their concerns. "Sometimes I wonder if the poor girl even knows how to crochet. She says she is a crochet designer, but from what I hear no one has ever seen her work."

"And did you see that mess she was making this morning?" Judy added.

"The poor thing." Melissa clicked her tongue. "It was just pathetic."

Veronica observed the activity at the front of the room for a moment. "Gloria doesn't seem to be too happy with her. Are they arguing?"

"It wouldn't surprise me. Gloria is always arguing with everyone," Judy replied. Then, having reached the front of the line, Judy turned back around and began filling her plate with fresh fruit.

The others quickly began filling their plates as well. "This looks wonderful," Veronica said as she picked up a cinnamon raisin bagel, cream cheese, strawberry preserves, and a cup of coffee. "Oh, look, they have a tray of petit fours!" Veronica exclaimed as she picked up a chocolate and raspberry treat.

"I see you're not shy about eating." Robert smiled. "I like that."

Veronica laughed. "If it's free food, I'll be there."

They took their morning snack back to the table and began eating. Other members of their table group gradually returned as well carrying plates piled high with mid morning treats. Ellen, having just finished her snuggle, left to join the refreshment line.

Veronica began looking around at all the snuggles on the table. They were beautiful. "I love the pink snuggle. May I ask who made it?"

Melissa proudly admitted, "I made that one. It is a random combination of shells and V-stitches."

"It is lovely," Ann agreed. "And Judy your blue, cabled, knitted one is exquisite!"

"So, why didn't anyone do a crocheted cabled one?" Gloria angrily asked as she stormed toward the table. "You can make beautiful cables with crochet." Gloria stood behind Robert and placed her hands on his shoulders.

"You can?" Veronica asked in surprise.

Gloria began massaging Robert's neck. "Of course you can. Exquisite cables!" she exclaimed, borrowing Ann's expression. Robert turned around in his chair breaking Gloria's embrace.

"I agree. You can," Sara chimed in. She set her bagel down on the table and smiled up at Gloria.

Margery walked over carrying a cup of steaming hot tea. "Gloria, what in the world are you arguing about now?" she asked. "I could hear you all the way over at the refreshment table."

Gloria turned to Margery. "I was just saying that

crocheted cables are as pretty as knitted cables." Then turning back to Veronica she added, "Prettier if you want to know the truth!"

"Would you be willing to teach me how to make them?" Veronica asked as she picked up a skein of yarn and a crochet hook so that Gloria could demonstrate.

Gloria just stood glaring at her. "Come on, Gloria, you brought it up. Prove it. Get down off that high horse of yours and show her how to make the stitch!" Margery exclaimed.

Dead silence fell over the room. No one moved a muscle.

Veronica quickly realized she had made a grave error asking Gloria such a question. She looked around at all the people who had suddenly appeared around their table. If only she could think of a way out of this mess.

"I'm not about to stand here and prove what everyone already knows is the truth. And I'm not giving free lessons to everyone in this room!" Gloria said through clenched teeth.

"Oh, come on, Gloria. Veronica is the only one who asked for a demonstration. She is a new crocheter. Show her how to do the stitch," Margery goaded her on.

Gloria smiled a forced smile then pointed her gloved finger at Veronica. "I'll show, you, in your room after the afternoon sessions. What room are you in?"

"203," Veronica replied in a hushed voice.

"Fine, I'll be there this afternoon." Gloria turned to Margery. "Happy?" she snapped.

Margery grinned. "Yes, as a matter of fact I am."

Gloria turned. Then with head held high, she marched away from the gawking on-lookers. Sara immediately stood up and ran after her.

When the audience went back to doing whatever they were doing before the show began, Veronica breathed a sigh of relief. This was one humiliating moment she was not soon to forget.

Ellen returned from the refreshment line and sat down. "You know, this is a little ridiculous," she commented.

"What is?" Duke asked.

"They served all these jellies and butters and creams and coffees to a group of people sitting at tables filled with yarns and designs."

Everyone looked at one another then immediately picked up their food and began holding it over their laps as the scenario of coffee and cream drenched yarn played through their minds. Ellen quickly followed suit. But as it would happen, the yarn was saved the clothes were not. Ellen groaned as she picked the strawberry jelly topped bagel up off her lap and tried to wipe off the stain. Unfortunately the more she wiped the worse it got.

Between the shyness and the embarrassment Ellen was becoming a nervous wreck. "I...I better go change," she stammered as she got up to leave.

"Actually, I need to excuse myself also," Duke said as he stood up to go. "In all the excitement I forgot to take my blood pressure medicine this morning."

Ann swallowed her last bite and stood up as well. "Yes, I think I'll go give my husband a call since we have a few minutes left. He wasn't feeling too well this morning."

"Well, since everyone seems to be leaving I... I think I will take this opportunity to go to the powder room," Judy mumbled.

"Yes, I'll go with you," Melissa said as she stood up as well.

"NO! Uh, no, I mean, uh, I, mean, the downstairs room only has one stall," Judy explained then quickly disappeared into the crowd of people milling about.

"Well, that was a fascinating bit of information, but I still need to go, so if the rest of you will excuse me I guess I will head up to my room for a minute." Melissa picked up her cup for a farewell sip of coffee then she was off.

"Veronica, do you need to call Jack?" Robert asked.

"No. He said he would be busy all day playing trains. He is fascinated with the Texas and Pacific Railroad. I don't expect him back till suppertime."

"Well, I'm fascinated with yarn." Robert pushed back his chair and stood up. "Think I'll go look around, see what kind of snuggles were created at the other tables. Would you care to join me?" he asked.

"I'd be delighted." Veronica stood up and followed Robert to the next table.

"Where's Duke?" Robert asked when they returned to their table.

"I don't know," Ann replied glancing around the room. "It can't take that long to swallow a blood pressure pill."

"Excuse me," a lady from the next table interrupted. "Are you talking about Duke?"

"Yes. We were wondering if he was all right. He said he had to go take a blood pressure pill, but he hasn't come back," Robert explained.

The woman shook her head. "You must be mistaken. Duke doesn't have high blood pressure."

"Are you sure?" Robert asked getting a little concerned.

"Yes. I'm his sister. We are rooming together this trip and I know for a fact he doesn't have any medical problems."

"I'm sorry. I...I guess I must have misunderstood. I'm sure he will be back soon," Robert replied, trying not to unnecessarily alarm Duke's sister. The woman, certain that Robert had the wrong person, went back to conversing with the people at her own table.

"Excuse me, Robert!" Tammy called out excitedly as she rushed up to the table. "We just got a call from Donna. Her flight was delayed and she isn't going to be able to make it. Would you be willing to take her place on the panel?"

"Tammy," Robert sighed.

Tammy quickly interrupted him before he could have a chance to say no. "I know you told us that you didn't want to do the panel discussion when we were first setting this up, but could I prevail upon you, out of the goodness of your heart, would you reconsider?"

Robert paused a few seconds then cleared his throat and stood up, "Well, if you will excuse me ladies, it looks like I am on the second panel." Robert winked at Veronica to assure her that he wasn't nearly as upset as he was letting on, then he followed Tammy to the front of the room.

"I wonder where Sara is," Melissa remarked.

"Probably still chasing after Gloria." Ann laughed.

"Ellen and Judy haven't returned yet either. Ellen I can understand, she had to completely change clothes and probably wanted to go ahead and wash out the jelly stain if possible, but Judy was acting really strange." Melissa lowered her voice. "I went ahead and went to the lobby powder room. There were plenty of stalls and she wasn't in any of them. When I came out, I saw her duck inside the elevator."

"Maybe she just decided to go up to her room," Ann suggested in the same hushed tone Melissa was using.

"That's what I thought, but then I noticed that the elevator was headed down into the basement."

"It is time to begin the second part of our morning session, if everyone will go ahead and find their seats please," Tammy spoke into the microphone.

Ellen quietly slipped back into her seat wearing a clean pair of jeans and a blue wool sweater.

Tammy continued, "I would like to introduce our panelists. Robert is the editor of *Crochet Elite* magazine..."

Veronica picked out a couple more skeins of yarn. She liked the pattern she had designed for the snuggle and decided to make another one just like it, but in different colors. Others in the room began picking up yarn as well, to either finish the snuggle they had already begun or to start a second one. Margery and Keira, now sitting at the next table, were busily working on the models for their classes.

Time passed away much too quickly for Veronica. Before she knew it the morning session was over and she was being hurried into the dining room, along with Ann and Robert, for a quick lunch. Standing at the entry of the dining room was Judy. "Hi, Judy!" Ann greeted her. "Are you ok? We didn't see you after the morning break and were getting concerned."

"Oh, I'm sorry. I didn't mean to worry anyone. I was there. I got there right after they started and I didn't want to walk in front of everyone to get back to the table so I stood up in the back."

"Have you seen Duke?" Robert asked.

"No. Why do you ask me that?" Judy asked looking a little uneasy.

"Oh, it's nothing. We didn't see Duke after the break either, just thought you might have seen him."

"No, I...I didn't see him." Judy appeared rather antsy. She twisted the strings on her belt a couple of times then, obviously trying to change the subject, she asked, "How come you were not on the editor's panel? You are a wonderful editor. You should have spoken."

"But I..."

"Excuse me, Robert," Judy interrupted. "I have to go find Donna." And with that she disappeared into the crowd.

"Oh, look, Duke is in the food line," Veronica said, pointing toward the front of the line.

"That's good," Robert sighed with relief. "I guess he must be ok then. I was just a little worried about him. Are you ready for lunch?"

After lunch they headed back to the conference room for the breakout sessions. For her three sessions Veronica picked; How to Make a Living with Fiber, Contracts – What They Really Mean, and a session called Book Proposals – Sketches, Swatches and More. Veronica wrote down page after page of notes. She loved the sessions and was gaining vast amounts of knowledge, but by day's end her head was spinning. She was beginning to understand what Margery meant by crochet overload.

Tammy walked over to the podium. "I hope everyone has

had a great time today and more importantly that you have all learned something new that will help you in your careers." Loud cheers arose from the audience. "Now, in east Texas slang I shall say, 'thanx yall fer comin!' By the way, whatever supplies are left on your tables you are welcome to take with you as our gift."

There was a mad scramble as everyone swooped skeins of yarn into their arms then began gathering hooks, needles and other supplies up off the tables before they bid one another goodbye and headed back to their rooms.

The elevator line seemed to be a mile long, so Veronica decided to take the stairs. Her room was only one flight up and she felt a strong need to get away from the crowd for a little while. Veronica walked to the end of the north hallway then opened the door on her left to enter the stairwell. "Oh, hi, Ellen!" Veronica exclaimed. "I see you decided to take the stairs as well." Veronica smiled at the timid woman.

"Yes," Ellen replied as she stepped up on the bottom stair.

Veronica followed close behind, but her arms were so loaded with yarns and supplies that she couldn't see where she was going. Suddenly, she felt herself tumbling backward onto the hard floor. Ellen turned around and hurried to her side. Veronica lay on the floor a few seconds before sitting up to survey the damage, one bleeding elbow and one sore backside. "Are you ok?" Ellen asked anxiously.

"Yes. I must have just lost my footing. Could have been worse, I guess," Veronica replied as she and Ellen began gathering the supplies strewn on the floor. When Veronica reached for the last ball of green yarn she noticed for the first time the blood on the floor then spotted the blood on the bottom stair and the fire escape door. Had she bled that much? Suddenly a wave of nausea rose up in her throat.

Ellen ran out in the hall and returned a few moments later with a young woman from housekeeping. "Are you ok?" she asked.

"Yes. But I have ruined everything. I am really sorry about the mess."

Working together, Ellen and the housekeeper helped Veronica to her feet. "Don't worry," the housekeeper assured her. "We can clean it up. No problem. I'm just glad you're alright."

Ellen added soothingly, "Perhaps you should take the elevator up to your room and rest. I'll go with you."

"Thank you," Veronica replied trying to hold back the tears. "That would be nice."

Veronica doctored her elbow, cleaned herself up then collapsed on the bed. She lay there thinking over the day's events. So many thoughts running through her head all at the same time, she was glad she had taken notes. She never would have been able to remember it all. Veronica was just about to doze off when suddenly she sat straight up in bed. "Gloria!"

She had almost forgotten about that little embarrassing situation. Learning crocheted cables would be a lot of fun, but she was quickly starting to dread the idea of Gloria's visit. She was tired and sore and she knew Gloria didn't really want to show her how to make the stitches. She had been tricked into doing it. Margery tricked her. Veronica sat on the side of the bed hoping that Gloria wouldn't show, but she knew it was a futile wish. Gloria's inflated ego would force her to come.

She got out of bed. No point in trying to sleep now. Veronica fixed herself a cup of coffee, hoping the caffeine would wake her up or at least settle her stomach. She opened the curtains then sat down beside the window to enjoy the hot brew. The view out the window was of an open field in the back of the inn. Veronica was enjoying the peacefulness of the scene when a movement caught her eye. She stood up to get a closer look. The movement occurred again. Veronica kept watching as the armadillo made its way across the field then slipped under a sunburst colored Element.

Veronica went and poured herself another cup of coffee. Something was wrong, but what was it? She went back to the window and watched the armadillo scratching at the ground beneath the car as she drank her second cup of coffee.

Gloria was late. Gloria...Gloria...that was Gloria's car! Veronica stood up and took a closer look. No, it had to just be one like it. Gloria said she always parked by the door. Judy had even seen the car parked by the door. Veronica sat back down and continued to wait, still no Gloria. She looked at her watch. It was after five. Jack would be returning soon. She hoped he had a nice day playing trains.

Veronica rubbed her back. The soreness was beginning to set in. Perhaps a hot bath and dinner in the room would be nice, she thought.

The armadillo walked out from underneath the car then scampered back across the field. Veronica stood up. Gloria obviously wasn't coming and the hot bath was calling to her. She started to close the curtains, but out of the corner of her eye thought she saw something. Veronica strained to see inside the car, was that the outline of a person? Surely not, but still...

Veronica walked outside, once again, feeling the intense heat from the sun. She made her way through the parking lot then into the roundabout. She could now see where one of the logs, marking the edges of the roundabout, had been knocked to one side as the car went through the borders and out into the field beyond. Veronica carefully walked through the weeds hoping there were no snakes about. As she neared the car she could see that there was definitely a person inside. Gloria.

Veronica knocked on the window. "Gloria!" she called out. "Gloria!" But there was no response. Veronica tried to open the door, but it was locked. Then she saw the blood and the nausea returned.

Veronica sank back away from the car, took out her cell phone and with trembling hands began calling for help.

Sirens seemed to be coming from every direction. Officers Andrews and Leal were the first to arrive on the scene. They broke into the car just seconds before the ambulance and fire truck arrived. Veronica, as well as several other designers who had gathered around, watched as Gloria was pulled out of the vehicle, her body wrapped in a bloodied and torn knitted shawl. The medics began trying to revive her, but it was to no avail. The Justice of the Peace arrived a few minutes later and pronounced her dead. From the looks of her body, he estimated the time of death to be around two that afternoon.

Police officers began to take statements from the onlookers. But no one had seen or heard anything. Everyone was at the conference lunch, inside the inn, from noon till one and at the breakout sessions between one and four-fifteen.

Of course the officers were told of the confrontation at the table earlier that morning and that Gloria had been extremely agitated and had walked out of the room. But that certainly didn't explain why she would have been in a car wreck around two when the breakout sessions were going on. Plus, although it was obvious that the car had gone through the barricade, the car didn't look damaged at all.

But the big question that seemed to be on every designers mind was: Why was Gloria wrapped in a knitted shawl? It seemed like a pretty petty thing to be wondering in lieu of the fact that the woman had died. But it was so out of character.

After Veronica gave her statement to the police she went back upstairs to lie down. Jack arrived a few minutes later and was told of the day's events. He held her in his arms until she was able to calm down. Then, while Veronica went to soak some of the soreness from her body in a hot bath, he ordered pizza delivery.

Veronica lay in bed staring at the ceiling. She couldn't sleep. She couldn't get Gloria's death off her mind. Something was missing, some key piece to the puzzle, but what? What was it? If only she could figure out what was missing.

Veronica rubbed her sore arm as she stared at the shadows on the ceiling, created by the glow of the streetlight shining through the open drapes. Think. She had to think. She rubbed her arm again, thought about the blood, the blood. Blood on the stairs...blood on the floor...blood on the exit door...blood on Gloria...blood on the knitted shawl...

Veronica sat up in bed. Could Gloria have fallen down the stairs just like she did? Veronica knew her elbow had bled, but there seemed to be more blood than injury. Was it possible, could some of the blood on the landing have been Gloria's blood? If Gloria had fallen down the stairs, could she have tried to drive herself to the hospital?

Veronica lay back down. No, if Gloria had fallen down the stairs, she would have gone to the lobby to seek help.

Veronica listened to the steady rhythmic sounds of breathing as her husband slept peacefully in the bed beside her. The air-conditioner came on and the smell of cool, clean air began to fill the room. Suddenly, Veronica bolted upright. What if Gloria had been pushed???

Twenty

—◆—

"Oh, I'm so glad to see you!" Veronica exclaimed, running up to her yarn shop friends.

"Hi," Audra greeted her. Then looking around she asked, "Where's Jack? Isn't he joining us for breakfast?"

"No. He left early this morning to drive to Uncertain. Said he wanted to see the sun rise over Caddo Lake. Took the camera so he could make photos of the cypress trees, the knees and the Spanish moss. He's thinking about making some models of the trees for a train layout he's working on. I expect he will be gone most of the day."

"Why do you say that?" Katy asked, a little confused. "Caddo Lake is only about fifteen miles from here."

"Because he doesn't know how to use the camera." Veronica laughed light heartedly. "Plus, he said if he got back in time he was going to go to the TC Lindsey store. He was told it was an authentic country store built in 1847 that was still in operation. Thought it would make an interesting model for a building on his layout." Veronica took a deep breath then continued, "And after that, if there was still time, he wanted to take a drive down Stagecoach Road."

"Stagecoach Road? Never heard of it. Do you know where it is?" Katy asked with interest.

"I'm not sure. All he really told me was that it was an original dirt road, about four and a half miles long, and that he thought a model of it would look great on his layout. Said that the road was probably created by the Caddo Indians then later used by the stagecoaches coming through Marshall."

"Changing the subject," Jenny said, interrupting the history lesson, "did you have a nice time yesterday?"

"Didn't you hear?" Veronica asked in surprise.

"Hear what?" Chrissy jumped in, wondering what bit of juicy gossip she had missed.

"We arrived late last night and went straight to bed," Katy explained.

"Let's get some breakfast and I'll tell you all about it." Veronica led a puzzled Audra, Katy, Jenny and Chrissy over to the buffet. They hurriedly filled their plates then quickly sat down at one of the empty tables in the back, anxious to hear the news. Veronica began explaining the events of the night before, carefully telling only facts and leaving out her suspicions.

"You're right, it doesn't make any sense," Chrissy agreed. She set her orange juice glass back down on the table then continued. "I'm not a professional, but even I know that Gloria wouldn't have anything to do with knitting. She wouldn't be caught dead in a knitted shawl! Oh, I...I'm sorry, that's not what I meant."

"It's ok," Jenny assured her. "We know what you meant." Jenny gave her little sister a reassuring hug. "Besides, you're right. Something is definitely not right about all of this." Jenny visibly shivered. "You know, it's probably just all this talk, but do any of you get the feeling we are being watched?" The others began looking around. While they had been deep in conversation the room had somehow magically filled to capacity with crocheters and knitters all eagerly awaiting their first class.

Audra grinned. "Better get used to it. Or else give me that peacock shawl you're wearing!"

Jenny lovingly petted the Soysilk fibers. "Never!" She laughed.

Veronica started to speak, but decided against it. For she also had the eerie feeling she was being watched...and she wasn't wearing anything crocheted.

Katy looked questioningly at Veronica. "You say the car wasn't damaged?"

"Not that I could tell," Veronica replied.

"Well, I'm sure the police will figure it out soon." Katy began gathering her belongings and stood up. "I'm sorry you had to go through all that and I wish I could stay and talk longer, but I have to get to my crochet sock class." Katy swung her bag over her shoulder. "Would all of you like to meet for lunch?"

"Yes. That sounds wonderful!" Veronica replied as she too stood up to leave.

How to Carve a Crochet Hook was Veronica's first class Thursday morning. Veronica was so excited! There were a few women in the class, but it was mainly a class of men. The teacher was a very friendly outgoing woman who cheerfully visited with each student as they walked into the room. Veronica was enjoying just being in her presence. Her exuberance for what she was teaching would make the class exciting as well as educational.

When everyone was seated she began explaining the differences in the different types of woods as well as the differences in the different brands of crochet hooks. She then allowed them to choose a stick from a variety of woods. Veronica walked over to the table to make her selection. She carefully picked out the prettiest cherry wood stick she could find, but all the while kept glancing over her shoulder unable to shake the feeling she was being watched.

Carving the stick was the next step. Veronica made her measurements, as per the teacher's instructions. She then picked up a tiny saw to make her first cut. After that, the real work began. Carving a piece of wood with a file took a lot more strength than she had anticipated. If it hadn't been for her sore arm, due to the fall on the stairs the night before, the carving might have been easier. Still in all, after a little over an hour, she had carved herself a fairly decent looking crochet hook.

Veronica dipped her newly carved hook in a vat of walnut oil to add the finishing touch. She was amazed at how pretty the hook looked after dipping. Veronica was still standing by the vat admiring her work and feeling quite pleased with herself when the instructor walked up. "That is beautiful, but you better go ahead and get started on your next one."

Veronica smiled. "You mean we get to make another one!"

"Of course!"

Veronica couldn't have been more pleased. She rushed over to the table containing the wood sticks excited about all the choices, but once again feeling the piercing eyes watching her every move, she hastily grabbed a birch stick and slid back into her seat.

There wasn't an empty lunch table to be had. Veronica and her friends stood by the wall to wait their turn. Judy, who was sitting at a table nearby with Sara and Ellen, motioned for Veronica to join them. Veronica pointed at her yarn shop friends. Judy waved again indicating there was room for everyone.

Audra, Katy, Jenny and Chrissy followed Veronica over to the table. Introductions were made, then the topic turned to what was really on everyone's mind—the car wreck.

"Has anyone called her brother?" Sara asked. "Will he be coming here?"

"I don't know," Judy replied. "I haven't heard anyone say." She poked a hole in her roll, filled the cavity with honey then took a large bite. "Delicious!" she said, licking the sticky goo off her fingers.

Veronica looked at Sara. "Sara, when you followed Gloria out of the room during the morning break, where did she go?"

"Why do you ask that?" Sara asked acting a little too defensive.

Veronica was taken aback. "I...I guess I'm just trying to figure things out. Did anyone see her after the morning break? Was she at the Growth Lunch? The Justice of the Peace said last night that he thought she had died around two. I just don't understand why she was in a car then."

Sara took a sip of her coffee giving herself time to regain her composure. "I don't know. I followed her out into the lobby, was going to try to console her. She told me she was fine and that she was just going to her room to freshen up. Gloria's was the only speech I was really interested in listening to. Since, according to the program, she wasn't going to speak again, I went to my room. I don't know what happened after that."

"Maybe she just decided to go out for lunch," Judy suggested. "Sitting in her room by herself couldn't have been much fun."

A waitress walked over, handed menus to Veronica and her yarn shop friends then took their drink orders. When she left Veronica continued. "Sara, you said Gloria was going to her room. Do you remember if she took the elevator or the stairs?"

"Neither," Sara replied shaking her head. "She was still standing in the lobby when I left."

"She took the elevator," Ellen whispered.

"That's right, Ellen, you left soon after Gloria did. Did you see anything?" Veronica asked.

"No," Ellen looked up timidly. Continuing to speak softly she added, "But Gloria would never take the stairs. Everyone knows she thought she was too good for that."

"Ellen's right," Judy quickly agreed in a loud voice. "Gloria would never take the stairs. Actually, I think I saw her get on the elevator when I went to the powder room." Judy ate the last bite of her honey filled roll, giving herself time to think. "Yes, I'm sure of it. I definitely saw her get on the elevator."

"Excuse me ladies," a deep voice spoke. Veronica turned around. Two police officers were standing directly behind her chair. "I am Officer Andrews and this is Officer Leal. Veronica, we need you to come with us down to police headquarters." Total silence fell over the room.

"Is something wrong?" Veronica nervously asked.

"No," Andrews replied trying to reassure her. "We just need to ask you a few questions. If you will please come with us now."

The room contained only a table and two hard chairs. Veronica was told to sit down and wait. She had tried several times to reach Jack on the cell phone, but he didn't answer. Either he had turned the phone off or most likely he was out of range. Veronica kept trying to think, but she couldn't imagine what the police would want to talk to her about.

A few minutes later a tall, handsome man, with slightly graying hair at the temples, walked into the room and introduced himself as Detective Edwards. He then sat down and requested that Veronica tell what had happened the day before giving every detail she could remember. Veronica repeated what she had already told the police then, because it was troubling her so, added her speculations of the night before.

"You're a very good detective." Edwards smiled at her. "Of course we don't have the autopsy report back yet, but it is obvious that Gloria didn't die in a car wreck." Edwards, absentmindedly, tapped his pencil on the table while he spoke. "I spent this morning at the inn and learned of the blood on the landing. Unfortunately the cleaning staff did a fantastic job of getting rid of the evidence. That is why you were brought in this afternoon. We wanted your opinion on the amount of blood."

"So, you think Gloria fell down the stairs just like I did and tried to go for help then fainted or something?" Veronica asked.

Detective Edwards hesitated a moment as if trying to decide how much he should tell her. "No. I suspect Gloria was murdered."

"Murdered?" Veronica gasped.

Edwards noted her shock. He then continued, "There are two doors on that landing; one leads into the lobby hallway, the other is an emergency exit that goes directly into the parking lot. I viewed a video of Gloria's speech. In it she announced that she always parks by the door. With the way the bushes are set up around the outskirts of the building, if Gloria was parked by the door, the killer could have easily taken her body from the landing, out the emergency door then placed her body in the car without being seen. The car could have then been driven through the barricade in a bumbling attempt to make it look like a car wreck."

"Murdered," Veronica repeated again still not quite believing what she was hearing. She had thought it last night, but to hear the detective actually say the word...

Edwards continued to speak, but Veronica could barely hear him. She felt like she was in a fog, fighting her way out. If only she could wake up and learn it was all some kind of horrible nightmare. Edwards voice droned on, "From what we hear she was not the most well liked person so it could have been a hate crime. Many people were jealous of her, which could have led to a crime of passion. She had no money on her at the time she was found so it could have been robbery." Edwards looked Veronica in the eye. "Do you know any knitters who would want Gloria dead?"

"Dead?" The initial shock was slowly beginning to wear off.

"Yes. Dead." Edwards repeated the question a little louder, "Do you know any knitters who would want to kill Gloria?"

"You think a knitter killed her?" Veronica asked, still having trouble grasping what was being told to her.

Edwards explained. "From what I learned this morning

about Gloria's hatred for knitting, it had to have been a knitter who committed the crime. Gloria couldn't stand knitting, yet her body was found wrapped in a knitted shawl. The shawl had to have come from the killer. I suspect the knitter was wearing the shawl or the shawl could have been in the knitter's yarn bag. After the murder was committed, the shawl was used to clean up the blood. Seeing how torn the shawl was, I also suspect it was probably used to help drag Gloria's body out to the car."

"Excuse me, did you say bumbling attempt?" Veronica asked.

"That's a rather delayed reaction." Edwards smiled. He cleared his throat then began to explain, "The killer made three mistakes. No fingerprints were found in the car, not even Gloria's. There was blood on the front passenger side of the car. And no one would die in a car wreck from such a small collision."

"I'm sorry. I don't think I am going to be of much help," Veronica replied. "I was at Growth Day, but I don't remember seeing anyone wearing the shawl I saw wrapped around Gloria and the only professional knitters I have met in person so far are Keira and Judy. ...Oh...Judy."

"What are you thinking?" Edwards asked sitting up straighter in his chair.

"Nothing," Veronica replied, suddenly realizing the ramifications of having even mentioned Judy's name to the detective. "Judy was just acting a little strange yesterday and she missed the second half of the morning session. But," she assured him, "she was at the lunch. I saw her. And she was also at all the breakout sessions that afternoon."

Edwards tapped his pencil a few more times on the desk. "So, presuming the JP was correct about the time of death she is innocent. But suppose his timing is off by a couple of hours."

Veronica was feeling horrible. She hadn't meant to say Judy's name. It had just sort of slipped out. "No," she assured him again. "Judy told me she saw Gloria get in the elevator during the morning break. Gloria couldn't have been in the elevator and in the stairwell at the same time. So, the murder had to have taken place later in the day."

"Judy said?" Edwards lifted one eyebrow as he looked at Veronica.

"I...I'm sorry...I really can't help you. I'm not feeling very well." The idea that Judy could have killed Gloria was simply more than Veronica could imagine. "Besides," Veronica continued, "there were a lot of knitters at the conference."

"I'm sorry. I didn't mean to upset you," Edwards consoled her. "There is still much we don't know. But we have to start the investigation somewhere. I will have the officers take you back to the inn now." Edwards handed Veronica his card. "If you think of anything else, please give me a call. Also, I would appreciate it if you would keep our little conversation in confidence for now. We don't know that Gloria was murdered."

It was too late to go to her afternoon class and Veronica didn't feel like being alone in her room. She went over to the coffee bar and helped herself to a cup of hot brew loaded with sugar and hazelnut cream, then realizing for the first time that she had missed lunch, grabbed a jelly filled doughnut. After a few bites the sugar rush kicked in.

Veronica noticed a group of people were crocheting in the lounge and decided to join them. She walked over to one of the chairs and sat down. Although everyone was crocheting, crochet was not the subject of conversation, Gloria's death was. No one seemed to believe she was in a car wreck. Veronica listened as she examined a lacey crocheted runner sitting on the table beside her.

A few minutes later, Ann walked over. "Hi, Veronica," she greeted her. "I'm going to take a trip to a yarn shop in Longview. Margery told me about it yesterday. It's called Stitches 'n Stuff. Would you like to go?"

Veronica thought about it for a minute. It did sound like fun. Plus, she felt like she needed to get away from the inn for a little while. "I would love to. Thank you for asking. I had better call Robert first though and make sure it is ok. I missed my afternoon class and since I am here on a scholarship..."

"Sure go ahead," Ann interrupted. "I'll go grab a cup of coffee."

Veronica punched in Robert's number and listened while the phone began to ring.

"Are you set to go?" Ann asked when she returned, a few moments later, with a steaming cup of coffee.

"Yes. Robert said it would be fine." Veronica grabbed her coffee and her yarn bag and stood up. "Jack and I are supposed to go to dinner with him and his wife tonight at seven-thirty though. Will we be back in time?"

"Oh, sure, that gives us plenty of time." Ann took a sip of her coffee. "Say, I know Gloria was supposed to give the keynote speech tonight. Have you heard what they are planning to do instead?"

"Robert said they are going to omit the keynote address completely," Veronica replied as they walked toward the door. "The yarn market will open at five instead and stay open until nine. People will have lots of time to shop that way. But he said he wasn't going. Said it would be less crowded tomorrow."

"Veronica!" a voice called out, just as she and Ann reached the exit door. "I've been looking for you. Are you ok? What did the police want?"

Veronica turned around and saw Sara followed by Ellen. "They just wanted me to clarify what I told them yesterday, Sara."

"Is that all?" Ellen asked.

"Yes. That's all," Veronica answered, trying to sound as nonchalant as possible.

Ann, realizing the topic of Gloria could delay her trip indefinitely, extended the invitation, "We're headed to Stitches 'n Stuff, would the two of you like to come along?"

"Yes. If you don't mind," Ellen answered.

Laughter could be heard all through the van as they drove the twenty or so miles to Longview. Veronica was so relieved that Gloria's name was not brought up again. It was so thrilling to be with a group of people who all had the same interests.

They arrived at the yarn shop around three in the afternoon. Veronica was quite excited. The only yarn shop she had been in before was the one in The Village back home and she was anxious to see another. Ann opened the door and the four women entered.

Once again Veronica was surrounded by yarn, sample sweaters, hooks and needles, but this store was distinctly different. Along the walls matching wood units were filled with colorful skeins of yarn. Off to the right they saw a fireplace with an ornate wood mantel. Two, velvet cushioned, hardwood, rocking chairs were placed in front of the fireplace enticing customers to sit and crochet awhile. Off to the left was a glass-shelving unit, which held porcelain China teacups and a bouquet of roses. Other glass units held balls of yarn as well as silver dishes and glass bowls containing various sundries. The shop, err boutique, calling it merely a shop would have been an insult, had an unmistakable elegance to it.

They wandered around the boutique admiring all of the yarn. Sara seemed to be having a wonderful time. She began asking questions about the different types of yarns. The young salesgirl on duty apologetically told her that the two sisters who owned the boutique were both gone for the week. She explained that they were professional designers and had gone to the ACAKA conference and that she was trying to help out, but didn't really know much about the yarns.

So, Ann began answering Sara's questions. She was doing a wonderful job of explaining things. In fact, Veronica was enjoying learning from her as well. But at the same time, Veronica couldn't help wondering if maybe Melissa was right about Sara. Veronica knew that she, herself, had much to learn about crochet and crochet designing, but even she knew more about crochet than Sara did. Sara didn't seem to know anything. What Veronica couldn't figure out though was why would anyone want to pretend they were a crochet designer?

Ellen, despite her shyness, seemed to be having a nice time as well and was becoming quite talkative. Veronica was flattered that Ellen was opening up to her. When researching the various designers she had come across several of Ellen's designs and it was obvious from what she had seen that Ellen was a famous, high fashion couturier.

After awhile Veronica and Ellen walked toward the back corner of the boutique. "Margery!" Veronica exclaimed in surprise. "I didn't know you were in here."

Margery, who was sitting on the floor going through a bin of sales yarn, looked up at Veronica. "Yes, thought I would do a little quiet shopping. Please don't get me wrong. I love the conferences, but it's nice to take a break from the noise once in awhile."

Veronica, taking the hint that Margery didn't want to chatter, began admiring the alpaca yarns, while Ellen stooped down to look at the wools. Suddenly several skeins of self-striping yarn caught Veronica's eye. She picked up a skein and began turning it over and over in her hand looking at the different colors. She knew it looked familiar, but couldn't quite place it. Then suddenly she realized what she was holding. The exact same yarn the killer had used to knit the shawl found on Gloria's body. Despite the fact that deep down she thought it sounded morbid, she felt she had to have that yarn. She picked up six skeins and started toward the register.

"What are you getting?" Ellen asked, looking up.

"Just some of this self-striping yarn. I thought it would be interesting to crochet with yarn that changes colors all by itself." Veronica knew she wasn't being totally truthful, but then on the other hand she wasn't really sure what the truth was. For whatever sick reason, she was just drawn to that yarn.

They arrived back at the inn around five-thirty. As soon as they walked through the door it was obvious that everything had change. Everywhere they looked people were walking around like zombies, not quite knowing what to do or say. It was almost as if a shroud had fallen over the inn and everyone in it. Ann went to the front desk to inquire what happened. It was then that the last of the conference goers learned the truth, Gloria was murdered and everyone was a suspect—especially the knitters.

Veronica quickly said goodbye to her friends then went up to her room praying that Jack would be there. He hadn't answered his cell phone all day. When she opened the door, to her dismay, he was still out. Veronica took out her cell phone and tried to call once more. When she heard the loud music coming from the sofa cushion she realized what had happened. All she could do now was sit and wait.

Veronica prayed that the thoughts running through her head would slow down. She had never been so terrified in her life. She was in an inn with over seven hundred people. She had made friends with several of them. And one of them was a killer. What was worse was the fact that everyone knew she found the body, plus, everyone saw the police take her in for questioning during lunch. What if the murderer thought she knew more than she really did? What if she was next?

Veronica heard a scraping sound at the door. Terrified, she jumped up and ran in the restroom quickly locking the door behind her. Had she forgotten to bolt the room door?

She knew she had. Veronica leaned up against the locked door. Then she heard the sound of the room door slowly opening. "Veronica, are you here?"

Veronica swallowed the lump in her throat. She swung the restroom door open and ran straight into Jack's arms, tears streaming down her face.

Twenty-One

"Where are we going?" Veronica asked as they drove north on Highway 59.

"Roseville. It's a bed and breakfast about five miles west of Marshall," Clara cheerfully replied. "Robert and I have been there before. The food is fantastic! Oh, sweetie, you're going to love it. It's a reservation only place. I wanted to be sure we were able to get in, so I made reservations last week."

Robert spoke up, "Clara is right, the food is fantastic, but that isn't the real reason we're going. There was a famous crochet and tatting artist named Florence Anthony who lived in Shreveport. She gave some of her work to the owners of Roseville. In fact they have her work displayed in every room in the house. I thought you would enjoy seeing it."

"Oh, yes. Thank you. That sounds lovely." Veronica viewed the scenery out the car window. Trees were lined up on both sides of the road creating a beautifully shaded street. She turned toward Clara. "Have you been having a nice time touring the town the last couple of days?"

"Oh, yes, sweetie," Clara answered excitedly. "I went on the Lale Trail today. It was wonderful seeing all the historic homes." Clara went on to tell all about her adventures on the trail then Jack shared his adventures of the last two days.

When the conversation died down Veronica asked, "Clara, you said you went on the Lale Trail today, but what did you do yesterday, while Growth Day was going on?"

"Oh, look, there's Roseville!" Robert interrupted.

Jack turned onto the long driveway. Clara began looking around, never answering the question.

It was a lovely home surrounded by a white picket fence. Clara and Veronica began admiring the beautiful daisies, daylilies, marigolds and perennials growing along the winding pathway up to the wraparound porch. Veronica spotted a little angel sitting amongst the flowers quietly watching over all who entered.

White wicker furniture and an enticing porch swing beckoned them to sit down for a moment to enjoy the landscape before going in to dinner. All was quiet except for the crickets chirping softly in the background.

A few minutes later the front door opened and a tall, distinguished man invited them inside. When they entered the home they found themselves in a charming little parlor. Veronica's eyes immediately fell upon the crocheted pineapple lace doily lying on the oak coffee table. Robert went toward the far wall to admire a framed crocheted pinwheel doily. "I see you are interested in the crochet pieces," the man said in a deep voice. "Feel free to look around. You will find several tatting pieces as well. In fact, I believe you will find something in all of the guest rooms."

They happily wandered from one open room to the next admiring Florence's work. "That is a lovely tatted piece," Veronica said pointing to a framed piece she found in a back bedroom.

Robert walked over to have a look. "No, that's crocheted." Noting her embarrassment, he smiled at her reassuringly. "Don't worry," he said as they headed back into the parlor, "sometimes even professionals get confused."

Upon their return their host led them into a formal dining room. "This isn't the room you will be dining in tonight, but I thought you would like to see the crocheted piece on the wall." He pointed toward the back wall to a beautiful, framed, filet crochet piece, depicting four angels and The

Lord's Prayer. As Veronica silently read the prayer, she felt a cold chill run through her entire body. Somewhere, someone, was definitely watching, watching and waiting...

Robert, Clara, Jack, and Veronica were led into what looked like a family room. French doors to the left led into one dining area, French doors to the right led into another. Their host directed them to the room on the right. The room held two large dining tables, both of which were draped with beautiful, full sized, crocheted tablecloths. A glass had been placed over the tops to protect the delicate work.

"This is all so impressive!" Robert turned to their host. "I was trying to remember, does the other dining room have crochet in it as well?"

"Yes. But there is a private party going on in the room at the moment," the man explained.

Robert chose the table with the crocheted flower trellis motif design and everyone sat down.

Veronica watched as the lights suddenly began flickering in the room. Then she heard the clashing sound of thunder followed by torrents of rain. Veronica began to quiver. Suddenly it was all just too much. She had fallen on the stairs, had found a dead body, had been taken to the police station, not to mention the fact that there was an unknown murderer running around. And now, here she sat, in an unfamiliar, large, historic home where the lights were threatening to go out. The host, totally unaware of the terror building up inside her, politely asked, "Would everyone like the house special, raspberry lemonade?"

The rain continued to pour outside. Oil lamps were brought into the room and lit as a precaution. A few minutes later, the lights went out. Jack held Veronica's hand until she calmed down. Then, despite the lack of light, they enjoyed a delicious meal.

After dinner, no longer feeling like she was being

watched, Veronica excused herself from the table. Taking a lamp with her, she walked down the hall and entered the powder room. She was surprised and amazed to learn it held hidden crochet treasures as well. Veronica examined the crochet work for a few minutes, her earlier fears completely forgotten.

As she was walking back to the dining room she noticed that the French doors, to the left of the family room, were now open. Deciding that the private party must have ended, she couldn't resist taking a peek. Veronica slowly walked toward the doors, ready to make a hasty retreat in case she was wrong.

She found herself standing in a dimly lit, long room with several small tables in it. To the near left was a large filet crochet piece draped over a chest. Veronica went over to look at it more closely.

When she turned around, she saw, for the first time, two people huddled together behind a bouquet of roses at the opposite end of the room. Feeling extremely embarrassed she quickly headed toward the doors.

"Veronica!" a voice called out as chairs slid back, scraping against the floor. Terrified, Veronica froze in her tracks. "Veronica," the voice came again sounding a little more urgent. "Please don't say anything to anyone!"

Veronica turned around and saw Judy coming toward her followed by Duke. "I...I won't say a word," she stammered.

"Neither will I," came a voice from the doorway. Veronica turned back around and saw Robert standing between the French doors, looking into the room.

She looked back at Judy. "I'm really sorry, Judy. I...I didn't mean to intrude."

Rich, dark chocolate cake and coffee were served for dessert. They began eating in total silence. "Well, I guess we have a pretty good idea where Judy and Duke disappeared to during Growth Day," Robert suddenly blurted out.

"Veronica, you haven't touched your cake. Is something troubling you?" Jack asked.

Veronica looked up. She watched for a moment as the glowing warmth from the lantern danced around the dark room. "I was just thinking about what Robert had said earlier."

"What did I say?" Robert asked taking another bite.

"That sometimes even professionals confuse the different crafts."

Robert smiled. "Yes, but I doubt it happens very often. Professionals pretty much know their craft forwards and backwards. That's part of what makes them professionals."

Clara immediately jumped in, "Veronica, sweetie, don't worry about having made a mistake in front of Robert earlier. Robert knows you are just learning. Hey." She laughed, trying to cheer Veronica up. "Don't even get me started, sweetie, on all the mistakes Robert has made!"

"No, no, it isn't that," Veronica said shaking her head. "Detective Edwards thinks that Gloria was killed by a knitter based solely on the fact that Gloria's body was found wrapped in a knitted shawl."

"Well, that makes sense doesn't it?" Jack asked.

"Yes. I guess. But I keep thinking, what if the shawl wasn't really knitted?"

Robert set his fork down. "What are you getting at, Veronica?"

"Well, the last time I was in the ACAKA chat room, Gloria said that she had invented a new stitch and that she was going to reveal it at the fashion show." Veronica lowered her voice, "What if she invented a crochet stitch that looked enough like knitting that it could fool people. What if Gloria actually crocheted the shawl she was wearing herself."

Robert contemplated the question while consuming another bite of cake. "I suppose it might be possible. But I kind of doubt it. Crochet and knitting both use yarn, but that's where the similarities end. They are two totally different crafts in the way the stitches are formed and they don't resemble each other at all when the stitches are completed." Robert took a sip of his coffee. He looked straight at Veronica then added, "Of course, you realize, if she did, that would mean the killer could be anyone, including a crocheter."

"Veronica, sweetie, did a lot of professionals see the shawl?" Clara asked.

"There were a lot of onlookers after her body was found, both knitters and crocheters I imagine. But no one really got a very good look at the shawl, it was so bloody and torn up." Veronica was silent again.

Jack touched her hand with his, "Veronica, what are you leaving out?"

"Nothing really." Veronica took a sip of coffee then tried to change the topic. After all, she reasoned, she didn't know for sure someone was watching her. It was probably all her imagination anyway. She hadn't felt the sensation since they had sat down to dinner. "I...I found the yarn that the shawl was made out of in Longview this afternoon. I purchased some. I'm not sure why."

Robert set his cup down on the table. "Well, Veronica, I was just thinking, you like playing with stitches and you have the yarn. If this is bothering you, why don't you skip your class tomorrow morning, gather up a few designers to help you and see what you can come up with."

Suddenly the lights came back on. "And let there be light," Jack spoke.

Veronica, realizing she hadn't eaten any of her cake, took a small bite and started contemplating the possibility. "Robert, I wouldn't know who to ask," she said after swallowing the delicious morsel. "As you said, if I'm right, the killer could be anyone. My friends, Ann and Ellen, both have classes tomorrow. Sara doesn't know enough about crochet to help. Margery is teaching. I wouldn't have any idea how to find Melissa and I couldn't possibly ask Duke, not after tonight. Those are the only crochet designers I know well enough that I would feel safe asking."

"You trust Robert," Jack suggested.

"I'm afraid I wouldn't be able to help you in the morning either," Robert replied. "Our magazine is hosting a Designer Show and Tell tomorrow and I have to be there."

"Veronica, what about your friends from the yarn shop back home?" Jack jokingly continued, "They can't possibly be suspects. Their plane didn't even land until late last night."

Veronica feigned shock. "Of course my friends are innocent!" she exclaimed. She took another bite of cake then explained, "But they're not designers. They have never expressed any interest in trying to invent stitches." Veronica paused. "I suppose I could ask them though."

"Sweetie, do you hear music?" Clara asked just as everyone was finishing up.

Robert placed the money for their meal on the table then they headed toward the parlor. There they saw their host happily playing, "Let Me Call You Sweetheart", on a player piano, by pumping two pedals up and down with his feet. Judy and Duke were slowly dancing to the music in the middle of the room totally oblivious to their surroundings.

As they quietly slipped out onto the porch Veronica noticed that the rain had cooled the evening off considerably. She took a deep breath. She loved the clean fresh smell after a rain. They stood on the porch a few minutes and once again listened to the sweet sound of crickets before getting back into the car.

"Robert, did we miss a turn somewhere?" Jack asked, looking a little concerned. "This doesn't look familiar at all."

"Maybe it just looks different because it's dark outside," Robert suggested.

"Maybe." They drove a little farther down the road. "Is there a cemetery around here?"

"Well, I see some tombstones," Robert replied. "Why do you ask?"

"Nothing," Jack replied a little too quickly.

Clara looked around, "It does seem a little spooky around here, doesn't it, sweetie."

"Why do you say..." Veronica never finished her sentence. As she looked out her window, she saw the foggy figures drifting slowly toward her.

Jack slowed down as the figures began to obscure his view of the road.

"I don't believe in ghosts!" Veronica said out loud, almost hoping that if they really did exist that they would hear her.

"I don't either," Jack announced as they drove out of the fog almost as suddenly as they had driven into it. "But you've got to admit that was a little strange." Lightning flashed across the sky, as if in answer. But no living sole spoke a word.

Creak *creak*. "Someone is trying to get in," Veronica whispered as she shook Jack awake.

Jack sat up in bed listening for the sound. *Creak creak.* The sound came again. Jack got out of bed and listened at the door. Hearing the sound once more he opened the door and looked out into the hallway. "No one is out here," he announced, sounding a little relieved. Jack shut the door and headed back to the bed. *Creak, creak,* the sound came again as he climbed under the covers.

"What do you think it is?" Veronica asked.

"I don't know." Jack shrugged his shoulders. "I didn't see anything."

"Jack, I'm scared." Veronica sat up in bed. "I couldn't say anything in front of Robert, but I'm really scared. What if the killer thinks I know too much? Or what if the killer wasn't just after Gloria? What if the killer is some kind of serial killer and Gloria just happened to be the first victim?"

"Honey, you are safe." He put his arms around her trembling body. "Remember I'm your knight." Jack kissed her sweetly on the forehead. "Now, do you honestly think I would let anything happen to milady?"

Veronica snuggled up closer to her husband as the creaking sound was heard once again. "Please stay with me tomorrow," she whispered.

Twenty-Two

Friday morning Veronica called her aunt. She decided not to tell her what was going on at the conference. Didn't want to worry her unnecessarily. She just needed to hear her aunt's voice. Fortunately, never suspecting there was a problem, Sally happily began regaling tall tales of Love's misadventures.

It seems Veronica had forgotten to warn her aunt that Love would climb the shelves in the refrigerator every time the door was opened. That he liked to sit in the kitchen cabinets on top of the freshly cleaned warm dishes. And that he enjoyed swatting bubbles while one was trying to take a private bubble bath. Veronica was glad to hear they were having so much fun together.

When the phone call ended Veronica packed the yarn she had purchased the day before in her crochet bag, then she and Jack set out to find Katy, Audra, Jenny and Chrissy by way of the breakfast room.

After breakfast, having not found them, Veronica decided they should look in the market. She wanted to see the market, plus, she thought, it would probably be helpful if she purchased a pair of knitting needles. That way, she could knit a sample square to compare with whatever they crocheted.

Veronica handed her ticket to the attendant at the door,

Jack paid for a ticket for himself, then they entered, *Fantasyland for Yarnaholics,* or as it was more formally called, The Market.

They went from one booth to the next admiring the yarns and crocheted designs on display. Veronica found one booth that offered sonokling wood, hand carved and hand painted crochet hooks. She purchased a size six-millimeter hook, which had a cat playing with a ball of yarn carved into it. A few minutes later she found a display of knitting needles and purchased a nine-millimeter set.

Veronica then located Vashti's booth, which was lavishly decorated in the same style as her shop back home in The Village. She asked Vashti if she had seen Katy or any of the other crocheters, but Vashti hadn't seen them either. She did however introduce Veronica to Destiny. Destiny apologized for not having been available to teach the last few weeks then told her all about the upcoming classes she had planned, including a crochet retreat to be held in the autumn. They visited for a few more minutes before Veronica continued on her mission. Several booths and quite a few yarn purchases later, her friends had still not been found.

"I don't think we're going to find your friends in here and if we don't get out of here soon I'm going to be broke," Jack complained, after more than an hour of shopping.

"I guess you're right," Veronica acquiesced. They started toward the door, but didn't quite make it. Veronica stopped dead in her tracks.

"What's wrong?" Jack asked.

"Don't you see it?" she asked pointing toward a large black box, with a small opening in the front, through which an eerie looking ghostly glow was emitting.

"I'm starting to feel like we're in the Twilight Zone around here," Jack replied. "Come on. There's got to be a logical explanation," he said as he led Veronica slowly toward the box.

Veronica and Jack cautiously peeped inside. "This is fantastic!" Veronica exclaimed.

The booth attendant began to explain. "These are our new in-line crochet hooks, called Susan Bates Smartglo. They store energy from daylight then, when placed in the dark, transform the energy into a glow that lasts about three hours. Takes about ten minutes of light to recharge them. We sell them in two packs, 'G' through 'K' and 'L' through 'P'."

Veronica reached her hand through the box opening and picked up a pack of the pale green hooks. "If there was a storm like last night and the lights went out, I would still be able to crochet!" she exclaimed. She carefully removed one of the hooks from the package and turned it over and over in her hand admiring the ingenuity of such a creation.

"Ok, I give up," Jack said with mock exasperation. "How many of them do you want?"

After all the shopping was done, Veronica and Jack got their hands stamped, for reentry purposes, then walked out into the lobby. There sat Audra, Katy, Jenny and Chrissy crocheting and chatting away with several other yarn enthusiasts. Veronica led them away as quickly as she could so that they could talk in private. "I need a favor," she whispered. "Jack wants to go to the local library and check out the train books..."

"And you want us to stop him," Audra interrupted.

"No. This is serious," Veronica replied in a pleading tone. "I want all of you to go with us so we can talk." Veronica looked over her shoulder to see who was about. "Talk without being overheard."

"Veronica, are you ok?" Katy asked.

"Yes. But I really need to talk to all of you." Veronica's voice was becoming shaky.

Katy put her arm around Veronica, "Sure, we'll go with you."

A few minutes later, with yarn bags still in hand, they all

piled into the rental car then Jack began driving them to South Alamo Street.

"Ok, Veronica, no one can hear us in here. What is this all about?" Jenny asked.

"Does this have something to do with the police taking you in for questioning yesterday?" Chrissy inquired.

"In a way, yes. Detective Edwards thinks that a knitter killed Gloria because of the knitted shawl she was wearing. Everyone knows Gloria was strictly a crocheter. She didn't even know how to knit. And being the purist that she was, she never would have worn an article of clothing that was knitted. So, since she was found wrapped in a knitted shawl, the obvious conclusion he drew was that the shawl probably belonged to the killer, a knitter. But, I keep thinking, the shawl was so bloodied and torn and no one really got a very good look at it, how is everyone so sure that the shawl was knitted?"

Audra replied, "Veronica, I have never actually knitted anything, but even I know how to tell the two crafts apart. Knitting is basically made up of two stitches, knit stitches and purl stitches. The various patterns, stockinette, garter, ribbing, etc. are created by mixing those two stitches, even cables are made by using a variation of the two basic knit and purl stitches. The knit and purl stitches have a very distinct look to them."

"Yes," Veronica conceded. "But Gloria was a professional crochet designer for years and I was told that she was well known for inventing unique stitches. She even posted in the ACAKA chat room that she had invented a new stitch."

Chrissy was beginning to catch on to where Veronica was going with this. "You want to know if it is possible to crochet something that looks like knitting?"

Veronica nodded in affirmation. "Yes. I want to know if someone who crochets could crochet something that looks enough like knitting to fool a group of fiber people. I want to know if Gloria could have invented some kind of stitch that looks like knitting."

Chrissy interjected, "So that the shawl found around Gloria's body could actually belong to Gloria and not the killer."

Jenny spoke up, "If the shawl belonged to Gloria then the killer could be anyone."

"That's true," Veronica replied. "That's why I'm so scared. Before anything else happens, I'm begging the four of you, I have to know, could Gloria have made that shawl herself?"

"Veronica, there are stitches called Tunisian knit stitches and Tunisian purl stitches, which are crocheted stitches that resemble knitted stitches. I guess from a distance they could fool someone. Especially if the item was bloodied and torn and the person was not touching it," Katy informed her.

"What do you mean by not touching it?" Veronica asked.

Katy went on to explain, "Well, Tunisian, or afghan stitches as they are sometimes called, are thicker than knitted stitches when they are worked up. If someone felt the stitches, they would know they were too thick to have been knitted."

"Did anyone who knows the difference between the two crafts actually feel the afghan?" Jenny asked.

"Of course not, Sis. Everyone knows you don't touch evidence. You would leave fingerprints." Chrissy turned to Katy for support, "Isn't that right?"

Katy grinned. "Fingerprints wouldn't show up on a shawl." The others in the car began to laugh as well. It was good to have some release from the tension.

Veronica concluded, "It doesn't matter anyway, Chrissy. Gloria wouldn't have made a shawl using Tunisian stitches. She had very specific interests in the field of crochet. If she couldn't make it using a regular crochet hook, she wouldn't make it. In fact, she got into an argument with Cecilia in the ACAKA chat room saying that Tunisian wasn't real crochet."

"Let me see if I've got this right." Audra sighed. "Using a so called 'real' crochet hook, you want us to invent a stitch in a couple of hours that a superstar designer like Gloria could have possibly invented?" Audra looked to the others for backup. "Veronica, I want to help you out, but that's impossible."

"I'm not asking you to invent the exact stitch," Veronica replied hoping to make the job sound easier than she knew it really was. "I just want to know if we can come up with something crocheted that might fool a few people. If we can, then I can tell Detective Edwards, because I really think he is looking for the wrong person."

"Why do you think that?" Katy asked.

Veronica thought a second. "I don't know. I just do. I can't explain it. I...I'm scared."

"Well, I'm willing to try. Sounds like fun," Chrissy said just as they pulled up to the library.

Audra looked at the others. "Ok," she agreed. "We're all in."

Veronica gave each of her friends a skein of the yarn she had purchased in Longview. "This is the exact same kind of yarn that was used to make the shawl," she whispered. She then removed the newly purchased pink knitting needles from their wrapper and carefully began knitting a small sample square in stockinet stitch. She explained as she worked that she thought they could study the knitted square for stitch placement and also use it to compare their work by.

When she finished the square, she bound off the stitches then cut the yarn. The piece was passed around for each one to examine. "What do you think?" she asked.

"Looks like knitting to me!" Chrissy laughed, when the swatch was handed to her.

"I mean..." Veronica began.

But before she could finish Jenny interrupted. "It's ok. We all know what you mean."

Katy picked up the swatch. She began stretching it in various directions trying to see how the stitches were formed while the others looked on. "It looks to me like the main difference is that knitted stitches go from bottom to top whereas crocheted stitches go side to side," she observed.

"What do you mean?" Audra asked.

"In knit, the stitches stay on the needle from one row to the next so the loops stand up straight. As they are worked, the loops form columns of V's. In crochet, the loops are pulled one through the other and laid down in a horizontal pattern," Katy explained.

Veronica's mind was racing. "Then why doesn't crochet look like knitting turned sideways?"

"Well, it would if there was only one row." Katy took out a crochet hook and quickly worked a few chain stitches. "See," she said, showing them. "It looks just like a column of knitted V's. But when we turn our work and poke the hook back through the stitch, it totally changes the appearance of it."

"May I see?" Veronica asked. She took out her crochet hook and worked a row of single crochet stitches back across. "If you work the stitches in the back ridge of the chain then turn the piece sideways you get two vertical rows of V's," she said handing the work back to Katy.

"Hey, I have an idea! Can I see that?" Jenny asked as she began digging through her yarn bag for a hook. A few minutes later she returned the piece to Katy with an additional row of single crochet stitches.

"How did you do that?" Katy asked in surprise when she saw it.

"I'm left handed remember? Without turning the work, I crocheted the single crochet stitches from left to right through the hump in the back of the stitches Veronica made. Here, Veronica, you make another row," she said handing the piece back to Veronica. "Keep the right side of the work facing you and work your single crochet stitches through the humps in the back of the stitches I made."

Veronica chained one and worked the stitches. She then

handed the piece to Katy. "It does look somewhat like knitting," Katy agreed.

Audra examined the swatch. "But in one column the V's go up, in the other column the V's go down. In knitting, all of the V's go up."

"Yes, but was anyone looking at the shawl close enough to notice something like that?" Chrissy asked.

"Let's try to come up with some more ways," Veronica suggested. "What would happen if we did something similar with slip stitches?"

Katy cut the yarn then worked a new starting chain. "Well, I've done my part," she said handing the chain to Veronica.

Veronica worked a row of slip stitches through the back ridges of the chains then handed the piece to Jenny so that she could slip stitch back across left handed through the humps.

Jenny stared at the piece for a few minutes. "What's wrong?" Audra asked.

"There's no hump when you slip stitch."

Veronica took the piece back and played with it a little while. "Oh, I see. When you work a single crochet stitch you insert the hook through the stitch, yarn over and pull through the stitch. Then you yarn over again and pull through both loops on the hook. The yarn over that you pull through the stitch forms the hump. With slip stitches, the yarn over that you pull through the stitch is also pulled through the loop on the hook. So, instead of forming the hump, it forms the front and back loops of the next stitch."

Audra looked at the piece, "I wonder what would happen if you just went through the back loop of the stitch?"

"Only one way to find out," Katy replied taking the piece from Audra and frogging it back down to its original chain. "Your turn, Veronica," she said handing it over.

Veronica worked a slip stitch in the back or top loop of each chain across then handed the piece to Jenny so that she could do the same working from left to right. They passed the piece back and forth a few times till they had enough rows worked that they could compare it to the knitted swatch.

"It does kind of look like knitting," Chrissy said. "And the V's are all going in the same direction, but I was just wondering, was Gloria ambidextrous? I mean surely she wouldn't have had a left-handed person crocheting every other row for her."

"But remember what Veronica was doing with the single crochet stitches in The Village," Jenny reminded her sister. "Sure, we've been passing the piece back and forth, but Veronica could have done the left handed rows just as easily by herself simply by turning the piece, placing the yarn in front and inserting the hook from the back to the front with her right hand."

"Yes. But Chrissy is right," Audra agreed. "We should probably try to come up with a knit look where the rows are worked in the normal back and forth manner."

"I was thinking, if we only had a third loop we could turn the work," Katy mused.

"What do you mean?" Audra asked.

"Well, if there were three loops, on right side rows you could work in the back loop and the two front loops would create the V's and on wrong side rows you could work in the front loop and the back two loops would create the V's."

"That's it!" Veronica exclaimed, a little too loudly to suit their library setting. "Sorry," she whispered. "But I just remembered. Ellen showed me how to do a half double crochet stitch. I thought it was a fascinating stitch because the yarn over made before inserting the hook in the stitch creates an extra loop so it looks like there are three loops going across the top instead of two. She told me that, once you turn your work, the first loop you see, the one created by the yarn over is called the front bar. The next loop is the front loop and the last loop is the back loop."

"Let's give it a try," Katy said enthusiastically. She fastened off the slip stitch swatch then created another starting chain. Katy worked a row of half double crochet stitches through the back ridges of the starting chains. She then worked a second row of stitches working only in the front bar followed by a third row of stitches working only in the back loop. Everyone looked at the swatch.

"No." Audra disappointedly shook her head. "The columns of V's are too far apart. That doesn't look anything like knitting."

"I have another idea," Veronica said as she began frogging the swatch. "The V's are too far apart because the stitches are too tall. If we altered the half double crochet stitch to make it short like the slip stitch the V's would be closer together."

"How are you going to do that?" Chrissy asked.

"By leaving off the last yarn over and pull through," she explained. Veronica wrapped the yarn around the hook, inserted the hook in the back ridge of the second chain from the hook, did a yarn over and pulled through the stitch and both loops on the hook. She repeated the process working a kind of altered half double crochet stitch in the back ridge of each chain across. She then turned her work and chained one. She repeated her altered half double crochet working her stitches through the front bar of each stitch across. On the next row she worked a chain one then worked her new stitch through the back loop of each stitch across. She repeated the last two rows a couple more times. Feeling very pleased with the results, she turned the piece over to Audra for examination.

"Well, you have the V's all going in the same direction and they are close together, but they aren't really lined up very evenly. All of the wrong side rows created V's, which sit slightly higher than the V's created on the right side rows. But it does look like knitting." Audra reviewed the swatches lying on the table. "In fact, I think all three samples resemble knitting," she declared.

"You're getting awfully agreeable all of a sudden," Katy said suspiciously.

"It's past lunch time. We have a class this afternoon." Audra winked at Katy. "If this doesn't look like knitting, Veronica is going to make us all starve."

Katy cleared her throat, "You know, you're right, they do all resemble knitting!"

As a, thank you, treat, Jack decided to take everyone to Gucci's for lunch before going back to the inn. The aroma of fresh baked bread greeted them as they stepped out of the car. Once inside they watched as a giant pizza was removed from a brick oven and placed on the buffet. "Forget the menu, I'm having the buffet," Jack whispered to Veronica.

"I think we all will," Audra chimed in.

They gorged themselves with pizza, pasta, and salad then went back to the buffet for a delectable dessert, blueberry pizza pie.

Veronica looked at Jenny and Chrissy, "I know Audra and Katy have classes this afternoon, but what about the two of you?"

"We didn't sign up for any Friday classes," Chrissy answered before thinking.

"Oh, you shouldn't have told her that," Audra jokingly admonished. "She's up to something. I can see it in her eyes."

Veronica laughed. "No. Not really up to anything. Just wondering. Would it be possible for each of us to make a small something out of the three stitches we came up with and just kind of show them around to see if we can fool anyone. If we could, then I could tell Detective Edwards that we had tested the theory. I don't want him to think I'm crazy."

"Sure, we'll help you. I'm kind of curious myself. Sounds like fun," Jenny agreed. "But Veronica, Edwards isn't going to think you're crazy. Keep in mind, in just a couple of hours we came up with three ways to make stitches that look like knitting and we're not even designers! Admittedly ours are not perfect faux knitting stitches, but they are certainly close. If we can do that, I'm positive that someone like Gloria could easily have invented a perfect replica."

"I guess you're right." Veronica grinned. "I hadn't thought about it that way! But I would still like to test the stitches out. Just to completely satisfy my own curiosity." Veronica sipped her soft drink. "Could the two of you come to my room to work? I might need some help working up a design. Then afterwards maybe we could show them around the lobby and in the market to see if people think they are knitted or not."

"Sure," Jenny replied. "Like I said, sounds like fun."

Twenty-Three

———◆—◆———

Jack placed the card key in the door then turned the handle. He gallantly opened the door to allow the ladies to enter. A few seconds later, he heard a loud gasp followed by a scream.

Jack ran into the room. The place was a shambles. The room had been totally trashed. After making sure the culprit was no longer in the room, Jack called the front desk and asked them to send for Detective Edwards down at police headquarters. Veronica began looking through her belongings trying to discover what was missing.

By the time the detective arrived both Jack and Veronica were totally baffled. Nothing was missing; money, a forgotten cell phone, digital camera, computer, everything was still in the room albeit not in the right location.

Jack told Edwards about the sounds they had heard the night before, explaining that he had investigated and saw no one.

Edward's took down their statements then looked briefly around the room. "Veronica, I'm sorry to say this, but my guess is that whoever killed Gloria thinks you know more than you do or thinks you have some kind of incriminating evidence. The person who searched the room obviously didn't find anything, since you say nothing is missing." Edwards scratched his head. "When you were out today, did you have anything with you that the killer might have been looking for?"

Veronica shook her head. "No. All I took with me this morning were my crochet hooks, some yarn, that type thing."

"Veronica, I'm scared," Chrissy was almost in tears. "If the killer broke in here, our room is probably next. People know we're friends. They have seen us together. And...and we've been helping you snoop..."

"What kind of snooping?" Edwards demanded, interrupting her.

Veronica pulled the swatches out of her yarn bag and showed them to the detective. "We were trying to come up with a crocheted stitch that looks like knitting. I was thinking that if the shawl Gloria was wearing was crocheted..."

"Veronica!" Edwards stopped her. "That is the same yarn the shawl was made out of that Gloria was wearing when she was found dead. This is incredulous!" he ranted. "Why would you put yourself in danger like this? How many people know you have that yarn?"

Veronica placed the swatches down on the desk. "Lots of people I guess," she replied, not quite sure why the detective was becoming so enraged. "It is just yarn."

Edwards started pacing around the room. "Veronica, the killer knitted the shawl with this yarn. The killer probably knows you purchased the yarn. For whatever reason, doesn't it make sense to you that the killer might not want you to have the yarn?" Edwards paced a few more steps then removed a notepad and pen from his pocket and placed them on the desk. "This is important, Veronica. I need you to write down the name of everyone who knows you have that yarn!"

Veronica cooperatively sat down at the desk and began trying to remember. Of course she had gone to the yarn shop with Ann, so Ann obviously knew. And Sara and Ellen had gone with them. The lady who sold the yarn knew and Margery. Was there anyone else in the shop? She couldn't remember.

"Detective, this is impossible." Veronica threw her hands

up in despair. "Anyone could have found out about the yarn. I wasn't trying to keep it a secret. I didn't think it was any big deal. In fact, it was completely visible in my bag today and I walked all over the market!"

"Don't worry about the market, restrict the list to those who knew you had the yarn yesterday," Edwards replied.

"Why?" Chrissy asked, still rather shaken.

Edwards explained. "Jack said it sounded like someone was trying to break in here last night. Which, if the theory is correct, means the person knew Veronica had the yarn yesterday."

"That's true," Jenny agreed. "Besides, if someone had seen it in Veronica's bag today, they would have known she had it with her and they wouldn't have bothered trashing the place. It had to have been someone who saw her with it yesterday and thought she might have left it in the room."

Veronica went back to her list. That night she had told Robert about the yarn. So, Robert and his wife Clara both knew. It was quite possible that Duke and Judy could have overheard the conversation. They were in the house. Had she told anyone else?

Veronica got up and handed the pad and pen back to the detective. "That is all I can think of."

Detective Edwards read the nine names to himself. "Well, we can probably rule out the checkout girl at the yarn shop. I doubt she was even around. That leaves eight possible suspects." He flipped the pad open to a blank sheet then with pen poised said, "Tell me what you know about them."

"I know they are my friends. And you can rule all of them out!" Veronica exclaimed defiantly, as she sat down on the sofa beside Jack.

"In that case," Edwards calmly retorted, "tell me what you know about your friends so we can get them scratched off the list as quickly as possible."

Veronica hesitated, but finally relented. "Ann has been very nice to me. She is a crocheter. I really like her. Her husband has been sick this week so she has been concerned about him. She is the one who offered to take me to the yarn shop yesterday when I was upset."

Edwards jotted down notes the whole time she spoke.

"Sara, I'll admit, is a little strange. She says she is a crochet designer, but she doesn't seem to know anything about crochet and Melissa told me that no one has ever seen any of her work. But even still, she is exceptionally kind. Plus, she thought the world of Gloria. She mentioned that Gloria had a brother and asked if he had been notified. Have you talked to him?"

Edwards looked up from his writing. "We haven't been able to get in touch with him. He lives in Deadwood, not too far from here. But no one seems to know where he is at the moment. Go on with the list."

"Ellen is a very famous, fashion crochet, designer. She's really shy, but very sweet. She's beginning to open up to me and we're starting to become good friends. Margery is a famous crochet designer as well. I met her on the train coming down. Talked to her most of the night about crochet stitches."

"Margery. That name sounds familiar," Edwards said as he began scrambling through his notes.

Veronica shook her head. "I'll save you the trouble, Detective. Margery is the one that got in the argument with Gloria at Growth Day. But she didn't kill her."

"We'll see," Edwards replied.

Veronica cleared her throat. "Robert is the editor of *Crochet Elite* magazine. His company paid for our trip to the conference. I know for a fact that he couldn't have killed Gloria. He was with me the whole time at Growth Day. Clara, is Robert's wife. She couldn't have done it either. She wasn't even at the inn that day. She has been taking day trip vacations every day while her husband works. Plus, she doesn't knit or crochet."

"Day trips?" Edwards replied skeptically, raising one eyebrow.

Veronica continued, "Duke is a crochet designer. I don't

know much about him, but to be honest he seems to be more of a lover than a killer."

"Crime of passion," the detective mumbled as he scribbled more notes in his little green notepad.

"Judy is a knitter. But I know she isn't guilty. I can't explain how I know. But I do." Veronica looked pleadingly at the detective, wishing with all her heart that he would leave her friends out of his investigation. He was wasting so much precious time when there was a real killer to be found.

"But the fact remains," Edwards concluded, "out of the eight people, Judy is the only knitter on the list."

"Yes, that's true," Veronica stood up as she spoke. "But as I was trying to tell you. My friends and I think there is a good possibility that the shawl wasn't knitted, that, in fact, it was crocheted by Gloria. We spent the whole morning working on stitches that are crocheted, but look like they are knitted." Veronica pointed toward the swatches on the desk. "We were going to make some designs with the new stitches and try them out this afternoon, to see if we could fool professional designers into thinking they were knitted."

Detective Edwards looked at the swatches again, then shook his head, finding it hard to believe how incredibly naive Veronica and her friends were. "If you do this, for your own safety, don't make the designs out of this yarn."

"We won't!" Chrissy assured him.

Edwards handed the swatches to Veronica, said his goodbyes and headed toward the door.

Veronica glanced at the swatches then quickly called out, "Detective! Is there any chance I could see the shawl that Gloria was wearing?"

Edwards turned around and looked Veronica straight in the eye. "Veronica, I want you to know that I appreciate your cooperation, but you do understand, this is getting dangerous."

"But I just noticed something very important," Veronica replied showing the swatches to Edwards once again. "Since we worked our knit look crochet stitches from side to side instead of bottom to top like real knitting, the color pattern on the swatches is different than if they had been knitted. If Gloria made the shawl and if she also had to work from side to side, that would mean, with this self-striping yarn, that the columns of V's would change colors rather than the rows of V's, just like it does on our swatches. If the columns change color on the shawl we would have positive proof that the shawl was crocheted!"

"I'll check with headquarters," Edwards replied. "Listen, Veronica, I don't want to give you the wrong impression. I actually think you might be on to something. When we checked the shawl for foreign substances to see if the killer had left any evidence entwined in the threads, we found nothing. All substances on the shawl were Gloria's. My wife does crafts, she spends hours, days, weeks, even months sometimes working on a single project. I don't see how the killer could have made anything as large as a shawl and not left some kind of evidence on it. If Gloria made the shawl, that would solve at least part of the mystery. So, I do appreciate your help. I just want you to be aware of the danger."

"I'm aware," Veronica replied, looking around at the disheveled room.

Edwards headed once again toward the door. "If your idea works, of course, I would appreciate it if you would let me know. In the meantime, I'm going to stick with the original theory and go talk to Judy. See if she has an alibi for this morning."

Jenny and Chrissy began helping Veronica straighten up the room. Jack followed the detective out the door, "Detective," he said once they were out of hearing range of the room, "I am a little uneasy with all this. What if this person decides to come back?"

"I will have people watching the building and your room." Edwards turned to face Jack. "Don't leave her alone."

Jack turned on the television then sat down on the bed to watch. He was quite pleased to learn one of the channels was showing an all day marathon of westerns and spent the rest of the afternoon happily critiquing the shows. It seemed none of them were using the correct trains for the era they were depicting.

After much discussion, Jenny decided to make a scarf with the slip stitches, Chrissy chose to do a belt with the single crochet stitches and Veronica decided on a purse for the altered half double crochet stitches.

Jenny and Chrissy sat on the sofa. Jenny pulled out a ball of light blue Jezebel wool from her yarn bag. Chrissy started working with a ball of sorbet Gianna.

Veronica looked through her yarns. She couldn't decide what to use. She tried out several of the new yarns she had just purchased from the market, but none of them seemed quite right. Then she remembered that she had packed the celery colored Moda Dea Bamboo Wool yarn, from her surprise bag that Vashti had sold to her the first time she had gone into the shop. She removed the skein from her suitcase and once again admired the softness of the yarn. Satisfied with her choice, Veronica settled herself into the desk chair and began to work.

After trying the altered half double crochet stitch with several sizes of hooks she finally decided that a size six point five millimeter hook would work best. The yarn over before inserting the hook made the stitches a little tight and the larger hook seemed to help.

Jenny explained to Veronica the easiest way to crochet an envelope purse then showed her how to increase by working two stitches in the same stitch and also how to decrease.

Decreasing was the difficult part, not only because she had never decreased before, but also because she had to pull the yarn through three loops all at the same time. Chrissy suggested that she pinch the loops off with her fingers. It worked great.

Armed with her new found knowledge of purse making skills, Veronica chained thirty-one then worked her altered half double crochet stitches in the back ridge of each chain across starting with the second chain from the hook. That gave her thirty stitches. Then, concentrating as hard as she could, she continued working till the piece was complete.

At the same time, Jenny and Chrissy were having fun passing their projects back and forth to one another, Jenny doing the left hand rows and Chrissy doing the right. Veronica was impressed that they could keep track, knowing if they were supposed to be doing a slip stitch or if they were supposed to be doing a single crochet stitch. But they seemed to be working it out with no problems.

Feeling a little queasy, Veronica went to the refrigerator and got soft drinks for everyone. After the beverages were depleted and she was feeling a little better, Jenny showed her how to alternate slip stitch decreases with a chain stitch across the ends of the rows to make them look nicer.

Once the ends were finished, Veronica folded the piece and sewed the sides to form the body of the purse then she added a chained, shoulder strap. Now all she needed was a way to fasten the flap down.

Veronica dug through her suitcase, for her emergency repair kit, and found a sew-on snap, which she attached. The purse was cute, she thought, but it needed some kind of decoration on the front. She began looking through her things. A kitty cat button on one of her jackets caught her eye. That would be perfect she thought. She removed the button from her jacket and sewed it onto the purse.

Jenny and Chrissy were just finishing up their projects as well. After expressing their sincere mutual admiration for one another's projects, they decided to go to the market and try them out. Jenny donned her scarf, Chrissy her belt and Veronica picked up her purse. "Jack, we're leaving," Veronica called out as they walked out the door.

Jack quickly flipped off the television set and ran after

them. "Wait!" he called out. "You can't leave your knight behind!"

"Veronica, where have you been? I've been looking for you all day!" Ann exclaimed, as she ran up to Veronica in the market.

"I decided to do some crocheting in my room this afternoon." Veronica moved the purse from her left shoulder to her right, in an effort to get Ann to notice it. "Did you need something?"

"I was hoping I would be able to talk you into entering the Designer's Contest with me tonight," Ann replied.

"Tonight?" Veronica had forgotten all about the contest.

"Yes. It starts at eight tonight and lasts till midnight." Ann began to explain, "They used to have it on Saturday mornings, but so many designers were teaching Saturday classes that they had to change it. So, now they are holding the contest on Friday night. The designs are still judged by secret ballot before the fashion show on Saturday." Ann paused. "Would you go to the contest with me? I really want to go, but I don't want to go by myself. By the way, just as a suggestion, you really shouldn't be carrying around a knitted purse. Everyone will think you are a knit designer."

Veronica smiled. Mission accomplished. "Thank you, Ann. I would love to go with you. I need to run a few errands first though and get a little supper. Could we meet in the lobby, say around seven-thirty?"

"Sure. That would be great," Ann agreed.

Veronica and Jack began looking for Jenny and Chrissy to see what kind of response they had received. When they found them in the back section, both were grinning from ear to ear.

They excused themselves to go get a bite to eat. As they walked out of the market and through the lobby, Veronica could feel the intense heat as the eyes bore into her. She held Jack's hand. They were making progress, but time was running out.

Twenty-Four

———◆◆———

Sitting in the car, on the way to supper, Veronica called Detective Edwards to share the results of the experiment. He informed her that he had obtained a photo of the shawl and invited her to stop by the station.

Edwards met Veronica and Jack at the door and showed them to his office. Veronica was amazed at how much his office looked like the detective offices she had seen in old movies, complete with clutter. Despite the mess, Edwards seemed to know exactly where everything was. He picked several photos up off his desk. "These are photos of the crime scene." He shuffled through them then handed one to Veronica. "This one shows the shawl the best."

Veronica carefully studied the picture for a few minutes. The shawl definitely looked knitted. The V's were all going in the same direction and they were all lined up perfectly. "Well, what do you think?" he asked.

"It's crocheted!" Veronica smiled.

"Are you sure?"

"Yes." She handed the photo back to Edwards. "Look, the color changes occur from one column of V's to the next, not from row to row."

Edwards looked at the photo. "I still don't know what you're talking about." He quickly held up his hand. "But I believe you," he added, just in case she was inclined to explain.

"There is something else you should know," Veronica added. "The shawl wasn't torn. One side of the shawl is completely missing. It looks more like someone took a pair of scissors and cut it off."

"How can you tell that?" Edwards asked, sitting down on top of his desk.

"Generally, when a design is finished the crocheter puts a border around the edges to make the design look more professional. This shawl only has a border on the top, bottom and one side," Veronica explained as she pointed to the various locations in the photo. "The fourth side, which appears to be cut, has no border."

"Maybe she just hadn't finished the last side," Edwards suggested, motioning for them to sit down in the two wooden chairs behind them.

Veronica and Jack sat down then Veronica continued, "I doubt she would have been wearing an unfinished shawl. But there are two other things to go by. The border on the shawl has more than one round. She wouldn't have begun the second round of the border without doing the first round on all four sides.

"Also, if you look real close you can tell it was cut by the fact that the side that is missing the border has several dozen tiny yarn ends dangling from it. Crochet uses one hook and works with one loop. So, unless she was working with several skeins of yarn, which she wasn't, there should only be one yarn end."

"Ok," Edwards replied. "You gave me two reasons. I'll give you two questions. Why would someone, in your opinion, want to kill Gloria and why would that person cut off a piece of the shawl?"

Veronica sat quietly contemplating the questions. "Well, it sounds ludicrous, but the obvious answer would be they wanted to steal the pattern."

"What type of person would kill someone to steal a pattern?" Edwards asked as he began strumming his fingers on the desk.

"I'm not sure." Veronica shook her head. "But in this case, it was someone who didn't know a lot about crochet or at least didn't think about what they were doing before they did it."

"Why do you say that?" he asked.

"Well, if the killer wanted to steal the pattern, he or she should have cut the bottom off the shawl, not the side. If the bottom had been cut, the killer could have gradually frogged the stitches to see how the V's were made. By cutting the side, all the killer got was a bunch of cut yarn ends."

Jack, who had been quietly listening to the conversation, spoke up, "Detective, you said you didn't find any substances on the shawl that would lead back to the killer, but couldn't it be possible that the killer got something on the side of the shawl and cut the shawl to get rid of the evidence?"

"Possibly. But as crazy as it sounds, I think Veronica might be right about the pattern stealing. If the killer had merely gotten something on the shawl, he or she would have got rid of the whole shawl not just part of it. Cutting the shawl took time and effort on the killer's part. It had to be deliberate. And leaving most of the shawl wrapped around Gloria, I imagine, was a calculated attempt to throw the investigation off."

"Well, at least this strikes Judy off the list. A knitter wouldn't want a crochet pattern," Veronica concluded.

"A knitter might not want a crochet pattern, but isn't it a possibility that they might also not want a crocheter creating such an exact replica of their craft?" Edwards challenged.

"I don't know." Veronica sighed. "This is all so crazy."

"Ok," Edwards said. "In lieu of what you have just told me, let's go down the list again of our possible suspects. In my opinion, Judy is still at the top of the list. On top of the fact that she is a knitter and knows very little about crochet, I talked to her this afternoon after your room was vandalized and she had no alibi. Clara and Sara look like good possibilities as well."

"What?" Veronica asked in surprise. "Why do you say that?"

Edwards reminded her, "Because you said it was probably someone who didn't know much about crochet which neither of them do. Plus," he went on to explain, "Clara disappeared that day. It appeared on the tape that Gloria was flirting with Clara's husband, Robert, which could easily have lead to a crime of passion. If not that, Clara could also have been working with Robert. Clara kills Gloria. Steals part of the shawl. Gives it to her husband, who just happens to be the editor of a very popular crochet magazine. And the next thing you know, he becomes even more famous for 'inventing' this knit looking crochet stitch. And the money comes pouring in."

Veronica's mouth dropped open. Could something like that possibly happen? Was crochet that cut throat of a business? Surely not...

"As for Sara," Edwards continued, "not only does she seem to not know anything about crochet, but according to the tape, she followed Gloria out of the room and didn't return. I'm not taking anyone off the list, and I strongly advise you not to be alone with anyone on the list, but for the moment, those are the top three suspects."

"I'll be careful," Veronica agreed. "But you're wrong about my friends."

Veronica felt a refreshingly, cool breeze on her face as she walked into the Subway restaurant. Ceiling fans were wonderful, she thought. She ordered a six-inch wheat turkey sandwich and a bottle of water. Jack placed his order for a foot long, subway melt, with the works. After receiving and paying for their meal they headed toward the dining area. Veronica spotted Ellen sitting all alone at a green marbled table in the corner of the restaurant near the ladies room. She led Jack over to the table so they could say hello.

Ellen looked up. She smiled sweetly then invited them to join her.

"How come you're here all alone?" Veronica asked. "Is everything ok?"

"Yes," Ellen spoke softly. "I just wanted to get away for a little while."

"I understand." Veronica pulled her sandwich out of the clear plastic bag then began removing the paper. "This is quite a change from eating at Roseville last night." Veronica smiled at Jack.

"Yes. Roseville has wonderful food," Ellen replied.

Veronica swallowed a bite of her sandwich. "I didn't realize you had been there before. Do you go often?"

"Yes." Ellen looked down at the floor.

Veronica tried again to draw her friend out. "Are you going to be in the Designer's Contest tonight?"

"No, I don't think so. I was in class all day today." Ellen sipped her soft drink. "I think I'm just going to go back to the inn and try to get some sleep. Are you going?"

"Are you kidding?" Jack exclaimed. "Milady would never miss out on a contest."

"You must like competition," Ellen said as she ate the last of her sandwich. "I hate it myself." Ellen turned to Jack, "Are you going with her?"

Veronica was confused as to why Ellen would think that Jack would go. "Is there something there for the spouses to do?" she asked.

"No." Ellen shook her head. "I just thought...well you know...with all the rumors that are going around."

Jack smiled reassuringly at her. "No, I think in a group that large she will be perfectly safe." Ellen looked back down at the floor. "Ellen, are you scared?"

"Yes...I mean...a little...I...I mean, I'm here all alone."

For some odd reason, Ellen's fright was making Veronica feel more confident. Putting aside her own fears she tried to console the shaking woman. "It's ok," she whispered. "You have us. You can hang out with either of us anytime you want."

"Thank you. That really means a lot. Would...would you mind if I sit here with you until you finish eating?"

"Of course not," Jack assured her. "We'll even follow you back to the inn. Veronica is going to the Designer's Contest, but we'll be back in plenty of time, we can even walk you to your room and make sure everything is ok before you go in."

"Thank you, but that's not really necessary," Ellen half-heartedly replied, obviously not meaning a word she was saying.

"Really, it's no problem," Veronica declared.

All was quiet as Veronica and Jack entered Ellen's room. She invited them to stay and have a drink, but Veronica reminded her that she had to get back downstairs for the contest. Veronica did however sneak in a request for an invitation back. She was becoming a big fan of Ellen's fashion designs and was just dying to see samples and learn more about designing from her. They made arrangements to meet for lunch in the dining hall after Veronica's Saturday morning class. After which, Ellen would show her some of the designs she was working on.

Veronica pushed the elevator button then she and Jack impatiently waited for the doors to open. "Do you think it is a bad idea?" Veronica asked.

"Is what a bad idea?"

"Going to see Ellen's designs tomorrow. Edwards said not to be alone with anyone on the list. Ellen is on the list. But I really want to see her work."

Jack gave her a kiss. "No, I think there are a few people we can scratch off that list of Edwards. I mean Clara couldn't possibly have done that silly scenario Edwards painted. I really think he is stretching..."

"But what about the jealous wife theory?" Veronica interrupted.

"I suppose that's possible. It sure would help if we knew if

Clara had an alibi during that time." Jack sighed. "She told us about the Lale Trail on Thursday, but she never did say where she was on Wednesday." Jack paused for a moment. "Well, anyway, we know Robert couldn't have done it. He was with you at the conference. Unless he is some kind of Houdini, he couldn't have been in two places at the same time. And poor Ellen was scared to death tonight of the murderer. She wasn't scared of herself. Also, despite what Edwards keeps saying," Jack smiled, "we both know what Judy and Duke were doing when they disappeared from Growth Day."

Veronica put her head down. "Guess that leaves Ann, Sara, Margery, and a possibly jealous Clara," she said sadly.

Jack placed his hand under her chin and gently lifted her head back up. "Or any number of other people," he replied. "Just be careful and use common sense."

Veronica and Jack wandered over to the mezzanine railing while they continued to wait for the elevator. Veronica spotted Sara and Ann standing in the lobby chatting away beside one of the elephant statues. Veronica smiled to herself. Edwards was wrong about Sara too. She was obviously going to the designer contest with Ann. She had to know how to crochet!

A bell rang and the elevator doors slid open. Seeing several other designers already on board, she and Jack went ahead and said their goodbyes. He kissed her on the forehead for luck then turned to go back down the hall to their room. Veronica stepped into the small box and the doors closed behind her.

"Hi, Ann. Hi, Sara," Veronica greeted her friends when she walked into the overly crowded lobby. "This is exciting."

"Hi, Veronica!" Ann responded. "The contest is going to be held in conference room 'A', same room as Growth Day. Let's go on in and find a seat. Sara I guess we'll see you tomorrow."

"Sara, aren't you going to be in the contest!" Veronica

exclaimed, as all hope of proving Sara really was a crochet designer suddenly evaporated.

"Sara has some work she has to do tonight. She's taking a class tomorrow, which requires homework and she hasn't done it yet," Ann spoke for her.

Sara looked down at her feet. "Look, could I talk to both of you, in private?" she asked. "Maybe we could go out to the pool area. There's no one out there at the moment."

Veronica's instincts immediately kicked into survival mode. Edwards had put Sara at the top of the list of suspects and here she was asking to speak privately to her. And around a swimming pool no less, the perfect murder weapon, one slip and you were gone. Veronica quickly started to object, but before she could find her voice, Ann agreed to the meeting and began leading her out the door. "Don't worry, we have time before the contest," Ann said seeing the worried look on Veronica's face.

Darkness filled the sky. Only the glowing light from the lanterns atop the iron fence surrounding the pool area lit their path. Sara opened the wrought iron gate and led them to one of the umbrella-covered tables beside the pool. Unfortunately, Sara was right, no one was about.

Veronica sat down on the edge of her chair, anxiously waiting for Sara to speak. She watched as the water cascaded over the rocks into the pool below. The soothing sounds of the waterfall along with the smell of chlorine enveloped her senses. If she wasn't so frightened, it would indeed be a beautiful sight.

Sara hesitated several times before she actually began, "I...I don't know how to say this, except to say I'm sorry. I know I have been deceiving everyone." Veronica noticed that Sara was shaking all over and wringing her hands as she spoke. "I...I don't know anything about knitting or crocheting or whatever it's called. I just wanted Gloria to introduce me to her brother." Sara looked up at Veronica. "He's so wonderful!"

She looked back down again then spoke wistfully, "We've lived in the same town for over a year now. I see him occasionally coming and going from various places, but he spends most of his time working at home, has his own business. I've tried to meet him on my own, but working at home the way he does, there just aren't a lot of opportunities."

Sara sat silent for a moment, trying to gather her thoughts. "Gloria and I went to high school together our senior year. Her brother had already graduated by that time. Anyway, since we had sort of kept in touch over the years, I guess I just thought, if I buttered Gloria up enough, if she liked me enough, maybe she would introduce us. They are...were...very close." Sara put her face in her hands and began to cry softly.

Ann got up and walked over to her. "It's ok, we understand. We've all done crazy things in the name of love," she said as she gave Sara a hug.

Sara lowered her hands and looked up at Ann. "After the news of her death I thought about going on home, but I was afraid if I did people would think I had killed her or had something to hide. Everyone saw me follow her out of the conference room." Sara looked pleadingly at Veronica. "But honestly, I didn't do it and I didn't see anything."

Veronica covered Sara's hands with her own, "We believe you," she whispered consolingly. Sara looked relieved. But unbeknownst to her, she wasn't half as relieved as Veronica was.

"Life is so strange," Sara mused. "I figured I needed to keep up the pretense so Thursday morning I went to the class I had signed up for just as if nothing was different. I had signed up for all of Gloria's classes. The ironic thing is, from the teacher who took over the class, I actually started learning the craft. I am enjoying it too. It is very relaxing. I'd never want to be a designer or anything like that, but I am enjoying the repetitive motions of the stitches.

"Anyway, I wanted you both to know the truth. I'm sorry I tried to fool everyone. Guess I wasn't really fooling anyone though."

"It's ok, Sara," Ann assured her. "Honestly, we understand."

Sara shook her head. "Yes, but I haven't told you the worst part." She looked Ann straight in the eye. "Despite everything that has happened, I...I still can't stop thinking about John."

"John. That's Gloria's brother?" Veronica asked.

"Yes."

"Sara, I want you to listen to me very carefully." Veronica leaned toward Sara and spoke softly to her, "I know this may sound silly to you, but I honestly believe that what is meant to be will be. If God has chosen John for your soul mate, you will eventually be together. You just have to be patient and have faith."

Twenty-Five

———◆———

Once again, Veronica entered the large conference room. The room looked basically the same as before except no yarn was to be seen anywhere. All the round tables sported crochet hooks, knitting needles, yarn needles, scissors, rulers, calculators, pencils, pens, lined paper, graph paper and sizing charts. The rectangular table at the front of the room held a large assortment of autumn colored buttons as well as a large display of ribbons, fasteners, purse handles, hooks, rings and beads. There were sealed cardboard boxes piled on the floor to the left and also to the right of the table.

Ann led Veronica to the same table they had sat at earlier in the week. Margery was already seated at the table. "May we join you?" Ann asked.

"Certainly, have a seat." Margery turned toward Veronica. "I want you to know how truly sorry I am. I should have said so when I saw you in the yarn shop yesterday, but I was just too embarrassed. I need to apologize to you about last Wednesday. I'm really sorry. I realized afterwards how much that must have embarrassed you. I shouldn't have goaded Gloria on like I did."

"It's ok," Veronica said as she sat down. "I know you weren't trying to embarrass me. It's partly my fault anyway. I shouldn't have asked her to show me how to make a crocheted cable."

"No!" Ann snapped. "You didn't do anything wrong, Veronica. You had no way of knowing that Gloria would react that way." Ann's anger grew steadily as she spoke. "Look, I'm sorry, I know she's gone, but that doesn't change what kind of person she was when she was living."

Deciding she had better try to change the subject fast, Margery asked, "Veronica, we have a little time right now, would you like me to show you how to make a cable?"

Veronica thought to herself, first she was to be taught the cable by Gloria because Margery goaded Gloria into it, now she was to be taught the cable by Margery because Ann's outburst had to be defused and Margery was feeling guilty. "Sure, that would be wonderful," Veronica replied, hoping cables were really worth it.

Margery pulled a skein of yarn out of her yarn bag. She worked a few chains then did several rows of single crochet stitches. "Cables can be made in many different ways. Probably the two most common methods are by; working long stitches such as treble crochets around the posts of stitches a couple of rows below and by working surface slip stitches on top of the rows, which is the way I prefer." Margery showed Veronica how to hold the yarn in back of her work, how to insert the hook from the front of the work to the back and then how to pull the yarn through. Veronica worked a few surface slip stitches. "This is fun!" she exclaimed, a little surprised.

"Now to make it look like a cable you..."

"Designers, we are about to begin, if you will all take your seats please." Veronica looked up and saw Tammy standing in back of the podium holding several sheets of paper, from which she was obviously planning to read. She began, "We have provided all needed supplies for your projects. If you would like to use your own hooks and needles that's fine, but remember, the only yarn you are allowed to use is the yarn in the box you choose and the only accessories you may use are what you find on the front table." Tammy looked up and glared at Margery. "If you have yarn with you, please put it away at this time."

Margery grabbed her yarn and stuffed it back in the yarn bag. "Sorry, Veronica," she whispered.

Tammy went back to her oral reading, "For those of you who may not know, this is not only a competition, but also a charity event. All of the money raised from the sale of the books, minus the printing and shipping costs, goes to charity. In years past the books have been very popular as I'm sure this year's book will be since, this year, the money will be benefiting not only the fiber arts, but kids as well. It has been decided that the funds from this year's book will be used to start up a kids ACAKA group." Applause broke out across the room. Tammy patiently waited for everyone to quiet back down. "A monitored Internet chat room will be set up for kids and we also hope to be able to offer classes next year, specifically geared toward children."

Tammy cleared her throat then tried to read a little faster. "Now how are winners chosen? Winners will be chosen by secret ballot. Everyone who attends or who is in the fashion show Saturday night will have a chance to preview the designs. On the back of their admission ticket they will write the name of their favorite crochet project and also the name of their favorite knitting project. Votes will be tallied during the fashion show and the winners will be announced at the conclusion of the show. Winners will then be given the appropriate title, Crocheter of the Year or Knitter of the Year. For those of you who have been asking, since the keynote address was cancelled, we will also be passing out the certificates of completion and pins, due to those graduating from one level of proficiency to the next, at that time." Several in the audience began to applaud. Veronica assumed they were the ones awaiting awards.

"A word of precaution, keep your projects small. This is a timed competition. All projects and written directions have to be completed within four hours. To help you out though, if you are doing booties, slippers, etc. you only need to make one for photography purposes. Also, if you make a clothing item, you need only write the directions for the size you have actually made the model for. If you need a suggestion of what to make, there is a list of possible designs on every table. Do not limit yourself to the items listed. They are only suggestions."

Veronica picked up the pink sheet and began reading to herself; place mat, coaster, hot pad, dishcloth, coffee cozy, preemie blanket, baby bootie, baby bib, child's vest, hat, mittens, scarf, headband, hair scrunchy, cell phone bag, small purse, pet snuggle, pet coat, small doily, flower, bookmark, finger puppet, ball.

"Most important, all directions need to be printed using clear large letters." Tammy looked up. "Did everyone hear me?" She wrapped loudly on the podium a couple of times. "I will repeat. All directions must be printed using clear large letters."

Veronica was starting to get a little antsy. Time was passing. She wished Tammy would stop reading and let them get started.

"This is a competition, but it is a friendly competition. If you wish to help one another out that's fine. Just be sure you are able to finish your own project within the time limit. And remember, no swapping. Whatever yarns you receive in your box, that's what you use. No exceptions."

Veronica glanced around. There were seventy-five to a hundred designers in the room all looking as impatient as she was feeling.

"After you're finished, place your project, your directions and all unused yarn back in the box and leave it on the table. Should you need them, the rules I have just stated are posted on every table."

Tammy looked out at her restless audience. "And, believe it or not, that's all that I have to read. At this time, please come pick up a box and begin." Tammy hit the top of a clock, which was seated on the podium, and a countdown timer began.

Veronica went to the front of the room, grabbed a box, then went back to her seat, where she quickly ripped open the cardboard and began to survey the contents. There were three skeins of yarn; Moda Dea Silk 'n Wool wasabi, TLC Essentials aran and Red Heart Casual Cot'n falling leaves. Veronica immediately knew what she wanted to do. The aran yarn would make a perfect background for the surface slip stitches Margery had just shown her how to make and the falling leaves yarn could be used for the slip stitches themselves. Veronica read through the list of possibilities again and decided a hot pad would be just the right size. She picked up her five point five millimeter hook and began to work her beginning chain stitches while, up at the front of the room, the commotion continued.

"What's going on?" Veronica asked Ann.

"Nothing." Ann smiled. "They are shaking the boxes, trying to determine if the box contains thread or yarn, that type thing, before they make their choice."

"I didn't know we were supposed to do that, I just grabbed a box," Veronica replied, wondering if she had already made a mistake.

"I did too," Ann said as she began digging through her yarn bag. Her search quickly became frantic.

"Is something wrong?" Veronica asked.

"I can't find my crochet hooks. I must have left them in my room," Ann moaned.

Veronica innocently asked, "Why don't you just use one of the hooks on the table?"

With a sour look on her face, Ann picked one of the steel hooks up off the table and started her beginning chain using the Opera parasol rose thread from her box.

"I can't do it," Ann declared a minute later. "I just can't do it. This hook just doesn't feel right. I've got to have my own hooks. Veronica, would you go with me?"

"Go with you?" Veronica swallowed hard.

"Yes, back to my room to get my hooks. I don't want to go by myself," Ann explained.

Veronica's thoughts began rushing again. She knew she was becoming paranoid. She knew Ann was her friend. But how well did she really know Ann? Edwards had warned her not to be alone with anyone who knew about the yarn purchase. Ann knew she had the yarn. And now Ann wanted to be alone with her, really alone, in the elevator alone, in a closed bedroom room alone. Of course she had already gone with Ann to the yarn store and also out to the swimming pool. If Ann wanted to hurt her she could easily have done it either time. But then, they were not really alone either time.

Veronica looked at Ann. She had been so nice to her. And Detective Edwards could be wrong about the yarn thing, probably was. It was silly to think that someone would want to hurt her just because she had purchased some yarn, yarn that anyone could easily purchase from any yarn shop. Maybe it wasn't even a designer who killed Gloria. Maybe it was a total stranger. She couldn't let Ann go out all by herself.

The decision made, Veronica put her hook and yarn down on the table and followed Ann out of the conference room.

Ann unlocked her room door then opened it for Veronica to enter. Ann immediately began searching the room for her missing crochet hooks, looking on the bed then going through the bed linens. Veronica was wondering if she should join in the search, but Ann had not given her permission to look around in her private things. In fact, Ann had hardly spoken a word since they left the conference room.

Veronica noted that Ann had the bedroom of a true artist; clothes, shoes, books, papers and yarn scattered everywhere. Realizing this could take awhile she made herself comfortable on the end of the already searched bed—the perfect position for spotting crochet hooks on top of a television set.

Ann gave Veronica a big hug and thank you. "I must have put them down when I turned off the T.V.!" she said, by way of explanation, smiling happily, now that the lost had been found. "Listen, I'm sorry to keep holding you up, but I really need to go to the little room before we go back down. I'll hurry."

Ann dropped the hooks on the bed, went in the restroom and shut the door leaving Veronica alone in the room. Veronica couldn't help thinking it would be the perfect time to search the room if she were so inclined to do so. She nonchalantly walked toward the nightstand, took a quick peek in the closet then glanced at the black leather suitcase sitting on the chair. Did she dare? Veronica slowly walked toward the suitcase. She reached down with one finger and gradually began lifting the lid, all the while, carefully listening for sounds that might indicate Ann was returning.

Suddenly, Veronica dropped the lid in shock, and began running for the door. No! She stopped herself. She had to have a better look. She couldn't just jump to conclusions. Veronica listened. She could hear the sounds of water running in the sink. She knew her time was running out, maybe in more ways than one.

Quickly she went back to the suitcase and opened it. There they lay, the gloves Gloria was wearing at Growth Day. Veronica picked up one of the gloves. The peach ribbon was missing, but there was no doubt in her mind, she was holding Gloria's white lace glove and Ann was the murderer. Trying not to make a sound, Veronica put the glove back in its resting place and lowered the suitcase lid just as Ann walked into the room.

"We better hurry and get back to the contest," Ann said as she retrieved her hooks from the bed then headed toward the door. Veronica shakily followed, praying all the while that Ann had not seen her uncover the damning evidence.

Everyone was busily working on their projects when

Veronica and Ann sat back down at the table. Veronica wanted to call Detective Edwards, she needed to talk to him, but if she left now, Ann would be sure to know what happened. Veronica kept telling herself over and over again to calm down. There was no way Ann was going to do anything in front of all those people. She was safe. But no matter how many times she told herself, her hands just wouldn't stop shaking.

"Veronica, calm down," Margery said sympathetically. "I know it's a contest and this is your first time, but there is nothing to get that nervous about. Would you like me to help you?"

Veronica began to feel safer. If people thought she was nervous about the contest that was fine. It was something to hide behind. Veronica turned her head to look at Ann who was calmly crocheting away as if she didn't have a care in the world.

"Yes. I would appreciate some help," she replied turning back to Margery. "I want to make an aran colored hot pad and then decorate it with the surface slip stitches you showed me."

"Oh, you don't need my help. You just need a piece of graph paper." Margery handed a sheet to Veronica. "Just draw on the graph paper, the design you want to make on the hot pad."

"Thank you," Veronica replied as she picked up a pencil and began to draw. It wasn't hard to figure out how to make a cable shape and she soon had a couple of cable looking patterns on her paper. She then crocheted a hot pad twenty stitches by twenty-one rows. Afterwards, the design she had drawn on graph paper, was recreated in stitch form onto her hot pad, with the falling leaves yarn.

Veronica was very pleased with the way it was turning out and the best part was she still had over two hours to go. Using the falling leaves yarn she added the final touch, a border with a little loop to hang the hot pad by. Then, on a blank sheet of paper, she began legibly printing out the directions for her decorative hot pad. When all was finished, she was amazed to learn she had an hour to spare.

She looked at Ann for only the second time since they had sat down. Ann had created a beautiful doily with little pink roses and green leaves. It was so delicate looking. How could a cold blooded murderer create such delicate work? It just didn't fit. But the evidence was all there, or rather in the suitcase. Gloria was wearing the gloves when she left Growth Day. Ann had supposedly gone to call her husband. Had Ann been lying the whole time? Was her husband really sick? Did she even have a husband? Veronica's stomach began to churn. She knew she was going to be sick. She jumped up and ran toward the lobby's powder room.

Seeing Veronica leave, Judy, who had been sitting at a back table, quietly got up and followed. Veronica knew she was being followed. She could feel the eyes...

Leaving the stall, Veronica walked right into Judy, who was standing by the stall door. Veronica began shaking all over. "Are you ok?" Judy asked. "You left the room in such a hurry, I was concerned about you."

"I...I just feel sick."

"Do you want me to take you back to your room?" Judy asked as she placed her arm around Veronica.

"No...I...I'll call Jack. He was supposed to come get me," Veronica said as she pulled out her cell phone.

But the truth was she was terrified to leave. She had felt the eyes following her again as she left the conference room. Ann's eyes, the eyes of a killer, and she was waiting, right outside the door.

"Veronica, I'm sorry you're sick," Judy sympathized, when Veronica got off the phone. "I'll stay here with you till your husband comes. We haven't really had much of a chance to visit." Judy led Veronica over to a jungle painted, wood bench and helped her sit down.

"Yes, I'm sorry I intruded on you and Duke," Veronica apologized.

"It's ok. It was our own fault. After all, we were in a public place. You see, Duke and I started talking on the Internet a few months ago. We were really looking forward to this conference. Not only because it's a great conference, but also because we wanted to spend some private time together." Judy brushed the hair out of Veronica's face. "Unfortunately everything changed at the last minute when his sister decided to come to the conference and room with him. I was already sharing room expenses with another lady. There was just no place for us to be alone." She walked over to the washbasin as she spoke. "The last couple of days we have been sneaking time together when his sister and or my roommate are gone, but that doesn't give us much time alone." Judy dampened a paper towel with cold water then handed it to Veronica, instructing her to wrap it around her neck to help with the nausea.

"Duke is a fantastic designer," Judy continued. "He has been teaching me how to crochet and I've been teaching him how to knit. I'm sure we'll go public with our relationship eventually. We just aren't ready to yet. I guess, in a way, I'm trying to protect his reputation as a designer. There are so few men who come to these conferences. I just don't want people to think…"

"Veronica! Are you in there?" Jack called through the door.

Back in the room Veronica explained to Jack the events of the evening. He convinced her to wait until morning to call the detective. She was sick. Ann wasn't going anywhere. And, according to Jack, she was probably wrong. As he pointed out, the JP said Gloria died around two in the afternoon. Ann was in the breakout sessions at that time. And even if the murder had taken place earlier in the day, Ann had only been gone for a few minutes, to call her husband.

Veronica agreed to wait. It would keep until morning. But she knew she was right. How else could Ann have gotten Gloria's gloves unless she had killed her?

Twenty-Six

———◆—◆———

Saturday morning came much too soon. Veronica slowly rolled herself out of bed instantly making the decision that breakfast would be skipped. Angry with her body for turning on her, she sat back down on the edge of the bed. Here she was at a crochet conference and she had only gone to one class. No, she wasn't going to skip another one no matter how bad she felt. Veronica stood up straight, put on a happy face, stretched then ran to the restroom just as the heaving began.

Class would be interesting, she thought while washing her face. It was the only class that Dave, the original recipient of the trip, had signed up for that Gloria was to teach. Veronica had no idea what would be taught in its place, but was looking forward to the class just the same.

Jack was standing by the door when she walked out. "Don't you think you should stay in bed today?" he asked.

"Probably." Veronica smiled up at him. "But it isn't going to happen. There are only two days left of the conference and I intend to make the most of them. I can recuperate when we get home. Right now, I am going to call Detective Edwards, then I'm going to go to a crochet class." Veronica picked up her phone then sat down Indian style on the sofa. "Was there anyplace else you wanted to go while we're here?"

"I thought I'd go to Adkisson Donut Shop over on Pinecrest and eat doughnuts." Veronica tilted her head sideways and looked at Jack trying to figure out if he was joking or if he was really planning a doughnut-eating day. Jack smiled. "And then, I think I will drive around and explore the town. I heard they have a remodeled park with a fountain."

"And where's the train?" Veronica teased.

Jack grinned. Veronica knew him a little too well. "Inside the park. It's a 1915 Texas and Pacific steam engine that was donated to the city by the T&P railroad years ago. Number 400. There's talk of trying to restore the locomotive so they can put it on display at the depot. It's a Baldwin 2-8-2."

Veronica started to ask what 2-8-2 meant, but decided against it. She was anxious to call the detective and knew better than to get Jack started on a long dialog about trains. "Sounds like you are going to have a great day," was all that she replied before dialing.

"Veronica, be careful. You don't know that Ann is the killer," Jack pleaded.

"Edwards speaking."

"Yes, Detective Edwards, this is Veronica."

"Oh, Veronica, I'm glad you called. I just got the coroner's report. It seems that Gloria did take a tumble down the stairs, but the fall didn't kill her. She suffered numerous bumps, bruises and cuts, a broken arm, several broken ribs, and apparently hit her head hard enough on the floor to cause a subdural hematoma, but she was alive when she was placed in the car. The report estimates that the fall took place three to four hours before her death."

"Which puts the fall during the time of the morning break," Veronica finished for him.

"That's correct."

There was a long pause. "So, you are saying Gloria wasn't murdered?" Veronica asked.

"No, no, no. I'm not saying that at all. Gloria was unconscious from the hit on the head. Therefore, she couldn't have got in the car by herself and she certainly couldn't have driven through the barricade. Plus, with the velocity with which she had to have fallen down the stairs, to sustain the injuries she received, there is no doubt in my mind that her fall wasn't an accident."

Veronica looked at Jack. Nothing was making any sense. She spoke into the phone, "But if she was alive when she was placed in the car and she didn't die from the fall, what happened?"

Edwards began to explain, "The car was left in full sun with the windows rolled up on a ninety-eight degree day. The temperature inside the car must have reached close to one hundred and sixty degrees. Between the heat and humidity we were experiencing that day..."

"I get the picture." Veronica stopped him, suddenly feeling sick again.

"Anyway," the detective continued, "I wanted to let you know that we are going to play along with the killer. A rumor is going to go out that the autopsy report shows that Gloria must have accidentally fallen down the stairs. Then, knowing she needed medical help, she tried to drive herself to the hospital. Maybe if the killer thinks the heat is off, he or she will slip up."

Veronica was hesitant, but knew she had to ask, "Detective, I was wondering, was Gloria wearing gloves? Or were any gloves found in her car or in her room?" Jack sat down on the sofa beside Veronica and put his arm around her.

"You are referring to the gloves she was wearing at Growth Day. No, they have not been located. Why do you ask?"

"I was in Ann's room last night..."

Edwards interrupted her, "Oh, and Ann showed you the gloves her great grandmother made."

"Her great grandmother?" Veronica asked in surprise.

"Yes. When I went to question Ann she volunteered to show me the gloves so that I could have a better idea of what the gloves Gloria was wearing looked like. Ann recognized the pattern immediately when she saw Gloria wearing the gloves at Growth Day."

Edwards went on to explain, "Ann shared with me that her great grandmother had crocheted the gloves many years ago from a pattern she found in the newspaper. She gave the gloves to Ann right before she died as a keepsake. Ann told me that she takes the gloves everywhere she goes as a way of keeping her great grandmother near. They are a real treasure to her."

Veronica sighed with relief then thinking fast she replied, "Yes. I...I just wanted to know if you had seen them. They are beautiful." Then, feeling extremely foolish, she ended the phone conversation as quickly as possible.

When she told Jack what the detective had said they both started laughing. "I think, milady, that you had better hope, for everyone's sake, that you become a great crochet designer, because a great detective you ain't!"

Jack stood up, pulling Veronica up with him, "Come on, I want you to try to put something in your stomach before you go to class. Maybe you could keep down some fresh blueberries or at least a little ginger ale."

Melissa, Ellen, Ann, Chrissy and Audra were sitting together at one of the long tables in the classroom when Veronica walked in. It was a pleasant surprise. Veronica greeted everyone then sat down between Ellen and Audra.

"Are you ok?" Ann asked, obviously concerned about her friend. "I tried to follow you when you ran out last night, but I wasn't sure where you went."

"I'm sorry I ran out on you. I haven't been feeling well the last couple of days. I almost feel like I have the flu, but it's the wrong time of year and I don't have any fever. I'm sure whatever it is, it will pass," Veronica explained.

"Oh, you poor dear," Melissa said sympathetically. "I'm so sorry you haven't been feeling well. I hope you are better soon."

"Veronica, I packed your design in the box for you, along with your unused yarn, the directions you wrote out and the chart you created. Your hot pad was beautiful," Ann complimented her.

"Thank you. I appreciate your doing all that for me. Your doily was fantastic!" Veronica returned the compliment. "I saw it right before I had to leave."

Chrissy began strumming the table impatiently. "Does anyone know what this class is going to be about?"

"All I know is that it was supposed to be Gloria's, Thread Crochet Unraveled class. I hope the class is still about thread." Audra laughed nervously. "If it isn't, I'm in trouble. All I own are steel hooks."

"It...it is," Ellen hesitantly assured her. Then, hardly above a whisper, she added, "Beth is teaching it. I just signed up for the class a few minutes ago when I found out. I have never met her before, but I have always admired her thread work."

"Good morning everyone," a cheerful woman greeted the class as she came bustling through the door carrying several bags. "Sorry I'm late! I had to go to Brookshire's on Pinecrest to pick up the eggs!" She placed her bags on one of the tables then hurriedly began removing the contents. "How many of you have blown eggs before?"

The room was completely quiet.

"Doesn't matter, doesn't matter! That's what we're here for, to learn!" The woman whom everyone presumed must be Beth, she hadn't actually introduced herself, began running around the room handing everyone an egg, a giant syringe with needle attached, and two cups—one empty and one half filled with vinegar. While she was passing everything out she excitedly explained that, after the shells were cleaned, they would learn how to crochet fancy decorative thread covers for them.

Ann leaned over and whispered to Veronica, "Have you ever seen anyone with so much energy and enthusiasm?"

When all of the students had received their supplies, the woman raised her right hand as if leading a charge. "Off to the washroom!" she exclaimed, as she headed out the door.

Everyone sat in complete silence. "Are we supposed to follow?" Chrissy asked, completely bewildered.

"Believe it or not, I think we are." Audra laughed.

The atmosphere at the inn had completely changed by lunchtime. Everyone was much more relaxed and at ease. Edwards' planted rumors had evidently spread like wildfire. There was no murder. Gloria had simply accidentally fallen down the stairs, and unfortunately, had the bad judgment to try to drive to the hospital. Being a little "out of it" from the fall she went to sleep in the car and passed away due to the heat outside.

Audra joined in on Veronica and Ellen's lunch date. They went to the snack bar, which had been set up inside the market, to eat. As they stood in line for their hoagies, chips, and drinks, Veronica held up her egg to admire. "Better be careful you don't drop that!" Audra teased. "You know how fragile eggs are!"

Veronica defiantly tossed her egg several feet up in the air and caught it. "Can you believe she made us do all that work to clean those egg shells then handed us a fake egg made out of wood!"

Audra laughed. "She was quite a character, I'll give you that."

Having received their food they sat down at one of the tables in the corner. Veronica stood her egg on the table using the one inch white plastic ring Beth had given her for a stand. She then continued to chatter away about the class, "It was just so exuberating and I learned so much, how to crochet in rounds with no beginning chain and how to make pineapples. Plus, it was my first time to crochet with thread." Veronica admired her egg again. "It isn't nearly as hard as I thought it would be."

"Now you see why I like it so much." Audra smiled. "And the great thing about thread is that it's small and light weight. It's easy to carry around. You can even slip it in a purse. It's also wonderful for making intricate stitches because the detail of the stitches show up so well in thread." Audra picked up Veronica's egg. "Look at how delicate and pretty the stitches look on your egg. But the biggest bonus is that in the summer you don't have a huge, hot, heavy, yarn project sitting on your lap and..."

"Ok, ok, ok, I'm sold. I agree, thread is wonderful!" Veronica jokingly interrupted her, just before taking a large bite out of her sandwich.

"Alright I'll stop spouting the virtues of thread," Audra conceded. "I agree with you about the class though, I've never seen anything like it before and I've been to a lot of conferences."

"Yes, I have always been impressed with Beth's work. And she was so outgoing and so much fun to be with. I wish I could be like her," Ellen replied sounding rather pensive.

Veronica started to speak some words of encouragement to her friend, but her mouth was too full of sandwich to get the words out.

"I'm glad you are feeling better," Ellen said a few minutes later as she watched Veronica swallow her last bite.

"I am too. That was delicious and I was starving! You know, Ellen, what you said about Beth, you may not have Beth's bubbling personality, but you are a very sweet, sensitive and compassionate person and those are wonderful virtues to have."

After the meal the three ladies toured the market together. Audra found the speed crochet and knit contest, which was being held in the opposite corner of the market from the snack bar, and insisted they stay and watch awhile. Several crocheters were fixing to compete for the Twinkle Fingers trophy. A cute little bronze statue of a hand shaped in such a way that the separate crochet hook could be inserted in either a knife holding position or a pencil holding position, whichever the winner preferred. Below the hand was a little plaque engraved with the words, ACAKA Twinkle Fingers, along with the year.

Veronica thought about entering the contest, just for fun, but decided against it. Audra didn't want to enter because it was a yarn speed contest and she wasn't used to crocheting with yarn and Ellen said she hated competition. So, Veronica stood behind the ropes and watched with her friends while, for three minutes, hooks flew with lightening speed.

After the winner was announced and awarded her trophy, they proceeded to another corner of the market where newbies were being taught how to knit and crochet. They observed the lessons for a little while then decided to shop the market. Audra wanted to show Veronica and Ellen a canvas bag she had seen earlier in the week. The bag had numerous pockets and could be unzipped so that it lay completely flat. She had been very impressed with the bag's versatility. Then Ellen took them to a booth, across the way, where she purchased the two cones of green alpaca thread she had been admiring. From there, they went on to explore other booths marveling at all there was to see.

After an hour or two or three, no one keeps track of time when they are in the market, Veronica reminded Ellen that she had promised to show her some of the designs she was working on.

"Oh, I almost forgot," she said. "Audra, did you want to come too?"

"Thanks, but I think I need to go rest up a bit. I don't want to fall asleep during the fashion show tonight!"

Sitting in Ellen's room Veronica felt like a little kid in a candy store. The opportunity to sit down and visit with a designer of Ellen's magnitude about crochet was just overwhelming. She knew Ellen would be able to give her all kinds of good pointers.

"I can't wait to see some of the designs you are working on," she urged Ellen on.

"They are over here in my suitcase." Ellen picked up the large black suitcase and placed it on the chair near the bed. She opened the case then lovingly began displaying her designs, one by one, on the bed. Veronica couldn't believe her eyes. They were all so exquisite.

"Are these all for a book you are doing?" Veronica asked.

"They were."

"Were?" Veronica was confused.

"I'm kind of at a time in my life where I'm starting to rethink my career," Ellen explained.

Veronica sat down on the edge of the bed so that she could get a closer look. "How long have you been designing?"

"I started crocheting when I was in my early twenties."

"Your work is beautiful!" Veronica exclaimed as she spied a sage green silk top.

"Thank you," Ellen replied looking down at the floor, obviously uncomfortable with the accolades that were being bestowed upon her. "Feel free to pick them up and look at them if you like."

Veronica didn't need to be asked twice, she quickly began going through the designs admiring the uniqueness of each one. There were tops, shawls, sweaters, skirts, hats and even a pair of lace gloves. Veronica picked up the gloves. They were definitely not Gloria's. The gloves were crocheted with a pretty cream colored thread, but as Veronica studied the lacy stitches, it became very clear that the same pattern was used. Veronica wondered if Ellen had a great grandmother as well. She placed the gloves back on the bed and picked up another design; an autumn colored, mohair blend, sweater. "I love this one. Autumn is my favorite time of year."

"Mine too," Ellen agreed.

When Veronica finished going through the crocheted models, Ellen began showing her some of the yarns she had brought to crochet with while at the conference, a whole suitcase full; solid, variegated, heather, she even had some balls of the same self-striping yarn that Veronica had purchased.

Veronica looked up at her, "This is amazing."

Ellen laughed. "Yes, I'm afraid I have YAS." Ellen picked up the two cones of alpaca thread she had just purchased and added them to her collection.

"YAS?" Veronica was puzzled.

"It stands for yarn acquisition syndrome. I'm a yarnaholic. I receive an overwhelming feeling of comfort and love when I hold a ball of yarn in my hands." Ellen looked at Veronica, "Be careful." Ellen laughed. "It's extremely contagious."

"Don't worry, I'll be careful."

Veronica spent the rest of the afternoon visiting in Ellen's room. She didn't garner any crochet designing tips, as she had hoped, but she did learn practically everything there was to learn about Backgammon.

Ellen, Veronica soon learned, spent half her time crocheting and the other half playing Backgammon on the Internet. Being as bashful as she was, she didn't have a lot of "in person" friends. But due to the advent of computers she was able to play Backgammon with people from all over the world via the various game rooms.

"This is interesting," Veronica observed after a few minutes of play.

"What's that?" Ellen asked, rolling the dice.

"I move my stones from your home table, going right to left. I crochet from right to left also. I was just thinking, about the only thing I do from left to right lately is read. It gets kind of confusing."

Ellen moved one stone six, hitting Veronica's blot and sending it to the bar. Then she moved another stone four, blocking the second point in her home table. "Actually, if we traded places, you would be moving your stones from left to right, in the same direction you read. In backgammon one player moves right to left from the opponent's home table and the other player moves left to right. We can trade places if you like."

Veronica took her turn at rolling the dice, two and six, both closed points. "No. Right to left is fine," she replied. "Actually I have been crocheting so much lately, in an odd way, going right to left is starting to seem more natural."

Several games were played that afternoon. Ellen won gammon or backgammon on the majority of them, but Veronica enjoyed herself just the same. Although, in Backgammon, mainly the roll of the dice determined the outcome, just enough strategy came into play that it made the game interesting for her. Before leaving to go back to her room she had already vowed to teach Jack the game.

Twenty-Seven

It was such an impossible decision! Nearly fifty crochet designs and an equally large number of knitting designs. How could she ever pick just one design from each craft? Veronica walked back and forth from table to table repeatedly checking every design.

"Veronica, if you don't decide something soon we are going to miss dinner and the show," Jack complained as his stomach began to rumble.

"Which did you pick?"

"Well, yours of course." Jack grinned.

"Which knitted piece did you pick?"

"The black stocking cap," Jack replied pointing to the next table over. "It was the only thing that looked really masculine to me."

Veronica sighed, "That's fine for you, but I'm a girl!"

"Yes, I noticed." Jack winked at her. "Now come on, I'm hungry."

Veronica checked the items out one more time then began writing her selection down on the back of her admission ticket.

"What did you finally decide on?" Jack asked.

"I picked the 'For Her' crocheted wash cloth with the little rosebuds on it and the knitted 'For Him' wash cloth. Even though they are two different crafts, they look like they should go together," Veronica explained as she finished writing.

Jack began applauding when she put the pen down. "Now let's go eat!" he exclaimed.

As Veronica and Jack walked through the door into conference room "A", they dropped their tickets into a large fabric lined wicker basket. They then began looking for a seat. The room had once again been transformed. The round tables were now covered with white tablecloths and set for the evening meal. First course, an Italian salad with hard rolls, was already awaiting the guests along with tall glasses of iced tea. A long runway had been set up for the models to stroll down and the wood podium had been placed at the head of the runway for the master of ceremonies.

Jack found an empty table near the runway. He helped Veronica with her chair then sat down beside her. Wasting no time, he began buttering his roll.

"Hi, Veronica," Ellen greeted her. "Is it still ok if I sit with you?"

"Of course it is," Jack assured her. "Like we told you last night, you're welcome anytime."

"Thank you," Ellen replied softly as she slipped into a seat beside Veronica.

Over the course of the next few minutes others joined them, Robert and his wife Clara then Ann followed by Audra and Katy.

Veronica looked around the room, "Katy, where are Jenny and Chrissy?"

"They're in the fashion show, remember?" Katy pointed to the long black curtain that had been hung behind the runway, concealing everything beyond. "They're backstage right now getting ready."

"Oh, that's right! I forgot." Veronica glanced around the room. "Actually it looks like most of the audience could get up and model," she added noticing that over half the audience was fashionably dressed in their latest crochet and knitting projects.

"Yes, seeing what the audience is wearing is always one of the highlights of the fashion show," Robert agreed with her. "In past years, I have purchased several designs for the magazine, as a result of seeing people wear them here at the show."

Clara turned to Jack. "Sweetie, while they talk shop, tell me, what did you find to do today?"

Jack wondered if Clara often felt left out. He swallowed the last bite of his salad then told her he had spent the day at the city park.

"Oh, sweetie, I went there early Wednesday morning, took my lunch and had a picnic!" Clara exclaimed enthusiastically. "I loved the fountain. But my favorite part was the beautiful leaf imprints in the sidewalk. Did you notice them?"

Jack nodded in the affirmative then winked at Veronica. Veronica caught the message. Clara's alibi, she was at the park. Might be difficult to find someone to back up her story, but certainly not impossible. There were always people roaming around in parks.

Waiters, dressed all in white, began passing out plates of filet mignon, twice-baked potatoes and steamed broccoli.

"This smells delicious!" Ann remarked, as a plate was set in front of her.

Veronica took a bite, but couldn't even taste it. Her mind was on the list. Someone had been watching her every move for the last few days. Someone. She began running through the names again. Clara... Robert... Judy... Duke... Ellen... Ann... Sara... A clashing sound was heard as Veronica dropped her fork...Margery. Margery was the only one left. Margery was arguing with Gloria on the Internet. Margery was fighting with Gloria at Growth Day. And Margery knew about the yarn. Veronica picked up her fork and tried to nonchalantly look around the room. Margery was nowhere in sight. She thought it had been Ann, but could it have been Margery's eyes that were watching her last night...waiting...for just the right moment to strike?

Veronica went back to eating, trying to brush the

horrifying thoughts out of her mind. The food really was good. After the main course, cups of coffee and plates of cheesecake drizzled with raspberry sauce were served. When everyone was nearly finished, Tammy walked up to the podium and began making announcements. Shutterbugs began positioning themselves around the stage. A few minutes later, as the first model sauntered down the runway, the slightly darkened room lit up with flashes of light.

Veronica was thoroughly enjoying the show. Designs from bikinis to wedding gowns and everything in between were being modeled. Veronica thought Jenny looked lovely in her black sequined shell. Of course Chrissy was cute as always twirling around in her burgundy silk skirt. And to top it off, Tammy was doing a fantastic job of emceeing the whole thing.

At the conclusion of the show, when all the applause died down, Tammy announced that it was time for the crocheter and knitter of the year awards. After much fanfare she proclaimed that Duke won the title, Crocheter of the Year, for his "For Her" wash cloth design and Judy won, Knitter of the Year, for her "For Him" wash cloth. Both received standing ovations. Then, once again, cameras began flashing as Judy and Duke stood arm in arm at the front of the room, posing with their winning designs.

That night, as Veronica lay in bed, she began thinking about all the wonderful things that had happened that day. Although she knew mentally that the rumor, which had lulled people into a false sense of security, was a lie, she too had felt at ease, happy and safe, for the first time since she had stepped off the train.

She had been so nervous going to dinner with Robert and his wife that first night...even more uptight at Growth Day due to the unexpected confrontation with Gloria...her fall on the stairs...and worst of all finding Gloria's body in the car the way she did. Thursday hadn't been much better, learning that Gloria had been murdered...being taken to the police station and interrogated by the detective...embarrassing herself, Duke and Judy at Roseville...seeing the ghostly figurcs outsidc thc car on their way home from dinner...and that night hearing someone trying to break in while they lay in bed. Friday was the climax though, coming back to their room and finding it vandalized...terrified when Sara wanted to talk to her out by the pool...not to mention finding the glove in Ann's room and thinking she was the murderer.

Yes, today had definitely been a welcome reprieve. Everyone was so relaxed and happy. She loved her egg class...lunch in the market...the speed crochet contest...shopping...visiting with Ellen...the dinner and fashion show.

The fashion show, the memories brought a smile to her face. She couldn't recall all of it, but she would never forget parts of it.

Realizing Margery was the only name left on the list, Veronica had gasped when she first saw Margery walk out on the runway. Luckily everyone in the audience thought she was just admiring the design. But the momentary embarrassment wasn't what Veronica would never forget. It was Tammy's description of Margery's design. Veronica recalled it, verbatim.

"Ladies and Gentlemen, we present to you an original top down design by Margery. But I don't want to 'pull the wool over your eyes' she had help. On Growth Day Margery asked me to be her 'swift' during the morning break so that she could turn a few of the necessary hanks for her sweater into useable balls of yarn. So, I want everyone to know, I take half credit for this creation. Crocheted with Berroco Ultra Alpaca Light, a blend of Super Fine Alpaca and Peruvian Highland Wool yarn, in color turquoise mix."

Margery...the last name on the list...she couldn't have killed Gloria...she was with Tammy.

Yes, all days should be like today.

Veronica didn't know who the murderer was, but at the moment she didn't care. Her friends were innocent. And she was safely tucked in bed. That was all that mattered. She still didn't know who had been secretly watching her, but tomorrow night it would be a mute point. At seven thirty-one, she and Jack would be back on the train to Missouri, safe and sound. Edwards could find the killer. He would have to start back at square one, but she felt certain he would eventually solve the case. Veronica rolled over, kissed Jack goodnight, then with a smile on her face she gently slipped into peaceful slumber.

Twenty-Eight

Sunday morning Veronica awoke before Jack. She lay in bed, once again feeling sick at her stomach. She had a wonderful time yesterday, but was grateful the conference was coming to an end.

She tried to sit up in bed, but only felt worse, so she went to the washbasin, prepared a cold wet cloth for her head then went back to bed. An hour later, Jack woke up. Seeing that his wife was once again ill, he tried to convince her that she really needed to see a doctor.

"I know," she replied. "But this is the last day of the conference. If I'm still sick when we get home, I can go then." Veronica slowly got out of bed and began dressing for the day.

"Veronica, that is ridiculous. You're sick. We're going to be sitting up all night tonight on a train and then we have the car ride back to Springfield tomorrow morning. You need to see a doctor now," Jack argued. "Maybe he can give you something to settle your stomach so that the trip home isn't so hard on you."

"Alright," Veronica reluctantly relented. "But if I have to skip one of my scheduled classes today, I'd rather skip the afternoon one. I've really been looking forward to the morning class. I'll tell you what, you go on to Marshall Pottery this morning like you planned, then you can take me to the doctor this afternoon."

"Milady, is very stubborn," was all Jack replied.

Veronica and Jack finished dressing then went downstairs for breakfast. After Jack had eaten they went to an early morning worship service. Jack tried several times more to convince Veronica to skip the crochet class and go on to the doctor, but she refused.

The class was titled, Everything One Needs to Know About Post Stitches. Veronica was excited. Margery had mentioned something about posts on Friday night. She had wondered then, what they were, but never got to ask.

Except for the teacher, the classroom was empty when she walked in. "Good morning," Eliza greeted her. "Welcome to the class. Just take a seat anywhere you like." Eliza seemed nice and pleasant, but not nearly as bubbly as Beth. Perhaps, she too, was ready to go back home.

The room soon filled with eagerly awaiting pupils, none of which Veronica knew. Eliza told the students that they would be making a purse for their project, but that they probably wouldn't have time to finish it in class. She explained that she would teach all of the necessary stitches so that they could complete it at home. One of the students began passing out the handout sheets. Veronica read through a few of the directions. She didn't know if it was because she was ill or if the class was just too advanced, but she knew she didn't understand one word written on the paper.

Eliza stood at the front of the room. Using a giant hook and very thick yarn, she began demonstrating how to work post stitches. Veronica was thankful, that once shown how, the stitches didn't seem nearly as difficult as she first thought. She took out the required sport weight yarn and her size "G" crochet hook, chained forty-two, then began.

The time seemed to pass very quickly. When Veronica finished the first side of her purse, there were only thirty minutes of class time remaining. She admired her cabled piece. It truly was beautiful with all its intricate intertwining threads.

Deciding there was no point in trying to start the second half of the purse, she began putting her things away. Besides, she thought, finishing the purse would give her something to do on the train ride back home. Hungry for the first time that day, she decided get a piece of fruit from the market snack bar to tide her over while she waited for Jack. Veronica thanked the teacher and left, but she didn't get far.

Detective Edwards was waiting for her right outside the classroom. "I need to talk to you," was all he said. Veronica followed the detective out to the pool area, this time unafraid.

"I've been trying to track down Gloria's brother all week. Yesterday, through his pet bird's babysitter, we were able to get an email address for him. I received a response this morning. Apparently he had to go away on an unexpected business trip. That I can understand, but the rest of the email has me totally baffled. I thought perhaps you could help," Edwards said as he pulled a folded piece of paper out of his pocket and handed it to her.

Veronica began to read.

> Detective Edwards,
>
> I am very saddened to learn of my sister's accident.
>
> I had to go to Florida very unexpectedly on business Wednesday morning. Of course, I want to return to Texas as soon as possible. My sister and I were very close, but unfortunately it will probably be a couple more days before I can get back.
>
> I would like to ask a favor of you, if I may. My cousin, Nelle, is one of the professional

designers at the ACAKA show. The same show Gloria was attending. I know there was a lot of bad blood between them, but in lieu of what has happened I thought perhaps Nelle might be willing to forgive Gloria for the pain and suffering she caused her.

I know Gloria's heart. It was good and kind. She was only acting out what mother had taught her from birth. Just as, Nelle, tried to do her mother's bidding. If my grandmother had only left the twins alone, but she didn't. Instead, she pitted one against the other, and they continued the fight through their own children.

But the war is over now. Sis is gone. There is no one left to fight.

Could you please talk to Nelle for me, explain my situation, and ask her if she would please be willing to go ahead and start making arrangements for the funeral? It would really help me out, and hopefully, through this act, Nelle might find some family peace as well.

Thank you so much.

John

"I don't understand. What's the problem?" Veronica asked wondering why the detective was asking for her help.

"There is no Nelle," Edwards explained. "I have checked every registrant here. Do you know Gloria's cousin?"

Veronica stared at the paper. "I didn't even know Gloria had a cousin. I haven't heard anything from anyone indicating that she had a relative here. It's odd...with her death...and all...it looks like..." Veronica stopped speaking in mid sentence.

"Are you all right?" the detective asked seeing the look of sadness growing on her face.

"I have to go. I have to go talk to someone," Veronica hastily said as she turned and ran back inside the inn leaving the detective not only bewildered, but also extremely suspicious.

Twenty-Nine

—◆—

Veronica knocked on the door. She knew she was wrong. Standing in the hallway she read the paper again. She had been wrong about everything so far. Jack was right. She was a lousy detective. Surely she would be wrong again. Unfortunately, this time the evidence was overwhelming. All of the pieces to the puzzle were suddenly coming together in her mind and sadly this time they all fit. She knocked on the door again, a little louder.

Slowly the door began to open. "Oh, hi, Veronica, come on in. I'm so glad you came by before you left. I was hoping we would get to say goodbye to one another and I was thinking, maybe sometime, if you like, maybe we could arrange to play Backgammon on the Internet together."

"Nelle, could I talk to you for a minute?" Ellen seemed a little startled, but welcomed her friend inside. They sat down on the sofa. "Ellen, the other day when I was here I asked you how long you had been designing. You never answered the question."

"Sure I did. I told you I started crocheting in my twenties."

"Ellen, we both know that crocheting is not the same thing as designing. You purposely changed the wording when you answered. I asked you when you started designing."

Ellen looked down at the floor. There was a long pause. "I always wanted to be a designer," she whispered.

"But you are a designer!" Veronica exclaimed. "I've seen your work in crochet magazines and books dating back at least ten years. I don't understand this. When you were showing me your designs, you showed me a pair of lacy cream-colored gloves. Why are you now pretending you have designed a pair of gloves, which you obviously copied from an old pattern?"

Ellen continued to stare at the floor. "I'm not a designer. I tried. I tried so hard. I worked and worked on ideas. I just couldn't seem to make them turn out right. Everything I did was compared to what my cousin, Gloria, was doing." Ellen looked up at Veronica, "Did I ever tell you she was my cousin?"

"No, you didn't," Veronica replied.

"I was constantly being told how great Gloria was." Ellen began to rhythmically chant like a little child. "Gloria created a new stitch. Gloria was in *Crochet Elite* magazine. Gloria wrote a top ten best seller. Gloria was sent on a book tour all over the world. Gloria was paid thousands of dollars to teach."

Ellen began to sob. "I...I just couldn't stand it anymore. I...I just couldn't."

"I don't understand," Veronica shook her head. "You have so many published designs. I've seen your designs in person. They are beautiful."

Ellen picked up a tissue and dried her eyes. "They were beautiful, weren't they," she said dreamily. Her voice suddenly lowered, "But they weren't mine."

"What do you mean, they weren't yours?" Veronica asked speaking a little too loudly.

Ellen calmly began to explain, "When we were kids, I was always competing with Gloria; grades, violin lessons, boys, praise from our moms. I just couldn't seem to be better than her at anything.

"Then Gloria started to crochet. We were a little older by then and I just thought to myself, this is ridiculous. So, I decided I wasn't going to compete with her anymore. Instead of crocheting, I learned how to knit." The anger in Ellen's voice began to creep through her calm facade. "Gloria was so snooty about it though. She vowed she would never have anything to do with knitting, said it wasn't as good as crochet. And from that day on, she insulted knitting every chance she got. I didn't care though. I was pretty good at knitting. At least that is what I thought. But my mom sure didn't think so. She still threw Gloria up in my face."

Ellen began to mimic her mother in a high-pitched voice. "Gloria is crocheting, you're just knitting. Machines can knit. You're no better than a stupid machine that has to be told what to do. Gloria is doing something machines can't do. And Gloria is designing her own crochet fashion clothes. You're just following directions out of a book. Anyone can do that."

Ellen let out a small nervous laugh. "Even when we weren't doing the same craft I couldn't get out from under her shadow." Ellen lowered her voice. "It was then that I realized if I ever wanted mom's respect I was going to have to do exactly what Gloria was doing, only better. I was going to have to learn how to crochet and I was going to have to learn how to design patterns, not just follow patterns out of a book."

"So, that's when you started crocheting and creating crochet designs?" Veronica asked.

Ellen looked at Veronica. "No. That's when I started 'trying' to create crochet designs. I tried so hard. I just couldn't do it. I even had some pretty good ideas drawn out on paper for designs, but, I don't know, somewhere between the paper and my crocheting the design got lost in the translation. I just couldn't do it."

Ellen stood up and began pacing around the room as she spoke, "Gloria got a book of crocheted sweaters published and I just couldn't stand it anymore. I knew I was never going to hear the end of it from my mom or from Gloria. Gloria was so arrogant and conceited about everything. I knew I was going to have to do something desperate."

"What did you do?" Veronica asked as she stood up as well.

Ellen stopped pacing and looked at Veronica just long enough to answer the question, "I went to an old used bookstorc and purchased the oldest crochet book I could find. It was so old the designs were actually back in style." Ellen smiled.

"Then I purchased some yarn that had just come out on the market. Of course I made sure the colors were different from what was shown in the book. So many people just look at color. Anyway, after that, I went home and started crocheting one of the designs out of the book. I was still living with mom at the time. Mom walked in when I was about half way finished."

Ellen sat back down on the sofa. She waited a few minutes before continuing, as if trying to recollect the past. Then she whispered, "She liked it. It was the first thing that I had ever made that she liked. I couldn't believe it! I told her I had designed it myself. She was so proud of me. For the first time in my life, she was proud of me."

Ellen was speaking so softly that Veronica had to sit back down on the sofa in order to hear her. "So, you started submitting other designers' patterns to magazines with your name on them as the designer?"

"Yes. I didn't really mean to do anything wrong. I just wanted mom to be proud of me. Of course Gloria wasn't proud of me. She snubbed me every chance she got. That was fine with me though. As long as she stayed out of my life I was happy to stay out of hers." Ellen looked at Veronica. "She wouldn't even stay in the ACAKA chat room when I was in there!"

"I didn't realize," Veronica replied quickly trying to think back to her chat room visits.

"Anyway, I found several more extremely old crochet

books and before I knew it people were looking up to me, calling me a professional crochet designer. I was becoming almost as famous as Gloria.

"Gloria never believed it though. I guess somehow she just knew.

"One day last year, during a family reunion at my house, she found the books and started looking through them. She was snooping. The books were hidden way back in the closet. It didn't take her long to figure out what I was doing. I should have suspected she was up to something when she showed up at my door."

"What did she do?" Veronica urged her to continue.

"Blackmail. She called me into the bedroom and confronted me. Told me she knew what I was doing and that she was going to announce to everyone there what a fraud I was.

"I pleaded with her not to do it. Told her I would do anything. I just couldn't stand the humiliation. I couldn't stand the look that I knew would be in mom's eyes.

"She just stood there, laughing at me, saying how pathetic I was. Then her laughter turned evil. She told me that she would keep my secret as long as I gave her fifty percent of everything I made.

"I had to agree. I had no choice."

There was dead silence in the room. Veronica waited, but finally grew impatient. "Then what happened?" she asked.

"Nothing," Ellen replied nonchalantly. "I sent her the money the first Saturday of every month."

"That must have been awfully hard on you losing half your income like that," Veronica said sympathetically.

"Very. But I had no choice. Anyway, life just went on as usual. In public Gloria continued to avoid me and I avoided her. People didn't even know we were related."

Veronica was starting to catch on to the turn of events. "But the ACAKA conference threw you together."

Ellen looked down and began wringing her hands. "Yes. I

just couldn't seem to get away from her at Growth Day. Before the morning session started, everywhere I turned, she was there, goading me on. Bragging about some new stitch she had invented. Telling me it was going to be revealed at thc Fashion Show on Saturday night and that her fame was going to skyrocket."

Ellen began twisting and squeezing her hands harder. "She just kept egging me on and egging me on. Then when her name was called to go up to the front she strutted out wearing those gloves. I don't know how she found out that I had crocheted those antique gloves in a cream color for my new book. Snooping again I guess. But she was going to make sure I knew, that she knew exactly what I was doing all the time and that she was in complete control.

"Then during the morning recess, when I was finishing up my snuggle, she came up behind me and told me that I was a day late with my blackmail payment and that ACAKA would be the perfect place to announce to everyone what a fraud I was."

Ellen's eyes began to well up again. "I tried to tell her I had mailed the payment on the first Saturday of the month just like always and that it was probably just held up in the mail somewhere. But she wouldn't believe me. She said to meet her on the stairway landing between the first and second floor before the break was over. I was to have the cash or else. Then she walked over to Sara and started arguing with her."

Ellen shook her head. "I didn't have that kind of cash with me. All I had was a little money for food and necessities."

"Necessities?" Veronica interrupted.

"The alpaca yarn I purchased in the market yesterday. Yarn necessities," Ellen explained.

"Go on," Veronica coaxed.

"Well, I knew, even if I gave her every cent I had, it wouldn't be enough. I don't have an ATM card and I knew no one would cash a check for me. Not for that kind of money anyway. I didn't know what to do.

"When you and Robert came back to the table I tried to act like nothing was wrong. I got up and went to the refreshment line. I got a bagel with jelly and a cup of coffee then sat back down at the table. I was so scared and my hands were shaking so badly I knew someone would eventually notice.

"But I had made up my mind. I would give her all the money that I had with me and just hope it would be enough to appease her. I knew I had to get out of there without anyone knowing why.

"Then I got an idea. I started talking about the food. I joked about how silly it was to serve jelly and hot liquids to people who were seated at tables piled high with yarn. I picked up the bagel to take a bite and dropped it in my lap getting jelly all over my clothes. I didn't want to ruin anyone's snuggle project."

Veronica thought back to that day. "Yes, I remember how upset you were. I think everyone just thought you were upset about getting jelly all over your pants."

"Yes. I excused myself saying I had to go change my clothes. I went to my room and got the money out of my suitcase. I headed straight to the stairwell, money in hand. Gloria was already there." Ellen spoke in an almost dream like tone, "It was strange. She had a shawl wrapped around her shoulders and she was petting it. She just stood there gloating and petting this shawl.

"Then I realized why it seemed so strange to me. The shawl was knitted. After all the insults she had hurled at knitting and there she was wrapped in it. Then this evil grin spread across her face."

Ellen started shouting, in a voice like Gloria's, "It's not knitting, it's crochet. It just looks like knitting."

In her own voice, Ellen went on, "I was just so confused. I reminded her that she had always said that she hated knitting. And I asked her why she would invent a crochet stitch that looks just like knitting?"

Ellen, once again, began to imitate Gloria's voice, "I don't hate knitting I think it is a beautiful form of art. I just hate you! This is my new stitch that is going to be revealed at the Fashion Show Saturday night. Now hand over the money."

Ellen whispered, "I reached out to touch the shawl. I just couldn't believe it was actually crocheted. It looked just like knitting. I just wanted to feel it. I just..." Ellen broke down sobbing.

"I didn't push her. I don't think I pushed her." Ellen stammered, "I... I don't know what happened. I... I saw her and that stupid crochet bag of hers tumbling down the stairs. I... I was so scared. I went down the stairs to where she was and saw all the blood. I... I thought she was dead. She... She just lay there in a heap on top of her shawl. I didn't know what to do."

"So, what did you do?" Veronica asked softly.

"I reached down and touched her, tried to feel her pulse. I was so relieved when I felt it. She was just unconscious." Ellen looked up and smiled remembering her obvious relief.

"Why didn't you go get help? Why did you put her in her car?" Veronica asked.

Ellen thought back. "I don't know. I guess I just thought maybe if, when she woke up, if she was in her car, she wouldn't remember what happened. That maybe she would think that she had been in some sort of car wreck or something. So, I took her keys out of her crochet bag. I wiped the blood off the floor with the shawl then I wrapped the shawl around her, leaned her up against me, and just kind of drug her out to her car through the fire escape door. Luckily her car was parked right by the door."

"How did you do all that without anyone seeing you?" Veronica asked.

"It wasn't hard. Everyone was at Growth Day. No one was around. Actually with the bushes planted on both sides of the fire escape door the way that they are, no one from inside the inn would have seen anything even if they had been looking."

"Then what did you do?" Veronica asked, encouraging her to continue.

"I put Gloria in the car, drove the car through the roundabout barrier, then put her in the driver's seat."

"What happened to the gloves she was wearing?" Veronica asked.

"I took them. She made those gloves to prove she could expose me at any time. I wasn't going to let her keep them. After I took the gloves I wiped my fingerprints off everything then shut the door."

"Why did you wipe your fingerprints off?" Veronica asked, having trouble keeping up with Ellen's logic.

"Because I knew, when she woke up, that if she did remember what happened, the blackmailing would become worse. If my fingerprints were in her car, she would have legal proof to use against me."

"And you cut the shawl?"

"Yes. Before I closed the door, I took her scissors out of her crochet bag and cut off the one end that had somehow remained clean. I guess I was hoping she wouldn't notice. The rest of the shawl was so bloody, I knew it was going straight in the trash."

"That doesn't make sense. Why would you do that?" Veronica asked, still trying to fit all the pieces together.

"I... I don't know. I guess I just wanted to see if I could take it apart and figure out how she made it. I took the piece back to my room and hid it, changed clothes as fast as I could, then went back to the conference.

"I was so scared. I kept waiting for Gloria to come back in and say she had been in a wreck or for someone to come in and say they had found her and took her to the hospital. But it didn't happen.

"Then during the breakout sessions I started getting worried that maybe I didn't get all the blood up and someone would see it. So, when Growth Day ended, I went back to the landing."

"That's when I walked in." Veronica was beginning to feel a little uneasy, but tried to remain calm.

"Yes. I couldn't let you find out what I was doing. I started up the stairs and you followed me. But then I stopped on the third stair. You didn't." Ellen smiled nervously. "You bumped right into me and fell down. It was perfect. I went and got housekeeping and with you sitting there bleeding, no one questioned if it was just your blood or if it was your blood and someone else's."

Veronica looked at Ellen warily, "You pushed me down the stairs to cover up for pushing Gloria down the stairs?"

"No, I, no, it wasn't like that," Ellen protested.

Veronica had a sinking feeling it was exactly like that, but knew she had to maintain her composure if she wanted to learn the whole truth. "Then what did you do?" she asked as calmly as she could.

"I didn't do anything. Housekeeping cleaned up all the blood. After I walked you to your room, I went back to mine. I took out the end piece I had cut off the shawl, worked half the night moving one little crochet loop at a time trying to figure out how she made the stitches, but I couldn't figure it out."

"So, you wound up all the little unraveled strands into balls and placed them in your yarn stash?" Veronica asked incredulously.

"Of course," Ellen replied. "The yarn was perfectly good. I told you, I have YAS."

A thought suddenly occurred to Veronica, "That explains why my self striping yarn was in skeins and yours was in balls."

Ellen ignored the oversight on her part and continued, "The next morning I heard that she was dead. I didn't know what happened to her. She was alive when I put her in the car. I heard that you had found her. I wanted to know how much you had figured out. But you were with your friends at breakfast then you went immediately to the hook making class. At lunch, before I could find out anything, the police came and took you away for questioning.

"I waited with Sara till you came back. She was lost without Gloria. Then we kind of got ourselves invited on the trip to the yarn shop. You were acting so normal. I figured you hadn't guessed anything, until you went and bought the same yarn that Gloria's shawl was made out of. That's when I knew, you knew more than you were telling me."

"Is that why you tried to break in my room?" Veronica asked.

"You had told us you were going out to dinner with Robert and Clara at seven-thirty. That's why we couldn't stay at the yarn shop very long. When we got back to the inn everyone was talking about murder and saying that a knitter had killed Gloria. I had to get the yarn you purchased. I couldn't take a chance that you might learn something from it. It just lucked out that I had a six-thirty dinner reservation at Roseville that I had made several weeks earlier. I decided to go ahead and eat, then, while you were gone later that night, I would get the yarn."

Ellen whispered, "I saw you reading The Lord's Prayer." A chill ran up Veronica's spine.

Ellen continued, "I left Roseville immediately, but it was raining so hard that I couldn't see where I was going. I pulled off on the side of the road and waited for the storm to pass. But I was so tired, I guess from staying up all night the previous night trying to figure out the stitch, that I fell asleep. The next thing I knew, several hours had passed. I drove back to the inn as fast as I could and went straight to your room to get the yarn, but it was too late. I heard you inside the room and realized you were already back."

"So, you broke in the next morning instead." Veronica concluded.

"I had to get the yarn back," Ellen explained. "I looked and looked, but I didn't find it. You stayed in your room all Friday afternoon. I was so scared. Then I saw you in the market. I tried to follow, but I lost you in the parking lot. I went to Subway just to get away from everything."

"And when we saw you at Subway, Friday night, and you told Jack you were scared, what you really meant was that you were scared of what we might know."

Ellen looked up pleadingly at Veronica, desperately craving understanding. "You and Jack were so nice to me, taking me back to my room and all. But I knew if anyone was going to figure all this out, it would be you."

"So, you were stalking me all day Thursday and Friday? Were you following me Friday night when I went to the powder room as well? And Saturday, you signed up for the egg class at the last minute, just so that you could continue to stalk me!"

Ellen looked down sadly, knowing she was losing one of the only friends she had ever had. "I needed to be with you. I needed to know if you knew anything.

"Saturday, when we got out of the class and we were told that the police knew it was an accident, I was so relieved." Ellen looked at Veronica and tried to smile. "I wanted to tell them the truth, honestly I did, but I was afraid they wouldn't believe me. I didn't kill her. She was alive when I put her in the car."

"Ellen, I don't understand. If you were so afraid I would figure things out, why did you show me the gloves Saturday afternoon?"

Ellen shrugged. "It didn't matter anymore. The police knew it was an accident. I told you I was rethinking my career. Gloria's dead. I'm not going to keep up this charade that I'm a designer. So, even if you figured out that I was claiming to have designed something I hadn't, it really didn't matter."

Veronica looked at Ellen, "What about the yarn you showed me in your yarn stash. Did that not matter either?"

"I didn't do anything wrong by cutting her shawl," Ellen replied innocently.

"You were going to steal her pattern!" Veronica blurted out. "You killed her and then you were going to steal her work!"

"No, no. I didn't kill her," Ellen screamed. "I didn't. She didn't die when she fell down the stairs. I felt her pulse. Even the autopsy report said so."

Veronica tried once again to remain calm. "Ellen, you put her unconscious body in a car, sitting in the sun, with the windows rolled up, when it was ninety-eight degrees outside. Temperatures in the car were close to one hundred and sixty degrees. Don't you understand? You killed her!"

"No. No. I didn't," Ellen sobbed. "I didn't. I couldn't have. She was my cousin."

There was a long chilling silence. Ellen stood up and then softly began to speak in a childlike voice. "Mommy is going to be so mad. Mommy won't like this. She'll send me to bed without any supper. She'll lock me in my room. She... she won't let me watch T.V. for a week."

In a complete daze, Ellen walked slowly across the room and sat down in the corner. Then she began to scream, "Mommy, Mommy, Mommy!" Ellen covered her face with her hands as she continued, "I didn't mean to do it mommy. I'm a good girl. I am mommy. I really am."

Hearing the screams, Edwards, who had been standing in the hallway, broke down the door.

Thirty

—◆—

Soon people from all over the inn were headed toward Ellen's room. The undercover officers, Edwards had placed around the inn, began working on crowd control. Veronica heard Jack's voice out in the hall and asked the officers to please let him in.

"Are you ok?" he asked as he ran toward her taking her in his arms.

"Yes. I'm fine."

"Come on. I'm going to get you out of here," he said as he began leading her toward the door.

"I'm sorry," Edwards said putting his arm out to stop them. "Veronica is going to have to go downtown and give a statement."

"I'll drive her down later," Jack declared firmly. "She has been sick most of the week and now this. I'm taking her to the health clinic. We'll stop by the station afterwards. Our train doesn't leave until seven-thirty."

"That will be fine, but for my own curiosity, Veronica, before you go, what was in the email that Gloria's brother wrote that tipped you off that Ellen was the killer?"

"I...I saw Ellen's name," Veronica replied shakily.

"Ellen wasn't mentioned in the email," Edwards corrected her. "All John talked about was some cousin named Nelle."

"Yes. That's true." Veronica went on to explain, "I don't know, I guess because I have been crocheting from right to left so much the last few days or maybe it's because I played Backgammon all afternoon yesterday from right to left, but for whatever reason, when I read the name *Nelle*, I read it from right to left, which made it *Ellen*. Then all the pieces, everything that has been happening the last few days, just started to fall into place."

Jack gave Veronica a hug, "I take it back. You are a great crochet detective."

"I agree." Edwards smiled. "And I appreciate your help. Go on now. I'll see you at the station this afternoon. I hope you feel better soon."

Jack pulled up to the Marshall Health Clinic. Once inside, Veronica registered to see a doctor then she and Jack sat down in the waiting room. Veronica continued to tell Jack about what happened until the nurse called for her to go into the examination room. Jack picked up a magazine and began to read. Several articles later, Veronica still had not returned.

Jack began pacing around the waiting room. He turned around when he heard the door to the examination area open. It wasn't Veronica. He turned back and began pacing again.

"Jack?" a woman called out.

"Yes," Jack replied, obvious concern on his face.

"Your wife would like to see you."

"Is she alright?" Jack asked.

"Come this way please." Jack followed the nurse to the examination room. The door was shut. "Just go on in. She is waiting for you."

Jack opened the door. Veronica was sitting on the end of the exam table. A single tear rolled down her check. She held out her arms. Jack went to his wife and hugged her. Bracing himself for the bad news, he leaned over and sweetly whispered in her ear, "Whatever it is, milady, your knight will be there for you."

Veronica looked up at her husband then, through tears of joy, she whispered back, "We're going to have a baby."

Dying to Crochet Patterns

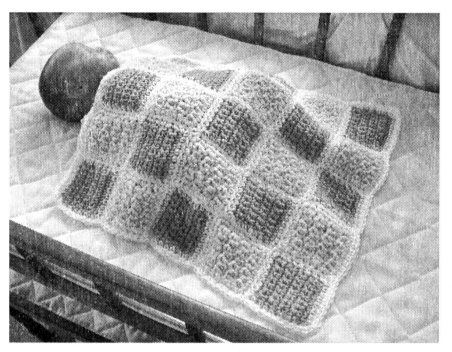

Veronica's 1st Design
Modeled After Floor Tiles

Preemie Squares Afghan
A Beginner Project

Designed by Bendy Carter

Finished Afghan: 14.25" wide by 15.5" long.

MATERIALS:
Red Heart® "Soft Baby™": Art. E705, Sport-Light 3, 100% acrylic, (7 oz / 198 g, 575 yards):
Amount: 1 skein each No. 7822 Sky Blue, No. 7624 Lime & No. 7001 White.
Yarn Needle.
Susan Bates® Crochet Hook: H-8 [5mm].

GAUGE: square before edging is added – 2.25" wide by 2.5" tall.
CHECK YOUR GAUGE. Use any size hook to obtain the gauge given.

SKY BLUE SQUARES (make 13):
Row 1 RS: Ch 9, sc in back ridge of 2nd ch from hook and in back ridge of each ch across; turn – 8 sts.
Row 2: Ch 1, sc in each st across; turn.
Rep Row 2 till 2.5" from beg. Fasten off.

LIME SQUARES (make 12):
Row 1 RS: Ch 9, sc through both lps of 2nd ch from hook, [sc in front lp of next ch, sc in back lp of next ch] 3 times, sc in both lps of last ch; turn – 8 sts.
Row 2: Ch 1, sc, [front lp sc, back lp sc] 3 times, sc; turn.
Rep Row 2 till 2.5" from beg. Fasten off.

EDGING (work around each square):

Attach white, ch 1, sc evenly sp around working (sc, ch 1, sc) in each corner to turn, join in beg st. Fasten off leaving long tail for sewing.

SEWING:

Sew squares together, alternating colors, so that there are 5 columns of 5 squares where 3 columns begin with sky blue squares and 2 columns begin with lime squares. Then sew the columns together alternating the colors.

FINISHING:

Rep Edging around afghan.

ABBREVIATIONS: beg = begin(ning); **ch** = chain; **lp(s)** = loop(s); **rep** = repeat; **RS** = right side; **sc** = single crochet; **sp** = space; **st(s)** = stitch(es); **[]** = work directions given in brackets the number of times specified.

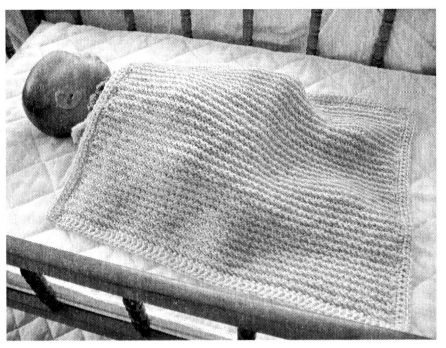

Veronica's 2nd Design
Sent in to Magazine

Preemie Slip Stitch Afghan (worked backwards) An Easy Project

Designed by Bendy Carter

Finished Size: approximately 14" by 16".

MATERIALS:
Red Heart® "Soft Baby™": Art. E705, Sport-Light 3, 100% acrylic, (7 oz / 198 g, 575 yards):
Amount: 1 skein No. 7730 Bright Pink.
Susan Bates® Crochet Hook: G-6 [4mm] & K-10.5 [6.5mm].

GAUGE: With larger hook – 15 sts = 4", 21 rows = 4".
CHECK YOUR GAUGE. Use any size hook to obtain the gauge given.

SPECIAL STITCHES:
Backward Slip Stitch = back sl st – Place yarn in front of work, with hook facing down, insert hook from back to front through indicated st, YO counterclockwise, pull through st and lp on hook, turn hook counterclockwise so that hook is facing up (yarn will be slightly twisted).

AFGHAN:
Row 1 WS: Using larger hook, ch 56, work back sl st in back ridge of 2nd ch from hook and in back ridge of each ch across; turn—55 sts.

Row 2 RS: Ch 1, work back sl st in back lp (the loop on top) of each st across; turn.

Rep Row 2 till 12.75" from beg ending with a **WS** row.

EDGING:

Rnd 1 RS: Using smaller hook, ch 1, sc in corner, *work 53 sc evenly sp across, work (sc, ch 1, sc) in corner, work 45 sc evenly sp across short end,* (sc, ch 1, sc) in corner, rep from * to * 1 time, sc in same corner as beg st, ch 1, join in beg st; turn.

Rnd 2 WS: Ch 1, sc in ch-1 sp, *sc in each st across to next ch-1 sp,** work (sc, ch 1, sc) in corner ch-1 sp, rep from * around ending at **, sc in same corner ch-1 sp as beg st, ch 1, join in beg st; turn.

Rnd 3: Rep Rnd 2. Fasten off.

ABBREVIATIONS: beg = begin(ning); **ch** = chain; **lp(s)** = loop(s); **rep** = repeat; **rnd(s)** = round(s); **RS** = right side; **sc** = single crochet; **sl st** = slip stitch; **sp** = space; **st(s)** = stitch(es); **WS** = wrong side; **YO** = yarn over; * or ** = repeat whatever follows the * or ** as indicated.

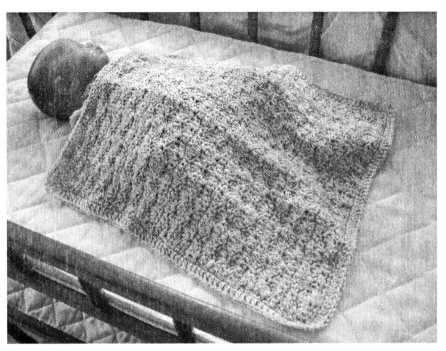

Veronica's 3rd Design
Made for Charity

Preemie Shell Afghan
A Beginner Project

Designed by Bendy Carter

Finished Size: 14" by 15".

MATERIALS:
Red Heart® "Soft Baby™": Art. E705, Sport-Light 3, (64% acrylic, 36% Nylon), (6 oz / 170 g, 430 yards):
    Amount: 1 skein No. 8680 New Mint Twinkle.
    Susan Bates® Crochet Hook: G-6 [4mm].

GAUGE: In pat – 17.5 sts = 4", 12.5 rows = 4".
    CHECK YOUR GAUGE. Use any size hook to obtain the gauge given.

AFGHAN:
Row 1 WS: Ch 56, sc in back ridge of 2nd ch from hook and in back ridge of each ch across; turn – 55 sts.
Row 2 RS: Ch 1, sc, [sk next 2 sts, work 5 dc in next st, sk next 2 sts, sc in next st] 9 times; turn.
Row 3: Ch 3 (counts as first dc), work 2 dc in same st as beg ch-3, *sk next 2 sts, sc in next st, sk next 2 sts,** work 5 dc in next st, rep from * across to last st ending at **, work 3 dc in last st; turn.
Row 4: Ch 1, sc in each st across; turn.
Row 5: Rep Row 4.
Row 6 – 9: [Work Rows 2 – 3] 2 times.
Row 10 – 11: [Work Row 4] 2 times.
Row 12 – 17: [Work Rows 2 – 3] 3 times.

Row 18 – 31: Rep Rows 4 – 17.
Row 32 – 39: Rep Rows 4 – 11.
Row 40 – 42: Rep Rows 2 – 4.

EDGING:

Rnd 1 RS: Turn to work down side, ch 1, sc in corner, *work 57 sc evenly sp across, work (sc, ch 1, sc) in corner, work 53 sc evenly sp across end,* (sc, ch 1, sc) in corner, rep from * to * 1 time, sc in same corner as beg st, ch 1, join in beg st.

Rnd 2 RS: Ch 3, *dc in each st across to ch-1 sp, work 3 dc in ch-1 sp, rep from * around, join in beg st. Fasten off.

ABBREVIATIONS: beg = begin(ning); **ch** = chain; **dc** = double crochet; **rep** = repeat; **RS** = right side; **sc** = single crochet; **sk** = skip; **sp** = space; **st(s)** = stitch(es); **WS** = wrong side; * or ** = repeat whatever follows the * or ** as indicated; [] = work directions given in brackets the number of times specified.

Veronica's 4th Design
Veronica's First Published Pattern

Backward Slip Stitch Scarf
An Easy Project

Designed by Bendy Carter

Finished Size: 4.25" wide, approximately 55" long.

MATERIALS:
Moda Dea® Vision™: Art. R196, Worsted-Medium 4, (65% wool, 35% Acrylic), (3.52 oz / 100 g, 155 yards):
Amount: 1 skein No. 2945 Sedona.
Susan Bates® Crochet Hook: L-11 [8mm].

GAUGE: 11.25 sts = 4", 13.33 rows = 4".
CHECK YOUR GAUGE. Use any size hook to obtain the gauge given.

SPECIAL STITCHES:
Backward Slip Stitch = back sl st – Place yarn in front of work, with hook facing down, insert hook from back to front through indicated st, YO counterclockwise, pull through st and lp on hook, turn hook counterclockwise so that hook is facing up (yarn will be slightly twisted).

SCARF:
Row 1 RS: Ch 13, work back sl st in back ridge of 2nd ch from hook and in back ridge of each ch across; turn—12 sts.
Row 2: Ch 1, work back sl st in back lp (the loop on top) of each st across; turn.
Rep Row 2 till all yarn is used ending with a **RS** row. Fasten off.

ABBREVIATIONS: ch = chain; **lp(s)** = loop(s); **rep** = repeat; **RS** = right side; **sl st** = slip stitch; **st(s)** = stitch(es); **YO** = yarn over.

Veronica's 5th Design
Baby Hat That Love Stole

Baby Hat
An Easy Project

Designed by Bendy Carter

Finished Hat: 14" circumference.

MATERIALS:
Red Heart® Luster Sheen™: Art. E721, Sport-Fine 2, 100% Acrylic, (4 oz / 113 g, 335 yards):
Amount: 1 skein No. 0517 Turquoise.
Yarn Needle.
Susan Bates® Crochet Hook: F-5 [3.75mm].

GAUGE: In V's-new-st pat – 13.5 sts = 4", 20.5 rows = 4".
CHECK YOUR GAUGE. Use any size hook to obtain the gauge given.

SPECIAL STITCHES:
Veronica's New Stitch = V's-new-st – Insert hook in st, YO, pull though, YO, insert hook through st in row directly below, YO, pull through and up even with current row, YO, pull through all 4 lps on hook.

HAT:
Rnd 1 WS: Ch 47, sc in back ridge of beg ch to form ring being careful not to twist ch sts, sc in back ridge of each rem ch; do not join this or any rnd – 47 sts.
Rnd 2: Sc in each st around.
Rnd 3: Sc, [work V's-new-st in next st, sc in next st] 23 times.
Rnd 4: Work V's-new-st, [sc in next st, work V's-new-st in next st] 23 times.
Rep Rnds 3–4 till 6" from beg ending with Rnd 3.

HAT SHAPING:

Rnd 1: Work V's-new-st, [sk next st, work V's-new-st in next st] 23 times – 24 sts.

Rnd 2: Rep Rnd 2 of Hat.

Rnd 3: [Sc, sk next st] 12 times – 12 sts.

KNOT RNDS:

Rnd 1 – 12: Rep Rnd 2 of Hat. Fasten off leaving long tail for sewing.

FINISHING:

Using yarn needle weave tail through sts of last rnd then pull tight to close.

Turn hat right side out.

Tie Knot Rounds in overhand knot.

Turn bottom of hat up 1.5" to create brim.

ABBREVIATIONS: beg = begin(ning); ch = chain; lp(s) = loop(s); rem = remaining; rep = repeat; rnd(s) = round(s); sc = single crochet; sk = skip; st(s) = stitch(es); WS = wrong side; YO = yarn over; [] = work directions given in brackets the number of times specified.

Veronica's 6th Design
Designer and Teacher Growth Day

Pet Snuggle
An Easy Project

Designed by Bendy Carter

Finished Snuggle: 14" wide, approximately 19" long.

MATERIALS:

Red Heart® Easy Tweed™: Art. E741, Chunky-Bulky 5, (95% Acrylic, 5% Nylon), (3.5 oz / 100 g, 143 yards):

Amount: 1 skein each No. 6653 Bright Teal & No. 6612 Black.

Susan Bates® Crochet Hook: N-15 [10mm].

GAUGE: 8.25 sts = 4", 4.75 rows = 4".

CHECK YOUR GAUGE. Use any size hook to obtain the gauge given.

SNUGGLE:

Row 1 RS: Holding 1 strand each of bright teal and black tog, ch 30, hdc in back ridge of 2nd ch from hook and in back ridge of each ch across; turn – 29 sts.

Row 2: Ch 1, hdc in front bar of st, [hdc in front lp of next st, hdc in back lp of next st, hdc in front lp of next st, hdc in front bar of next st] 7 times; turn.

Row 3: Ch 1, hdc in back lp of st, [hdc in front lp of next st, hdc in front bar of next st, hdc in front lp of next st, hdc in back lp of next st] 7 times; turn.

Rep Rows 2 – 3 till all yarn is used ending with a **RS** row. Fasten off.

ABBREVIATIONS: ch = chain; **hdc** = half double crochet; **lp(s)** = loop(s); **rep** = repeat; **RS** = right side; **st(s)** = stitch(es); **tog** = together; * = repeat whatever follows the * as indicated.

Veronica's 7th Design
To Show Crochet Can Look Like Knit

Envelope Purse
An Easy Project

Designed by Bendy Carter

Finished Purse: 6.5" wide, 4" tall (excluding strap). Strap is approximately 27" long.

MATERIALS:
Moda Dea® Bamboo Wool™: Art. R167, Worsted-Medium 4, (55% Rayon from Bamboo, 45% Wool), (2.8 oz / 80 g, 145 yards):
    Amount: 1 skein No. 3620 Celery.
    Yarn Needle.
    1 Sew on Snap: Size No. 1.
    Sewing Needle & Matching Thread.
    1 Decorative Hank Button.
    Susan Bates® Crochet Hook: H-8 [5mm] & K-10.5 [6.5mm].

    GAUGE: In pat – 15.25 sts = 4", 16 rows = 4".
    CHECK YOUR GAUGE. Use any size hook to obtain the gauge given.

SPECIAL STITCHES:
    Altered Half Double Crochet = A-hdc – YO, insert hook in indicated st, YO, pull through st and both lps on hook.
    Altered Half Double Crochet Decrease = A-hdc dec – YO, insert hook in indicated st, YO, pull through st, insert hook in next indicated st, YO, pull through st and all three lps on hook.
    Slip Stitch Decrease = sl st dec – Insert hook in indicated

st, YO, pull through st, insert hook in next indicated st, YO, pull through st and both lps on hook.

NOTE:

Make a row of A-hdc sts then turn work. When looking at the top of the A-hdc, one will see three loops. The first loop is called the front bar, this loop is created by the YO made before inserting the hook into the stitch. The second loop is called the front lp and the third loop is called the back lp.

PURSE:

Row 1 RS: Using larger hook, ch 31, work A-hdc in back ridge of 2nd ch from hook, work A-hdc in back ridge of each of next 4 ch (place marker in last st), work A-hdc in back ridge of each ch across (place marker in last st); turn – 30 sts.

Row 2: Ch 1, work A-hdc in front bar of each st across to last st, work 2 A-hdc in front bar of last st; turn – 31 sts.

Row 3: Ch 1, work 2 A-hdc in back lp of first st, work A-hdc in back lp of each st across; turn – 32 sts.

Row 4 – 11: Rep Rows 2 – 3 last row will have 40 sts.

Row 12: Ch 1, work A-hdc in front bar of each st across; turn.

Row 13: Ch 1, work A-hdc in back lp of each st across; turn.

Row 14 – 15: Rep Rows 12 – 13.

Row 16: Rep Row 12.

Row 17: Ch 1, work A-hdc dec over back lp of next 2 sts, work A-hdc in back lp of each st across; turn – 39 sts.

Row 18: Ch 1, work A-hdc in front bar of each st across to last 2 sts, work A-hdc dec over front bar of next 2 sts; turn – 38 sts.

Rows 19 – 26: Rep Rows 17 – 18 last row will have 30 sts. Fasten off.

EDGING (work for both ends):

With **RS** facing, using smaller hook, attach yarn to end of row, sl st dec over ends of first 2 rows, *ch 1, sl st dec over ends of next 2 rows, rep from * across. Fasten off.

SIDE SEAMS:

Fold piece so that right sides are facing and marked stitches on first row are touching each other. Using yarn needle, sew seam on both sides of purse then right side purse out.

STRAP:

Using smaller hook, attach yarn inside purse at side seam, ch 120, sl st inside purse at side seam on opposite side of purse. Fasten off.

FINISHING:

Fold flap down over front of purse, mark desired location for snap then sew snap in place. Sew decorative button on front of flap.

ABBREVIATIONS: ch = chain; **dec** = decrease; **hdc** = half double crochet; **lp(s)** = loop(s); **rep** = repeat; **RS** = right side; **sl st** = slip stitch; **st(s)** = stitch(es); **YO** = yarn over; * = repeat whatever follows the * as indicated.

Veronica's 8th Design
Designer Contest Entry

Decorative Hot Pad
A Beginner Project

Designed by Bendy Carter

Finished Hot Pad: 7.25" wide, 6.75" tall.

MATERIALS:

TLC® Essentials™: Art. E514, Worsted-Medium 4, 100% Acrylic, (6 oz / 170 g, 312 yards):

Amount: 1 skein No. 2313 Aran.

Red Heart® Casual Cot'n Blend™: Art. E723, Chunky-Bulky 5, (61% Acrylic, 29% Cotton, 10% Polyester), (4 oz / 133 g, 140 yards):

Amount: 1 skein No. 3952 Falling Leaves.

Susan Bates® Crochet Hook: I-9 [5.5mm].

GAUGE: 12.75 sts = 4", 14.5 rows = 4".

CHECK YOUR GAUGE. Use any size hook to obtain the gauge given.

HOT PAD:

Row 1 RS: Using Aran, ch 21, sc in back ridge of 2nd ch from hook and in back ridge of each ch across; turn – 20 sts.

Row 2: Ch 1, sc in each st across; turn.

Row 3 – 21: Rep Row 2. Fasten off.

SURFACE CHAIN STITCHES:

Using Falling Leaves, work Surface Chain Stitches according to chart beginning with number 1 and continuing in numerical order.

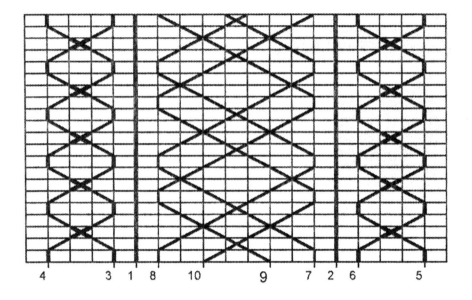

EDGING:

Rnd 1 RS: Attach Falling Leaves, in top right corner, ch 1, sc evenly sp around working 3 sc in each corner to turn, do not join.

Rnd 2 RS: Sl st in next st, *ch 1, sl st in next st, rep from * to top left corner, ch 5 (for hanger), sl st in same st as last sl st, **ch 1, sl st in next st, rep from ** around, ch 1, sl st in beg sl st. Fasten off.

ABBREVIATIONS: beg = begin(ning); **ch** = chain; **rep** = repeat; **RS** = right side; **sc** = single crochet; **sl st** = slip stitch; **sp** = space; **st(s)** = stitch(es); * or ** = repeat whatever follows the * or ** as indicated.

Veronica Saturday Morning Class
The Art of Egg Decorating

Pineapple Thread Egg
An Easy Project

Designed by Bendy Carter

Finished Egg: 2.5" tall.

MATERIALS:
Coats® Aunt Lydia's® Classic Crochet Thread: Art. 154, Size 10 Thread, 100% Mercerized Cotton, (350 yards):
Amount: 1 ball No. 0487 Dark Royal.
Egg: 1 Realistic looking Wood Egg – Approximately 5.25" circumference measuring around middle, 6.25" circumference measuring from end to end, 2.5" tall when standing upright.
Egg Stand.
Susan Bates® Steelites® Crochet Hook: US 6 [1.6mm].

GAUGE: First 8 rounds = 4". **Note:** Measure across shell stitches.
CHECK YOUR GAUGE. Use any size hook to obtain the gauge given.

SPECIAL STITCHES:
Beg Shell – Ch 3, work (dc, ch 2, 2 dc) in same ch sp as last sl st.
Shell – work (2 dc, ch 2, 2 dc) in indicated ch sp.

PINEAPPLE EGG:
Rnd 1 RS: Ch 4, work 15 dc in 4th ch from hook, join in top of beg ch-4; do not turn this or any rnd – 16 sts.

Rnd 2: Ch 3 (counts as first dc now and throughout), *dc in each of next 2 sts, ch 3, sk next st,** dc in next st, rep from * around ending at **, join in top of beg ch-3 – there are 4 groups of 3 dc sts.

Rnd 3: Sl st across and into ch-3 sp, work beg shell, *ch 3, sk next 3 dc,** shell in next ch-3 sp, rep from * around ending at **, join in top of beg ch-3 – there are 4 shells.

Rnd 4: Sl st across and into ch-2 sp, work beg shell, *ch 3, sk ch-3 lp, work 9 dc in ch-2 sp of next shell, ch 3, sk ch-3 lp,* work shell in ch-2 sp of next shell, rep from * to * 1 time, join in top of beg ch-3.

Rnd 5: Sl st across and into ch-2 sp, work beg shell, *ch 3, sk ch-3 lp, [sc in dc st, ch 3] 9 times, sk ch-3 lp,* work shell in ch-2 sp of next shell, rep from * to * 1 time, join in top of beg ch-3.

Rnd 6: Sl st across and into ch-2 sp, work beg shell, *ch 3, sk ch-3 lp, [sc in next ch-3 lp, ch 3] 8 times, sk ch-3 lp,* work shell in ch-2 sp of next shell, rep from * to * 1 time, join in top of beg ch-3.

Rnd 7 – 10: Rep Rnd 6 decreasing underlined number by 1 each rnd.

Insert egg in crocheted piece then work rem rnds.

Rnd 11: Sl st across and into ch-2 sp, work beg shell, *ch 3, sk ch-3 lp, [sc in next ch-3 lp, ch 3] 3 times, sk ch-3 lp,* work shell in ch-2 sp of next shell, rep from * to * 1 time, join in top of beg ch-3.

Rnd 12 – 13: Rep Rnd 11 decreasing underlined number by 1 each rnd.

Rnd 14: Sl st across and into ch-2 sp, ch 1, work 4 sc in same sp as last sl st, work 4 sc in ch-2 sp of next shell, join in beg st – 8 sts. Fasten off leaving long tail for sewing.

Sew sts of last rnd tog to close opening.

ABBREVIATIONS: beg = begin(ning); **ch** = chain; **dc** = double crochet; **lp(s)** = loop(s); **rem** = remaining; **rep** = repeat; **rnd(s)** = round(s); **RS** = right side; **sc** = single crochet;

sk = skip; **sl st** = slip stitch; **sp** = space; **st(s)** = stitch(es); **tog** = together; * or ** = repeat whatever follows the * or ** as indicated; [] = work directions given in brackets the number of times specified.

Veronica's Sunday Morning Class
Everything One Needs to Know About Post Stitches

Post Stitch Purse
An Intermediate Project

Designed by Bendy Carter

Finished Purse: 9" wide, 10" tall.

MATERIALS:
Red Heart® Designer Sport™: Art. E744, Sport-Light 3, 100% Acrylic, (3 oz / 85 g, 279 yards):
    Amount: 2 skeins No. 3301 Latte.
    Susan Bates® Crochet Hook: G-6 [4mm].

GAUGE: 18.25 sts = 4", 17.5 rows = 4".
CHECK YOUR GAUGE. Use any size hook to obtain the gauge given.

NOTES: dc – YO 1 time, tr – YO 2 times, dtr – YO 3 times.

PURSE FRONT & BACK NOTES: Leave st behind post st un-worked. All post sts are worked around post of st 2 rows below.

SPECIAL STITCHES:
Front post double treble over cross = fpdtr over cross – sk next 2 sts, fpdtr around post of next st, sc, with hook in front of post st just made, fpdtr around post of first sk st.
    Front post double treble under cross = fpdtr under cross – sk next 2 sts, fpdtr around post of next st, sc, with hook in back of post st just made, fpdtr around post of first sk st.

Double front post double treble over cross = d-fpdtr over cross – sk next 3 sts, fpdtr around post of each of next 2 sts, sc, with hook in front of post sts just made, fpdtr around post of first sk st, fpdtr around post of next sk st.

PURSE FRONT & BACK (Make 2):

Row 1 RS: Ch 42, sc in back ridge of 2nd ch from hook and in back ridge of each ch across; turn – 41 sts.

Row 2 and all even rows: Ch 1, sc in each st across; turn.

Row 3: Ch 1, sc, fptr, sc, *fpdtr over cross, [sc, fptr in each of next 2 sts] 2 times, sc,* [fpdtr over cross, sc in each of next 3 sts] 2 times, rep from * to * 1 time, fptr, sc, fpdtr over cross, sc; turn.

Row 5: Ch 1, sc, fpdtr under cross, sc, fptr, sc, d-fpdtr over cross, sc, [fpdtr over cross, sc in each of next 3 sts] 2 times, fpdtr over cross, sc, d-fpdtr over cross, sc, fpdtr under cross, sc, fptr, sc; turn.

Row 7: Ch 1, sc, fptr, sc, *fpdtr over cross, [sc, fptr in each of next 2 sts] 2 times, sc,* fpdtr over cross, sc, sk next 2 sts, fpdtr around post of next st, sc in each of next 5 sts, fpdtr around post of st 2 sts to right, sc, rep from * to * 1 time, fptr, sc, fpdtr over cross, sc; turn.

Row 9: Ch 1, *sc, fpdtr under cross, sc, fptr, sc,* d-fpdtr over cross, sc, fptr, sc, fpdtr under cross, sc in each of next 5 sts, fpdtr under cross, sc, fptr, sc, d-fpdtr over cross, rep from * to * 1 time; turn.

Row 11: Ch 1, sc, fptr, sc, fpdtr over cross, *[sc, fptr in each of next 2 sts] 2 times, sc, fptr, sc,* fpdtr under cross, sc in each of next 5 sts, fpdtr under cross, sc, fptr, rep from * to * 1 time, fpdtr over cross, sc; turn.

Row 13: Ch 1, *sc, fpdtr under cross, sc, fptr, sc,* d-fpdtr over cross, sc, fpdtr over cross, sc in each of next 3 sts, fpdtr around post of st 2 sts to right, sc, sk next 2 sts, fpdtr around post of next st, sc in each of next 3 sts, fpdtr over cross, sc, d-fpdtr over cross, rep from * to * 1 time; turn.

Rep Rows 2 – 13 for pat till there are a total of 35 rows. Fasten off.

SEWING:

With **RS** facing, sew sides and bottom of Front & Back piece tog.

PURSE TOP NOTE: All post sts are worked around post of st 1 row below.

PURSE TOP:

Rnd 1: With **RS** facing attach yarn at side, ch 4, work 81 tr evenly sp around opening, join in top of beg ch-4; do not turn this or any round – 82 sts.

Rnd 2: Ch 2, *fpdc, bpdc, rep from * around to last st, fpdc, join in top of beg ch-2.

Rep Rnd 2 till 2" from beg of Purse Top. Fasten off.

FIRST DRAWSTRING:

Cut 2 strands yarn 120" long. Put strands tog and fold in half. Tie ends in knot. Slip knotted end onto a stationary object the diameter of a pencil. Put looped end on finger. Make strands taut. Twist strands 120 times. Put one finger in center of strands, fold in half letting the 2 sides twist tog. Holding ends tog so that they stay twisted, weave drawstring through tr sts of Rnd 1 on Purse Top starting and ending at right side of purse. With purse wide open, tie both ends of the drawstring tog in an overhand knot to form a tassel knot at the top of the purse (when purse is pulled shut, tassel knot will come down farther on purse). Trim tassel ends as desired.

SECOND DRAWSTRING: Work same as first drawstring weaving drawstring through tr sts of Rnd 1 of Purse Top starting and ending at left side of purse.

ABBREVIATIONS: beg = begin(ning); **bpdc** = back post double crochet; **ch** = chain; **dc** = double crochet; **dtr** = double treble; **fpdc** = front post double crochet; **fptr** = front post treble crochet; **Pat** = pattern; **rep** = repeat; **rnd(s)** = round(s); **RS** = right side; **sc** = single crochet; **sk** = skip; **sp** = space; **st(s)** = stitch(es); **tog** = together; **tr** = treble crochet; **YO** = yarn over; * = repeat whatever follows the * as indicated; [] or = work directions given in brackets the number of times specified.